T0358843

BY SHERRILYN KENYON

THE DARK-HUNTERS

Night Pleasures
Night Embrace
Dance with the Devil
Kiss of the Night
Night Play
Seize the Night
Sins of the Night
Unleash the Night
Dark Side of the Moon
The Dream-Hunter
Devil May Cry
Upon the Midnight Clear
Dream Chaser
Acheron
One Silent Night
Dream Warrior
Bad Moon Rising
No Mercy
Retribution
The Guardian
Time Untime
Styxx
Dark Bites
Son of No One
Dragonbane
Dragonmark
Dragonsworn
Stygian
Shadow Fallen

DEADMAN'S CROSS

Deadmen Walking
Death Doesn't Bargain
At Death's Door

THE LEAGUE

Born of the Night
Born of Fire
Born of Ice
Born of Shadows
Born of Silence
Born of Fury
Cloak & Silence
Born of Defiance
Born of Betrayal
Born of Legend
Born of Vengeance
Born of Rage
Born of Blood

CHRONICLES OF NICK

Infinity
Invincible
Infamous
Inferno
Illusion
Instinct
Invision
Intensity

Hero for the Holidays
Season of Magic

SEASON
OF
MAGIC

SHERRILYN KENYON

St. Martin's Paperbacks

Published in the United States by St. Martin's Paperbacks, an imprint of St. Martin's Publishing Group.

SEASON OF MAGIC: ONE SILENT NIGHT copyright © 2008 by Sherrilyn Kenyon and LOVE BYTES copyright © 2001 by St. Martin's Paperbacks.

For information, address St. Martin's Publishing Group, 120 Broadway, New York, NY 10271.

www.stmartins.com

ISBN: 978-1-250-31989-0

Our books may be purchased in bulk for promotional, educational, or business use. Please contact your local bookseller or the Macmillan Corporate and Premium Sales Department at 1-800-221-7945, ext. 5442, or by email at MacmillanSpecialMarkets@macmillan.com.

Printed in the United States of America

St. Martin's Paperbacks edition / October 2024

10 9 8 7 6 5 4 3 2 1

ONE SILENT NIGHT

Do not seek death. Death will find you. But seek the road which makes death a fulfillment.

—DAG HAMMARSKJOLD

PROLOGUE

In the beginning, the world was made of beauty and of magick. Before there were humans, there were gods and those who served them and did their bidding whatever their bidding was. At war with each other, the gods fought among themselves until a new breed was born out of their senseless violence. Chthonians by name, these new creatures came from the earth that flowed red with the blood of the gods.

The Chthonians rose up and divided the world between the gods—they split the world among themselves.

To maintain the peace, the soldiers of the gods were ordered to be put down. None were to survive. Chthonian law took precedence and together they were able to bring peace to the world once more and to protect the new life-form of mankind.

But the Chthonians were not without corruption. Nor were they infallible.

It wasn't long before they bickered, too.

And so time moved forward. Mankind matured and learned to dismiss the gods and the magick that existed in their world. Unable to fight on their own, mankind chose to ignore it.

"Poppycock." "Hokum." "Fantasy." "Fairy tales." Those

were some of the many words man used to denigrate that which couldn't be explained by their so-called science. Empiricism became its own religion.

There were no shadows stalking innocent victims. It was nothing more than a human mind playing tricks. An overactive imagination.

Wolves can't turn into humans and humans can't turn into bears. All the ancient gods are dead—relegated to mythological tales that we all know are untrue.

And yet . . .

What was that sound outside the window just now? Was it the howling of the wind? A stray dog perhaps?

Or something more sinister? Something truly predatorial?

The subtle hair rise on a neck could very well be nothing more than goose bumps. Or it could be the sensation of the dead walking near. The sensation of the hand of an unseen god or servant passing through.

The world is no longer new. It's no longer innocent.

And the old ones grow tired of being ignored. The winds that whispered through the yard earlier weren't the tender caress of a climate change. They were a siren's call that can only be heard by certain preternatural species.

Even now, those forces gather and unite.

This time, they want something more than the blood of the gods and one another.

They want us . . .

And we are at their mercy.

1

Stryker paused as he looked around Tartarus. His father, the Greek god Apollo, had brought him here once, eons ago, when he'd been a small child to meet his great-uncle Hades, who ruled the Greek Underworld and oversaw the ancient dead. On that day his father had also bestowed a rare and beneficial gift on Stryker. The ability to come and go from the Underworld so that Stryker could visit his uncle. As a child, Stryker had been terrified of the dark god whose eyes had only softened when he looked at his wife, Persephone.

Luckily, Persephone was here with Hades now and the god was too occupied by her to notice the fact that there was an uninvited demigod in his domain. Hades could be extremely temperamental over such insults.

Especially when the uninvited demigod carried a vial of potent blood with him. More to the point, Typhon's blood. The son of the primordial god Tartarus, whose name was given to this very part of Hades' domain, Typhon was deadly and lethal. His power enough to take down even Zeus, the king of the gods. At least until the Olympian gods had banded together to trap Typhon under Mount Aetna.

"Thank you for not being able to kill him," Stryker

said, holding the vial up so that he could see the luminescent purple blood he'd taken from the trapped Titan. With this, Stryker could wake the dead and bring back the most potent of scourges.

War.

Gripping the vial tightly, Stryker headed to the lowest part of Tartarus. This level was relegated to the beasts and gods that the Olympians had defeated. To the ones they feared above all others.

But it was the tomb in the back Stryker had accidentally found as a child that drew him now. In the darkness around him, he could still see the look of fear in his father's eyes. . . .

"What's that, Father?" Stryker had pointed up at the statues of two men and one woman.

Apollo had knelt down by his side. "They are what's left of the Machae."

"The what?"

"The spirits of battle." Apollo had pointed to the tallest in back. Huge in stature and built like a warrior, the statue had made a seven-year-old Stryker gasp in fear of his coming to life to hurt him. "That is War. The fiercest of the Machae. He was created by all the gods of war to kill the Chthonians. It's said that he and his minions pursued them to the brink of extinction. In one final battle that lasted for three full months, War held the last of the Chthonians down until they tricked him. Beleaguered, he screamed mightily as his powers were bound by spell and then he was cast into his current stasis. Here he remains until someone reawakens him."

It had seemed a rather harsh punishment to Stryker's boyish mind. Ignoble and cruel. "Why did the gods not kill him?"

"We weren't strong enough. Even with our powers combined, we still lacked the ability to end his life."

None of that had made sense to Stryker at the time. "I don't understand why the gods fear the Chthonians so. They are human."

"With the powers of gods, child. Never forget that. They alone can kill us without destroying the universe and return our essence to the primary source that birthed us."

"Then why don't the Chthonians kill all the gods and replace them?"

"Because when they kill us it weakens their own powers and makes them vulnerable to each other and to us. So instead they police us and we obey out of fear of dying." Apollo had looked back at War then, his eyes harboring a morbid fascination. "War alone was immune to their powers. Unfortunately, he's also immune to ours. When Ares and the other war gods realized how powerful he was, they decided it was best that he remain hidden here for the rest of eternity."

"Did they not understand his power when they made him?"

Apollo had ruffled Stryker's short blond hair. "Sometimes we don't realize how destructive our creations are until it's too late. And sometimes those creations we make turn on us and seek only to kill us even though we loved and succored them."

Stryker clenched his teeth at the memory of his father's words. How true they'd proven. Stryker had turned on his father and his son had turned on him.

Here they all were. At war.

War . . .

Stryker opened the dank tomb that smelled of fresh earth and mold. He held his hand up and used his powers to light the cobwebbed torches that hadn't been lit in centuries. The light was bright as it flickered against the walls and the remains of the last three Machae.

He paused by the woman. Petite and frail in appearance, Ker was the personification of cruel, violent death. Merciless and able to multiply herself into numerous she-demons called the Keres, she'd once haunted battlefields and ripped the souls out of the dying. It had been her powers that had inspired the Atlantean goddess Apollymi to save the cursed Apollites and give them a chance to circumvent Apollo's unjust curse.

All hail Ker for her powers. . . .

The next statue was the spirit Mache. Battle. The right hand of War. It was the plural of his name that had been given to all the spirits of conflict. He was their backbone.

But compared to War, he was weak.

Like Ker, he was only a by-product of the one destructive force that Stryker sought.

A slow smile curled his lips as he stepped past the two lesser beings to approach the one he needed to awaken. No longer a giant to him, War was actually several inches shorter—which, given the fact that Stryker was six foot eight, wasn't surprising. War's body was as heavily muscled as Stryker remembered from eleven thousand years ago. Even in stasis, War's presence and power were awe inspiring and undeniable. Stryker could feel it in the air. Feel it from the chills that went down his spine in warning. This creature meant death to any who crossed his path. Dressed as an ancient soldier, the god wore a cuirass decorated with the head of Echidna.

Stryker reached out to touch War. The moment Stryker's fingers brushed the stone, light flashed through the room, turning the white marble to flesh. The cuirass was made of steel overlaid with gold, and a gold-studded black leather battle skirt and cloak completed the fearsome ensemble. The sword in War's hands that was halfway out of its black leather sheath flashed to steel.

Black eyes bored into Stryker.

Then all returned to marble. White. Cold. Eerily pristine. War was again asleep and yet Stryker could feel his consciousness rippling in the air around him. War was salivating for release.

"You want out," Stryker whispered to the spirit. "I want revenge against a god I can't touch." He pulled the cork from the vial and lifted it. "From the blood of the Titans to the blood of the Titans, I, Strykerius, return you to form in exchange for one act against my enemies."

He tilted the vial so that the purple blood only marked his fingertip. The feral power of it burned his flesh. Yes, Typhon's blood was as potent as the once-feared god. His eyes narrowing, Stryker wiped the pad of his finger over the lips of the dormant spirit. "Do you accept my terms, War?"

The lips alone turned to flesh. "I accept."

"Then welcome back to the living." Stryker poured the blood into the spirit's mouth.

The moment he did so, a violent shout rang out, extinguishing the torches and drowning them in darkness. "NO!"

Stryker laughed at Hades' indignant cry. It was already too late. A vicious wind cut through the room as War came to life with a battle cry so fierce it echoed through the chamber and caused the caged damned around them to cringe. The torches exploded back to life, flooding the room with so much light that Stryker had to shield his eyes.

Hades appeared with Ares by his side. The gods tried to blast War, but it was futile.

War laughed before he returned their attack. The force of it sent them scattering to the ground like leaves in a storm. The joy in his black eyes said the spirit took great pleasure in his cruelty. His lips twisting into a smile, War turned to face Stryker. "Who do I kill for you?"

"Acheron Parthenopaeus and Nick Gautier."

War sheathed his sword. "Consider it done."

Stryker caught his arm as he started to vanish. "One word of caution, the world isn't what it used to be." He handed the spirit a small messenger bag that contained a pair of black jeans, a black shirt, and boots. "You might want to lose the skirt and armor. Just a thought."

War sneered at him, but in the end, he took the clothes and vanished. Stryker turned toward the gods. Ares had been knocked unconscious while Hades shook his head to clear it.

The dark god of the Underworld glowered his displeasure and rage as he stood over Ares, trying to revive him. "Have you any idea of what you've unleashed?"

Stryker was ambivalent to his condemnation. "Cruelty, pestilence, wrath, violence, ultimate suffering . . . what other *gifts* did the gods bestow on him?"

"You hit the highlights. But before you released him, you should have bothered to learn that he always destroys the one who commands him. You won't be an exception." Hades gestured toward the room. "Look around you. This hole we call Tartarus is all that's left of the primordial god. His death at the hands of War is what caused all the pantheons to combine their powers with the Chthonians' to contain him. And that was back in the day when we were worshiped and held our full powers. We're not that strong anymore."

Well, there was something Stryker hadn't bothered to contemplate. Not that it mattered. He was more than ready to lay down his life—provided he took his enemies with him. "Oops," he said, his voice thick with sarcasm. "Guess I screwed up. Inability to see the consequences of our thoughtless acts must run in the family. So much for my father being a god of prophecy, huh?"

Hades' eyes turned bright red. "He will destroy the humans."

Stryker sneered at him. "I didn't see you standing up to defend the Apollite race when my father cursed *us* to feed off each other's blood and die painfully when we were only twenty-seven years old because a handful of Apollites had killed his worthless whore. As I recall, all of you turned your backs and left us to the darkness like rats you wanted to forget existed."

Hades shook his head. "I would kill you, but a better fate is to leave you to the thing you just unleashed. I'll see you back here when you're no longer living."

Stryker didn't comment as he watched Hades rouse Ares. Bored with them both, he returned to Kalosis, which was where he'd go after his death. The Atlantean hell realm had been his home since the day he'd turned his back on his father and sided with the goddess who ruled this domain. Apollymi owned his soul. He'd gladly consigned it to her the day his father had cursed Stryker's entire race for something only a handful of soldiers had done.

Stryker wanted nothing to do with the Greeks ever again.

Bitterly amused by the fact that Apollymi would most likely enjoy his eternal torture even more than Hades, Stryker returned to his office, where he kept the sfora orb that would allow him to spy on his enemy. At least on Acheron.

As for Nick, Stryker could see through his eyes any time he wanted to. It was one of the perks he'd claimed when he bound the bastard to him. Unfortunately, though, there wasn't much to see with Nick, as he'd taken to keeping himself isolated from the world and everyone Stryker wanted to spy on.

He was bored with Nick's moping.

For now, Stryker wanted to see Acheron's demise. Waving his hand over the orb, he watched as the clouds cleared to show him the one god he wanted most to bury . . .

Apollymi's most precious son.

Stryker curled his lip as he found Acheron in a bizarro Norman Rockwell scene. How quaint. Acheron was at home on Katoteros, the Atlantean paradise realm, trimming a Christmas tree with his girlfriend, Soteria. There was something almost twisted about an ancient god humoring a human custom to placate his lover. The two of them looked so happy and sweet it was enough to make him puke.

That was all about to change.

Leaning back in his chair, Stryker waited.

"Ooo, *akri,* can the Simi eat that?"

Ash Parthenopaeus paused as he heard the voice of his demon behind him. Turning around, he saw Simi eyeing the glass angel in his hand.

Dressed in a black-and-red plaid Goth skirt and corset top, Simi had a Santa hat on her head that covered her small demon's horns. Like Ash, her hair was solid black in color and fell all the way to her waist.

Before he could answer, Soteria gave Simi a sweet, tolerant smile that melted him. Her brown hair was pulled forward into two pigtails, and in total contradiction to Ash's dark Goth style, she was dressed in a pair of winter white pants and a red sweater with white reindeer on it. Ash's long-sleeved T-shirt was black with reindeer skeletons pulling a twisted sleigh.

"Um, please, Simi," Soteria said, "don't eat that. That's been my angel on the tree since I was a little girl. I picked it out at a Christmas store in Greece with my parents."

Simi pouted. "Then can I eat the chocolate?"

"Absolutely."

Simi squealed before she grabbed the Hershey's chocolate bar Soteria had left on the coffee table near them and ran off to savor it.

Soteria laughed. "Dang. I was going to share that with you later."

Ash put the angel on top of the tree, which given the fact that he was six foot eight in height was an easy reach for him. "It's okay. I despise the taste of chocolate."

Soteria pulled silver tinsel from the bear ornament in her hand. "I would ask for an explanation, but every time I ask why you have an aversion to something the answer always breaks my heart. So I'll just make sure not to get you any for Valentine's Day."

"Thanks."

Closing the distance between them, Ash pulled her into his arms for a quick kiss. His lips had barely touched hers before a bright flash blinded him. He drew a breath in to chastise his steward, Alexion, for the intrusion, but before he could speak something slammed into him and knocked him off his feet.

Soteria turned to face an intruder. Expecting to find the Greek goddess Artemis there, she was stunned to see a tall, extremely well-built man. The brutality on his face was only matched by its beauty. Dressed all in black, he walked past her as if she were nothing more than a piece of harmless furniture, toward Acheron.

She summoned her powers to blast him, but when she tried, she found her powers worthless against him. It was as if she were human again. The blast left her and seemed to be absorbed somehow by his body.

The man seized Acheron from the floor and threw him against the far wall as if he were nothing more than a straw dummy.

Dear God, the man was going to kill Ash!

Ash couldn't breathe as he tried to fight and couldn't. It was as if something had wrapped itself around him like a steel band, paralyzing him. Pain ripped through his body with potent talons. No one had been able to kick his ass this badly since he'd been human.

No sooner had that thought gone through his head than he had crystal clarity of who and what was attacking him.

War. The ultimate warrior.

Shit.

"No!" Ash shouted as Soteria started to attack War at the same time Simi manifested into the room by her side to fight. War would tear the two of them apart. "Take Simi and get out. Now!"

As Simi launched herself toward War, Soteria grabbed

her. Tory gave him a look to let him know that she didn't want to stand back, but that she trusted him enough to listen.

Alexion appeared with a sword that he tried to stab through the spirit. Instead, it went through War's flesh and tore into Ash's abdomen. Ash hissed as more agony poured through him.

Alexion's face paled. "I'm so sorry, boss."

He should try being the one with the gaping wound. But Ash wouldn't hold that against his steward. The most important thing right now was to save all their lives. "Go! Take Danger, the demons, and Tory, and get the hell out of here."

War seized him by his throat. Ash choked, trying to remove the tight grip. He met Alexion's gaze. Loyalty gleamed bright, but his friend knew what Ash did. He couldn't fight while distracted.

"I'll meet you at Neratiti." Gathering the women, Alexion disappeared.

Ash pounded at War's hand, trying to knock his grip loose. When that failed, Ash shot a blast at the god that didn't faze him in the least.

"What do you want?" Ash gasped.

War cocked his head in an impersonal gesture as he tightened his grip even more. "Your death."

Ash's ears buzzed as the airflow to his lungs was restricted. He tried to breathe, but it was futile. His grip on the spirit weakened as everything slid to black.

2

Stryker smiled as he watched Acheron turn blue and for once it wasn't his natural skin tone. The bastard was one gasp away from death.

At least until the Chthonian Savitar flashed into the room with twenty Charonte demons to attack War and drive him away from Acheron. Stryker's anger ignited as the winged demons attacked en masse. They lifted War up from the floor and slammed him against the wall even as he blasted at them.

Savitar ran to Acheron to revive him.

Damn. Why couldn't the Chthonian bastard stay on the beach where he lived? No, Savitar had to bring a demon army out to defend Acheron.

Not to sound childish, but it just wasn't fair . . .

And it seriously pissed him off.

"Strykerius!" Apollymi's shrill scream ripped through the air, piercing his eardrums and making the hair on the back of his neck stand at attention. An instant later, she was standing in front of him with her white blond hair flying around her beautiful face. Like him and Acheron, her eyes were a pale, swirling silver. And they were filled with fury as she glared at him.

He should probably be scared, but it wasn't worth the

energy it would take to rise to the occasion. Besides, he'd had the worst things done to him. Torture, dismemberment, and death would be a welcome relief to his current state of nothingness.

"Is something . . . wrong?" he asked nonchalantly, knowing the tone would only enrage her more.

Apollymi wanted to shriek at his patronizing tone. She wanted to blast the bloodsucking Daimon lord before her into oblivion. If only she could. But for an act of weakness on her part centuries ago, she would free herself of him once and for all. However, he'd been fatally wounded by his father, and to strike back at Apollo she'd shared her blood with Strykerius and fortified him. While that act had saved his life, it had also tied their life forces together.

If he died, she died. It was why her son would never really harm Strykerius no matter how angry the Daimon made him.

It was why she couldn't kill Stryker herself.

Ironic, really, she was a goddess known for lacking compassion and the handful of times she'd actually shown some had come back to bite her harshly.

There was nothing to be done for it now. Her real son was under attack and her adoptive one, Stryker, was most likely to blame for it.

"What have you done?" she demanded.

Stryker leaned back in his chair and folded his hands behind his head as he eyed her cautiously. "Mulling mostly coupled with a shot or two of reminiscing and a drop of regretting a few past decisions. Some might even call it moping, but I'd kill anyone so stupid as to suggest that of me." He was more a plotting kind of Daimon.

Her hair rose even higher around her like ribbons

twisting in a strong wind, letting him know she didn't appreciate his sarcasm. "Apostolos is under attack. Did you provoke it?"

He didn't know why it bugged the shit out of him for her to call her son Apostolos when the rest of the world knew him as Acheron, but it did.

And honestly, he hadn't provoked dick. He'd directly caused it. *Big* difference.

However, he wasn't stupid enough to tell her that. Their life forces might be tied together, but when it came to her real son and his well-being, Apollymi lost all self-restraint and sense of survival.

She'd kill them both to protect Acheron.

"No," Stryker answered honestly. He slid his gaze down to the sfora that was hidden from Apollymi's view. The moment Stryker focused on it, he saw War surrounded by the Charonte demons who were actually doing damage to the spirit. Acheron was on the floor coughing and wheezing. A little worse for the wear, but alive nonetheless. *Worthless bastard.* Savitar was shouting to the demons, but sound wasn't available to Stryker while Apollymi was here.

Damn them.

Careful to shield his expression, he returned his gaze to Apollymi's. "So what can I do for you, Matera?" he asked, using the Atlantean word for mother.

Apollymi drew a long, slow breath as she tried to detect the truth from him. Strykerius had always been a convincing liar. At one time the two of them had been a united force against Apollo. But those days were gone and now the two of them danced around each other in a complicated battle of one-upmanship.

She would cast him and his Daimons out of here, but

for all their aggravation, they provided her with company and an army that allowed her to still have power to affect the human realm. Not to mention the small point that so long as they worshiped her, they fed her powers.

Unlike her small group of priestesses who still lived and served in the human world, the Daimons held much more power. They could provide her with a means to protect Apostolos.

"I want your Daimons to subjugate War. Immediately."

"It's daytime and until the sun sets he's beyond our reach. You wouldn't want one of *us* to die and deplete your strength now, would you?"

She wanted to knock that smug look off his handsome face. Unlike the rest of his blond Daimon horde, his short hair was as black as his heart. Perfectly dyed to keep him from looking exactly like his father. "Protect him, Strykerius. Your existence hinges on his. Remember I *will* kill you to protect him."

Stryker forced himself to wait until she was gone before he curled his lip in repugnance. He couldn't believe that he'd ever been dumb enough to think that Apollymi loved him as a son. That she would protect and care for him the same way she cared for Acheron. And every year that had passed since the moment Stryker took his own son's life to prove himself to her and had been forced to see the truth of his relationship with "his" mother had only made his bitterness grow.

"Tear him apart, War," he said, glancing back to the sfora. He wanted blood. Unfortunately, there was nothing there. No sign of War, Acheron, or Savitar.

Growling in anger, Stryker slung the orb against the wall, shattering it. Where the hell had they gone?

* * *

"War's broken out."

Artemis looked up at Ares' angry declaration as he appeared in the center of the Hall of the Gods where she and the rest of the Greek pantheon were having a small feast.

Her father, Zeus, cursed as he rose off his throne. "What have you done?"

Tall and blond, with muscles honed by his daily training, Ares held his hands up in surrender. "I did nothing. It was Apollo's son, Strykerius, who released him."

Artemis felt the color fade from her face at the mention of her nephew. If Stryker was involved, there was only one target he'd have.

Acheron.

And like as not, Acheron's mother along with Acheron would blame *her* for his attack. As if she'd dare . . .

Athena shot to her feet. She moved so fast that her actions startled the owl on her shoulder, causing him to take flight to the hall's rafters. Gold armor covered her instantly as she turned to face Zeus. "We should summon as many of the other pantheons as we can muster. It won't be long before War turns his sights on us again."

Zeus nodded in agreement. "Fetch Hermes and send him to them. As for the rest of us, let's prepare for war."

Artemis ignored her father's pun as she made her way out of the Hall of the Gods to her own golden temple. As soon as she was alone in her bedchambers, she used her powers to locate Acheron. He was alive but in pain. She let out a breath in relief.

Though he hated her and was planning to marry

another woman in a few weeks and she wanted desperately to hurt him for that, she still loved him and the last thing she wanted to see was him killed after all they'd shared these past centuries. Their daughter's heart would be broken if Artemis allowed him to die. But how could she protect him when he wouldn't even speak to her?

No sooner had the question entered her mind than she knew how to stop Stryker once and for all. . . .

Zephyra.

The demoness had taken refuge in one of her sanctuaries centuries ago, before Apollo had cursed the Apollite race. At first Artemis had wanted to turn her out, but sympathy for the woman had swayed her. She, too, had been betrayed by men, and at the time Zephyra had begged her for shelter Artemis had been angry at Apollo and had wanted to strike back at her arrogant brother. In a rare moment of sympathy, she'd allowed Zephyra to stay in Greece.

Little had she known how beneficial that decision would one day be.

"Zephyra?" she said, summoning the woman to her.

She instantly appeared in the room.

Where Artemis was extremely tall, Zephyra was petite. Even so, her preternatural powers gave her an advantage over any except those who were divinity. Her long blond hair was braided down her back, and to the uninformed she looked like any twenty-seven-year-old woman and not the eleven-thousand-year-old warrior she was.

She lowered her head respectfully. "My goddess?"

Artemis narrowed her gaze on the smaller woman. "I have a mission for you. One I think you'll enjoy."

"And that is?"

"Kill Strykerius."

Lifting her chin, Zephyra's black eyes widened. "The son of Apollo?"

He was also the man who had betrayed Zephyra centuries before. And while he was Artemis's nephew by blood, she had no more love for him than he had for her. The two of them had battled too long and too hard for there to be anything other than hatred in their hearts.

It was time to finish it and him. "Yes."

Zephyra's obsidian eyes glowed with relish. "Show me where he is, goddess, and I will make you proud."

Stryker held the bolt holes open, calling out to his Daimons the world over to summon them to Kalosis. Apollymi thought he did it in accordance with her orders to protect Acheron. The truth was Stryker intended to use them as pawns to get at Nick and Acheron. If nothing else, they'd keep the two of them occupied while War slit their throats.

Blood for blood.

Nick had killed Stryker's beloved sister and Acheron had to die because it wasn't in Stryker's nature to let that bastard win after all these centuries. Apollymi had destroyed him. It was only fair he return the favor to her. She had taken Stryker's son. Stryker would take hers.

Another flash of light denoted a new arrival. Stryker waited to see the mettle of this Daimon recruit. As typical, the Daimon landed flat on his back with a loud "Oof!" Then the man actually whimpered like a child as he writhed on the floor, whining over his pain. "I think I broke my arm."

Stryker let out a long, agitated breath. He missed the old days when the Daimons and Apollites were warriors. When they would appear in his hall on their feet, ready to battle. These new generations were almost as pathetically weak as the humans they fed on.

It was a supermarket world with a supermarket mentality. Since mankind no longer trained for war and huddled together in cities where loose morals made them easy pickings, today's Daimons didn't have to fight for food. All they had to do was stroll into any bar or nightclub, find a drunk woman or man, and take them outside to rip their stupidly willing soul out of their body to feed themselves. There was no fighting. No coaxing.

Fast food even for them.

The only challenge they had left was avoiding the Dark-Hunters and Acheron in particular.

It was why Stryker had treasured his sister so much. Aggravating to the extreme, Satara had always been plotting something. Always trying to betray someone or screw them over. Even him. It had kept him on his toes and sharpened his skills.

Now he would grow as worthless as all the others.

Weary of their weakness, he turned to find Kessar approaching his throne. A Sumerian gallu demon, Kessar looked more like a human fashion model than the lethal killer he was. Even his brown hair was swept back from his red eyes in a manner so perfect he could run for political office. His features were finely boned and as razor sharp as the demon's cruelty. Like Stryker, the demon used his good looks to his advantage whenever he stalked human prey.

Human women were weak. Susceptible. They would do anything for the attention of a handsome man. Gods, how he loved the weak-minded. They all deserved the painful deaths they got.

He looked over at Kessar. "If you want to make that one your lunch, I won't stop you."

A slow smile spread over Kessar's face before he flashed across the room, grabbed the Daimon up from the floor, and ripped out his throat.

Survival of the fittest. Stryker's people had been very Spartan in their beliefs. If you weren't fit to fight, you weren't fit to live. Simple and perfect. Just like Stryker's new plan.

Kessar cursed as the Daimon he'd tried to feed on evaporated into dust. "I hate that gritty taste between my fangs—like feeding in a sandstorm. Not enough blood in the world to clear the palate after that."

Stryker shrugged. "It's what you get for being greedy. You know what happens when you kill one of us. You should have just drunk his blood and left him breathing."

Kessar spat on the floor. "You're in a foul mood. Someone piss in your blood?"

Before he could answer, the light flashed again. Stryker ground his teeth in expectation of the next round of Weak and Pathetic Losers.

At least that was what he thought until the blur of black landed on the floor in a deadly crouch. He could barely make out the fact that she was female before she attacked him with a ferocity and vigor that would have made a rabid tiger proud. Her first kick knocked him out of his seat. He barely had time to grab her wrist before she decapitated him with the oversized dagger in her hand.

She head-butted him hard, knocking him back. Stryker shook his head to clear it. She shoved him into the wall.

He caught her arms and rolled with her, throwing her away from him.

Exposing his fangs, he was just about to rip her throat out when his swirling silver gaze locked with her black one.

Zephyra.

In that one instant, he was taken back eleven thousand years ago to the day they first met. The sea air had been blowing her blond curls around her delicate face. Slender and small, she'd been as beautiful as a goddess.

And when he'd reached for her, she'd turned on him with a curse more foul than any man's as she'd kneed him in the groin for daring to touch her without an invitation.

Which she again tried to do. But this time he was expecting it. He barely moved out of the way of her knee as emotions tore through him. Happiness. Anger. Joy. Confusion.

All these centuries he'd assumed her dead.

He could barely get his bearings over the reality of her being alive and well. She'd survived Apollo's curse and managed to live out eternity . . . just like him.

"What are you doing here?"

She answered his question with a stroke of her dagger that narrowly missed his throat. "I thought we'd catch up on old times. Maybe play Parcheesi."

Stryker caught her arm and spun with her, pinning her to the wall again. He tightened his grip until she was forced to drop her dagger. Closing one hand around her neck, he held her in place. "I can think of much better games to play." He was about to say, *Strip Poker,* when something hit him hard across his back, knocking him away from Zephyra.

He turned with a feral growl on his new attacker, intending to kill whoever was dumb enough to interfere with him, then froze as shock riveted him to the spot. It was an exact duplicate of Zephyra. Same blond curls. Same black eyes. Same height and weight.

He would think her a twin sister, except that he knew for a fact Zephyra was an only child.

"Get your filthy hands off my mother."

3

"Mother," Stryker repeated under his breath an instant before Kessar grabbed Zephyra's daughter. The demon opened his lips to taste her throat. Stryker barely had time to call out to the demon before he killed her. "Stop!"

The demon's red eyes flared bright before he curled his lip and released her with a snarl. "Let them tear into you then. Not like I give a shit if you live or die."

Zephyra ran at Stryker, drawing a hilt that she extended to a sword to stab him. Stryker took a step back as he used his powers to manifest a sword of his own. He caught her blade with his. The sound of steel rang out, echoing through the room as she met him stroke for stroke. Every parry, every thrust. She was there as if she knew exactly what he was going to do.

Stryker smiled. It'd been too long since he'd fought someone other than Acheron who could match his skills. Yet here she was, the daughter of a peasant, fighting with the expertise of a trained soldier. He wondered who had taught her so well. "I always knew you were good at handling a man's sword, love, but I had no idea that extended to those made of steel, too."

She growled an instant before she kicked at him, catching him in the side.

Stryker grunted at the pain that simple move caused. But to be fair, she held her temper.

"At least this sword doesn't disappoint. I don't have to worry about it going soft on me."

"I never went soft on you."

She rolled her eyes as she blocked his slice. "Trust me, baby, you weren't *that* good. I was just a better actress than you were actor."

"Ew!" her daughter groaned as she gave them more room to fight. "No offense, Mum, I don't want to know who you've slept with. Kill the sexual bantering and him before I go deaf from it."

Zephyra's eyes darkened as one side of her mouth quirked up into an evil smile. "You shouldn't be so prudish, Medea. After all, you've always wanted to meet your father. Happy Birthday, baby. Sorry the reunion's so short. But trust me, he's no loss."

Stryker staggered under the weight of the news. His attention deflected from the fight, he glanced at his daughter and her startled expression to take in the subtle differences in her features from her mother's. That lapse cost him, as Zephyra stabbed him straight in his chest, narrowly missing his Daimon's mark. . . . Had she been a single millimeter up, he would have burst into dust.

As it was, it hurt like hell.

"Stop!" Medea cried as she ran at her mother and pulled her back.

Stryker cursed as he covered the wound with his hand and tensed against the pain.

Zephyra shoved Medea away, moving back toward him. He brought the sword up, ready to fight. Medea shot between them again and forced her mother back.

"Is he really my father?"

Zephyra threw the sword at him. Stryker quickly moved out of the way. He felt the heat of the blade as it skimmed his cheek to bury itself in the wall behind him.

Furious, he went at her.

Medea turned on him with an expression so purely Urian that it stunned him completely.

Urian. His most treasured child. The one son who'd meant everything to him, and in that moment he knew that Zephyra wasn't lying.

Medea was his.

That one reality slammed into him and almost drove him to his knees. He had a daughter and she was alive. . . .

Medea swallowed as she studied him. "Are you Strykerius? The son of Apollo?"

Stryker nodded.

She started for him only to have her mother grab her arm and pull her to a stop. "Don't you dare embrace him. Not after he left us for dead."

"I never!" he snarled. "You're the one who lied and told me you'd lost the baby."

"Because I didn't want to tie you to me. I wanted you to stay because you loved me. But I alone wasn't good enough for you, was I? You went belly-crawling to your father and for what? So he could curse everyone who held a drop of Apollite blood in their veins? I told you then your father didn't give a damn about you. You should have listened to me."

She'd been right, but that didn't excuse *her* lie. Her betrayal was every bit as great as his father's.

"You kicked me out."

She rolled her eyes. "You were always such an idiot."

Kessar laughed out loud. "Finally, someone who agrees with me."

Stryker glared at the demon, whose presence he'd completely forgotten about. "Why are you still here?"

"The entertainment value of this is beyond measure. I've never seen a man get his ass kicked so badly by a mere woman." He'd barely finished the words before Medea slung her arm out. Something black flew from her hand and it wasn't until it wrapped itself around Kessar's throat and dropped him to the floor that Stryker realized what it was.

Asfyxen. Reminiscent of a bolo, it was much smaller and much deadlier.

Medea stalked toward the demon with a warrior's lope. She snatched one of the golf-sized black balls and pulled the demon toward her while he choked and gasped, trying to loosen the wire that was strangling him. "Never underestimate a woman, demon. In this world, *we* rule."

Stryker felt a chill go down his spine. She was Urian . . .

Only female.

He couldn't be prouder.

Shoving Kessar back, she jerked the wire free with a graceful arc. "Next time, think before you lose your head."

Kessar's eyes glowed with his fury. "You and me, little girl, are going to dance again. One day soon."

She tucked the asfyxen back down her sleeve. "I'll bring the music."

Kessar vanished.

Medea turned back to face them with a satisfied smile.

Stryker hid his amusement. "You do know he is the most dangerous of his kind."

"He's nothing to her," Zephyra said proudly. "Medea has powers you can't conceive of. Not that it matters to you."

Before Stryker could open his mouth to respond, she head-butted him. He saw stars an instant before darkness took him under.

Zephyra drew the dagger out of her boot as she knelt on the ground beside Stryker, intending to kill him. But as she plunged the knife down, Medea caught her wrist.

"What are you doing?"

Medea's determined gaze locked with hers. "He's my father. Could I at least speak to him before you kill him?"

Zephyra snorted. "Your father's an asshole, honey. Take it from someone who used to sleep with him. You're not missing anything, and if you don't let me kill him now, you'll only do it yourself later."

"Then let me do it later. I want to have at least five minutes with him."

Zephyra snatched her hand out of Medea's grasp. "Don't be ridiculous. Artemis wants him dead. But for her, you and I wouldn't be here now. Your *father*," she spat the word, "abandoned us."

"I know. You've told me that enough that it's permanently seared into my brain. Still, he's a part of me and I'd like to have closure."

"You really need to stop watching *Oprah*. You're an abbadonrani, girl. Act like it."

In one swift, graceful move Medea twisted the dagger from her hand and had it pressed against Zephyra's throat. "You're right, Mum. Get up and step back. I'm taking custody of him."

Zephyra smiled proudly. Then she disarmed her daughter. "Just remember, sweetie, while you may command demons, you don't command this one." She tilted her head down as she felt her eyes shift from those of a Daimon to vibrant orange.

Stryker came awake to a deep throbbing ache in his head. For a moment, he couldn't remember what had happened to cause it. But as he opened his eyes to find himself chained to a wall, he had complete clarity.

His first wife had returned with a vengeance.

Furious, he pushed himself to his feet and yanked at the thick chain that held him to a steel anchor in the wall. There were bands on each wrist and ankle, and while he had freedom of movement, he couldn't go far.

But that was infinitely better than the man who was chained to the wall across from him. Tall and lithe, he looked like someone had put him through hell. Literally. Dirty, matted dark auburn hair fell just past his shoulders. Completely naked, his body was covered with bruises and bite marks. The fact that they were visible through the thick black tribal tattoos that marked his torso, arms, and thighs attested to just how deep and vicious they were. Unlike Stryker, he was held standing up, with his arms stretched high above his head. His finely boned face was covered by a thick, unkempt beard.

"What the fuck did they do to you?"

The man laughed as he twisted his hands in the chains holding his wrists and leaned his head back against the wall to stare at Stryker, who drew his breath in sharply at the sight of the man's yellow eyes ringed by a narrow band of bloodred. "They feed from me. My guess is you're their next course."

Stryker was confused. "You're neither Daimon nor Apollite. There's nothing to be gained from feeding off you."

He laughed bitterly. "Tell *them* that."

Stryker frowned as he noted the thin black band wrapped around the man's throat. It was a containment collar of some sort. "What are you?"

"I'm misery."

No doubt. The man more than looked the part. "Do you have a name?"

"Jared."

"I'm—"

"Strykerius, but you go by 'Stryker.' You hate the goddess you serve and you seek to kill her only son and claim vengeance on the former human who murdered your sister."

Stryker froze as the creature laid bare his plans. "How do you know that?"

"I know everything. I feel every heartbeat in the universe. Hear every scream for mercy and feel every tear of pain."

And he was spooking the shit out of him.

"Sorry," Jared said. "I do that to a lot of people."

"Do what?"

"Spook them."

"Can you hear my thoughts?"

Before you have them, I hear them. This time, he didn't speak. His voice was loud and clear in Stryker's mind.

"Stay out of my head."

Jared gave him a taunting grin. "Believe me, I would love to. It's a mess in there. But you're too close physically to me for me to block it." He banged his head against the stone wall. "Pain is the only way to keep your thoughts out of my head."

"Is that why they beat you?"

He gave Stryker a cold "duh" stare. "Mostly they just do it for fun."

Stryker honestly felt sorry for the creature, who had to be in absolute agony. There was something about him that seemed familiar, and yet Stryker couldn't place it. "How long have they held you here?"

Jared let out a tired breath. "Medea is coming."

The words had barely left his lips before the door opened to show her. Dressed in a red blouse and jeans, she was beautiful. No father could ask for a more perfect child.

A more loving one, perhaps, but not one more beautiful.

Her gaze went to Jared, where sympathy flashed for an instant but was quickly hidden behind a wall of stoicism. Jared's look, however, was angry and defiant.

She turned her attention to Stryker. "I'm sorry about your current position."

Jared scoffed. "Yeah, she's a basketful of sympathy. One glance at me tells you exactly how deep it runs."

"Shut up."

A leather muzzle appeared over the lower half of his face. Jared growled as he tried to jerk free of his chains or remove the muzzle, but it was useless. His muscles bulged as he fought against his restraints.

"Is that really necessary?" Stryker asked his daughter.

She ignored Jared's shouts and Stryker's question. "You should be more concerned about your own well-being."

"Why? You intend to kill me?"

"I'm sure Matera will the first chance she gets."

"Then why am I here?"

Folding her arms over her chest, she shrugged. "Curiosity. I want to understand where my powers come from and how to better channel them. I know I didn't get them from my mother. . . . She was psychic, but she didn't have the ability to summon the things I can."

Her words intrigued him. What exactly were his daughter's powers? "What kind of things?"

Me. He heard Jared's voice in his head.

Medea turned toward Jared and shot a blast into his chest. He hissed in pain as a black circle smoldered and burned his flesh. His entire body drew tense and taut.

"Stay out of this."

Stryker ground his teeth as a single red tear of pain slid down Jared's cheek. How strange that he cried blood. Stryker had never heard of such a creature. But regardless of what he was, Jared didn't deserve this.

Stryker glared at his daughter. "You know, as cold-blooded as I am, I've never been one for torture. Either kill him or free him."

She shook her head. "My mother would never allow that."

"Then leave him alone."

"You really don't care for torture, do you?"

"No, I don't. It's one thing to strike out in anger, another to cause agony for the hell of it. I'm a soldier, not a coward."

"Are you calling me a coward?"

He looked back at Jared, who was panting to cope with

the agony of his wound. His chest was still smoldering as the blast continued to burn his skin. "You should always give your opponent a fighting chance. Let the best fighter win, and if it's not you, then die with dignity."

She arched a brow at him before she turned toward the other prisoner. "Jared? Is he lying to me?" She held her hand up and the leather muzzle vanished.

"No," he said, his voice strained and weak. "He lives by a very screwed-up moral code."

The creature and his powers intrigued Stryker. "What is he? Your personal lie detector?"

She gave him a flippant smile. "Something like that."

Jared scoffed. "Why don't you tell him the truth? I'm your pet dog you keep chained up so he won't piss on your floor."

She threw her hand out again and his muzzle returned to cover his face. "Why do you push me so?"

Jared jerked at his restraints as he shouted something indecipherable.

His strength was admirable. Stryker even noted the light of respect for the creature in his daughter's eyes.

"You two lovebirds fight like this all the time?" Stryker asked her.

She snorted. "I don't fight with him at all. He's merely a tool I use."

"Use how?"

She didn't respond. "Matera says I should let her kill you for abandoning us."

"But?"

"I want to understand how it is that you could leave the woman you loved and never once look back or regret it. I find that kind of selfishness baffling."

Stryker froze as her accusation stung him deep inside. Not regret it? He'd regretted the loss of Zephyra every day of his life. But he'd been raised to believe that duty came before love.

Always.

His father had demanded he divorce Zephyra and marry a priestess to fulfill the destiny his father had planned for him and he'd done it. No, it wasn't just that. Zephyra had all but kicked him out the door when Apollo told her what the god thought of her and her lowly birth.

"The daughter of a fisherman married to the son of a god? Are you out of your minds? There are whores for you aplenty, Strykerius. I didn't save you from slaughter to see you marry this and beget worthless children from lesser genetic stock."

Stryker should have defended Zephyra. He'd known it at the time. But at only fourteen, a prime marital age in the ancient world, he'd been scared of his father's powers. Scared of disappointing the god who'd meant the world to him.

"Well?" Medea demanded. "Answer me. Why did you leave us?"

Stryker deadened his features. He was no longer a frightened youth. He was an eleven-thousand-year-old general. "I don't answer to anyone, and I damn sure don't answer to my daughter. What happened then is between me and your mother."

"Are you willing to die then?"

"I'm a warrior, Medea. I accepted death as inevitable the moment I picked up my first sword to fight. I killed my own son for betraying me. It seems somehow fitting that my daughter should kill me for perceived similar actions. My only regret will be not knowing better the child who is so similar to me that she could execute me so swiftly and without regret or hesitation."

She lifted her arm up. Stryker expected her to kill him. Instead, the chains holding him broke loose from his wrists and ankles.

"Come with me."

Stryker followed her as a new plan formed in his mind. Little did she know he was no docile pup to be commanded by any person.

When he reached the door, he turned back to see Jared hanging limply from his restraints, his muzzle firmly in place. A wave of sympathy went through him.

Don't feel sorry for me, Stryker. I didn't choose to be here.

Those ominous words echoed through his head as he followed Medea out of the room and she closed the door, blocking his sight of Jared.

"Is he a prisoner?"

"No. He was a gift."

"A gift?"

She nodded without any further explanation.

"From?" he prompted.

She opened a door and led him inside a cold, austere room. "Jared's presence isn't something we talk about. Ever."

Perhaps . . .

Medea started down the hallway. Now that Stryker was free of the room, he felt his powers soaring. There must have been some sort of dampening spell on the room. Now that it was gone . . .

Invigorated, he rushed to his daughter and grabbed her from behind.

Eyes wide, she gasped.

"I'm a leader, child. I follow no one." Tightening his hold, he flashed her out of the building and back to Kalosis.

4

Medea shrieked in anger as she tried to flash herself out of Kalosis.

Stryker tsked at her. "I've closed the channel. You can't get out until I open it again."

Her black eyes flared with fury, reminding him all the more of her mother. "Matera will kill you for this."

He released her and took a step back. "She was going to kill me anyway. What difference does it make?"

"Her plan hadn't included torturing you first. This . . . this will make her change her mind."

He shrugged nonchalantly. "You wanted to spend time with your father. Here I am." His features hardened as he met her gaze and showed her his resolve. "You should know one thing about me. I do nothing on other people's terms. I am and will always be a commander. No one tells me what to do." The last person he'd obeyed— his own father—had betrayed him. Since that night, he'd vowed that in the future his life was his own and no one else's.

Medea curled her lip. "Matera was right. You are an asshole."

Her anger amused him. "Not true. An asshole would throw you to his demons. I am your father, and honestly,

I miss having my children with me. That weakness is the only reason you're still alive after threatening me."

He reached out to cup her face in his hand. The way she tensed, he was actually surprised she didn't sink her fangs into his palm. Instead, she continued to glare her contempt at him. She reminded him so much of his daughter who'd died eleven thousand years ago. Only Tannis had never been a fighter. She'd never shared her brother Urian's love of life. Not like Medea.

Tannis had blithely allowed herself to decay on her twenty-seventh birthday while Stryker held her in his arms, begging her to take a human life so that she could live another day. She'd steadfastly refused. And her screams for mercy echoed in his ears to this day.

Medea turned her face into his hand, then kneed him hard in the groin.

Cursing, Stryker caught her hand before she could hit him again and shoved her back. His body aching, he wanted to kill her for what she'd done. But she was her mother's daughter.

And his.

Using his powers, he pinned her to the wall behind her. "You've no idea how lucky you are that I've been regretting killing my son for doing a lot less to me than you just did. But for that, you'd be dead already."

"I love you, too, Dad." The sarcastic tone was acerbic and cold.

But at least she wasn't like Urian, telling him how much she hated his guts and wanted to kill him.

"Davyn!" he shouted, calling in one of his commanders. He stood upright and refused to let his man see the fact that he was in pain. No one would ever know his weaknesses.

Davyn entered the room. "My lord?"

He jerked his chin toward Medea. "Take our guest to my quarters and lock her in until I have time to deal with her." He lifted his hand, letting her fall free from the wall before he manifested a pair of shackles on her wrists.

She sucked her breath in as she tried to break them. "I'll get you for this."

"And your little dog, too," he added snidely.

Davyn wisely ignored their comments. "Yes, sir. I'm on it."

Medea didn't speak as the handsome man stepped forward. To his credit, he didn't touch her.

"If you'll follow me." He held his hand out toward the door.

As if she had a choice? Bugger bastards!

Furious, she glared at her father before she allowed Davyn to lead her from the room. "You always obey him?" she asked as soon as they were alone.

Davyn glanced back at her over his shoulder. Tall and blond, he had short hair and a small goatee. "If I didn't want to live, I'd stop taking human souls and expire. It would be a lot less painful than crossing Stryker."

"So you fear him?"

Davyn snorted. "Everyone fears him. The man killed his own son."

"So he keeps telling me."

"Yeah, well, I was there when it happened. We were facing our enemies when Stryker walked up to him all calm and collected, hugged him close, then cut his throat and left him to die."

That description actually sent a shiver down her spine. How could any father be so cold-blooded? The fact that he was hers was even more chilling.

Davyn turned left and headed down another hallway. "Urian was one of my best friends and he loved his father more than anything. He'd served him for centuries with absolute loyalty. Believe me, he didn't deserve what he got."

What had her half brother done to cause so severe a punishment? "Why did Stryker kill him?"

"He married one of our enemies behind his back."

She stumbled at his low words, unable to believe so slight an offense would be worth taking a life over, never mind that of one's own child. "That was it?"

Davyn paused to open a door. "That was it."

Unable to believe the man's cruelty, Medea hesitated as she sensed something about her escort. "You're Anglekos." They were Daimons who only preyed on evil humans. Daimons who vowed to take only the souls that deserved to die. Pedophiles. Rapists. Murderers. The lowest of the low.

He blanched. "How do you know that?"

"I can sense the souls inside you. You took three kills recently." It was then she realized another fact about him. He wasn't like her father. He still had a heart that hadn't been destroyed.

Yet.

"I know why you pick the ones you do, but let me give you some advice. Those souls will wear you down. They will corrupt you until you become the very thing you feed on."

Davyn watched her warily. "How do you know?"

That was one question she had no intention of answering.

* * *

Stryker sat in his office, watching Zephyra pace furiously through his new sfora. That woman moved like liquid silver. Hot. Fluid. Graceful. It made every hormone in his body fire into overdrive as he remembered how she'd felt in his arms. How it felt to make love to such a hellbrand. Her scent and touch were seared into his memories.

He'd always loved it when she was angry. One time not long after they'd married, he'd pissed her off by flirting with another woman. When they'd returned home, she'd grabbed him and shoved him to the floor, then made love to him until he'd all but gone blind from the pleasure of it. He'd had rug burns on his knees for a solid week afterward.

"You ever look at another woman and I'll claw your eyes out."

Instead, she'd clawed most of the skin off his back as they made love the entire night. His heart raced at the memory of her skills and he was instantly hard as he ached for another taste of her.

Walking away from her had been the hardest thing he'd ever done. But had he stayed, his father would have mercilessly killed her. There was no way Apollo would have allowed them as mortals to defy his divine plans. He was even less forgiving than Stryker was.

And so he'd done the noble thing. The right thing. Rather than try to fight a losing battle that would have cost them both their lives, he'd left her alive, thinking that she'd be able to find a man worthy of her.

And in all these centuries since then, Stryker had thought of her every day and missed her. He'd regretted every moment they had been denied.

But he'd never regretted saving her life from his father's wrath.

Unable to stand being away from her for another instant, Stryker flashed himself to her temple in Greece. One of the last remaining temples of Artemis that was still used to worship her, it was as cold and timeless as the goddess herself.

As soon as Zephyra felt his presence, she turned on him with the full weight of her fury. Her black eyes blazing, she snatched the dagger from its sheath in her boot and advanced toward him.

"Don't," he said calmly, even though his body was on fire for a taste of her. "Kill me and my men will destroy Medea."

Zephyra's grip tightened on the dagger as she froze before him. "You would use your own daughter as a bargaining chip?"

He shrugged. "Agamemnon killed his just to sail a ship to attack his enemy. We are ancient Greeks, are we not?"

"You were a half Greek pig. I'm an Atlantean Apollite." She returned her dagger to its sheath, then straightened. Her tough stance let him know that she was more than ready to fight. "So what do you want?"

Before he stopped himself, he jerked her into his arms to kiss her.

Zephyra had thought she'd stab him the moment he touched her, but the instant his lips were on hers she remembered why she'd married him. Insufferably arrogant, dismally loyal, and unbelievably sexy, Stryker had always made her hot. No one kissed like he did. No one felt the way he did. His warrior's body was sculpted by hard, taut muscles that moved like water. Muscles that beckoned to be stroked and licked.

And with his arms around her, she could forgive him anything.

Almost.

She shoved him back. "That won't work with me any-more, asshole. I'm not the little girl you left behind."

His swirling eyes darkened. "No, you're not. She was beautiful, but you . . . you're a goddess."

Retrieving her weapon again, Zephyra held her dag-ger against his neck, just below his Adam's apple. She wanted to slice his throat and yet some foreign part of her couldn't quite complete the task. What was wrong with her? She never hesitated. "Don't come any closer."

His gorgeous features taunted her. Gods, but no man had ever been born more handsome. Black eyebrows arched over a pair of pale swirling silver eyes. And his lips . . . all too well she remembered how well they'd pleased her and for how long. He'd been an insatiable, skilled, and thoughtful lover. One who'd never left her wanting.

"Would you really cut my throat?" he asked, his voice dropping an octave.

She stood strong against her volatile emotions. "Re-lease my daughter and you'll find out."

He rubbed his neck against the sharp blade, letting it cut a fine line into his skin. Zephyra stared at the blood, her mouth watering for a taste of it. That was one of the things she hated most about what Apollo had done to them. The lure of Apollite blood was a madness that made them have to feed whenever they smelled it. It was a compulsion no one born of her race could deny.

Unable to stand it, she pulled the dagger back, grabbed Stryker by the hair, and drew him close.

Stryker sucked his breath in sharply as she clamped her fangs into his skin. Chills spread through his body while he welcomed her arms holding him close. The sensation of her breath on his neck heated his entire body.

"Gods, how I've missed you."

She bit harder, drawing the blood into her mouth until it pained him. "I hate you with every beat of my heart."

Those words hurt him more than her feeding. Yet he took pleasure from the pain. He deserved her hatred. "I wish I could go back and change the night I left."

Zephyra pulled back with a curse. "You were always a coward."

He grabbed her arm and jerked her closer. "Never a coward. A fool maybe, but I've never run from anything."

"If you really think that, you're even dumber than I thought. Now give me Medea."

He shook his head. "My daughter stays with me."

Growling, Zephyra went for his throat.

Stryker caught her and held her back. "Still so unreasonable." But worse, she was delectable and he wanted her with a madness that was all-consuming. He leaned close enough to her hair that he could inhale the delicate scent of valerian mixed with lavender. That smell slammed into him. Gods, how he wanted her. "I'll tell you what. You want me dead and I want to taste you. What say we settle this like the warriors we are?"

"How so?"

"We fight and if you win, you kill me."

She cocked her head suspiciously. "If I lose?"

"You give me two weeks to win you back. If at the end of two weeks you still loathe me, I'll let you execute me."

Zephyra froze at his offer. She eyed him suspiciously. "How do I know I can trust you?"

"I'm a man of my word. Of all people, you know my

honor means everything to me. If I haven't won you back in two weeks, then I deserve nothing better than to die by your hand."

"You know I'm not the same weak-kneed fool who couldn't cut her own meat that you married. I *will* kill you."

"I know."

"Then I accept your terms." She stepped back. "Now prepare to die."

Stryker manifested two ancient Greek swords and handed one to her.

Her eyes glowing with anger, she took it from his hand and readied herself. Stryker saluted her with his.

She charged, slicing at his throat. He caught the blade with his and forced her back. Twirling, he changed hands to catch her on an upswing that almost succeeded in disarming her. But she was quick and strong. And like him, she changed hands, and drove him back with the ferocity of her attack.

"You're incredible," he breathed, impressed with her skill and passion.

"And you're not." She scissor-kicked him back and swung the blade at his neck.

Stryker felt the burn of it as he dodged left and dropped to the floor, where he swept her feet out from under her. Cursing him, she flipped to land back on her feet before she thrust at his outstretched arm. Stryker smiled in appreciation as he continued to press his attack. She feinted left, then right. He caught her blade with his and swung it high, out of her grasp.

She shoved him back, sank her teeth into his arm, then rolled on the ground so that she could scoop the hilt back into her hand and rise with the sword held at ready.

Stryker cursed as he covered the wound on his arm with his hand. "You bit me?"

"We use what we have." She came at him swinging.

"That's such a girl move," he said, disappointed that she'd used those tactics.

"But it works. Maybe if you fought like a girl and not a stunted baboon, you'd actually win."

His arm throbbing, he caught her blow and pressed her to his left. Out of instinct, he lifted his hand to strike her face, then stopped.

He would never lay hand to the mother of his child. Never lay hand to the woman he'd once loved more than his own life.

That hesitation cost him, as she jerked the sword free and laid open the skin on his shoulder. Hissing in pain, he staggered back. Like a true warrior, she pressed her advantage, slamming her sword against his over and over again.

The ferocity of her attack did more than just damage his injured arm. It cut him deep in his heart. "You really want me dead?"

"With every part of me."

Unwilling to concede that to her, he renewed his attack, sweeping his blade under hers and then wringing it from her hand. It arced up.

Pushing her away, he yanked it from the air and then angled both blades at her throat.

"Yield."

Her eyes flared with anger. "I hate you, you bastard!"

"And I've won in all fairness. Concede the fight."

She spat on the ground at his feet. "I'll abide by my word, but you will *never* win me back. Believe me, in two weeks I will slice open your throat, drink from your blood, and then pierce your heart and laugh while your body explodes into dust."

"Beautiful imagery. You should write for Hallmark." He used his powers to dissolve the swords. "I want you to know that I fought you fairly. Equal to equal. I could have used my powers against you, but I didn't."

She gave him extremely sarcastic applause. "Should I warm the oven and bake you a batch of hero cookies?"

He let out a long breath. "I have my work cut out for me where you're concerned, don't I?"

"Not really. Hate you today. Will hate you tomorrow. What say we don't waste any time? Give me the sword and let me have your throat now. You told me once that you'd die for me. How about you keep that one promise?"

He scoffed at her rancor. "Why keep one now after I've broken so many?"

That brought color to her cheeks as her eyes glistened with her rage. "Just as I thought. A liar and a coward. You'll never submit yourself to me in two weeks, will you?"

"This isn't about promises. It's a matter of honor. I've never sacrificed my honor for anyone."

"No, only your love," she sneered. "Tell me something, Strykerius. Was it worth it?"

That was always the one question in life, wasn't it? One of the priestesses who'd tended him when he was a child had once told him the biggest regrets were those that hadn't been done. And she was right. He wished he'd never left Zephyra.

His heart softened as he remembered the past. "I had ten beautiful children. Strong. Determined. And I loved every one of them. How could I ever regret that?"

"And your wife? What of her?"

She had been beautiful, too. Docile and quiet. Never questioning. A true lady of the ancient world. "She was dutiful and faithful. I would never besmirch the honor of or insult the mother of my children."

Her eyes flared an even darker shade. He'd struck her without meaning to.

And he would never take away from her what they'd had between them. "But she was never you, Phyra. Not in face, form, or passion. You were always the light in my darkness."

Zephyra moved toward him slowly. Cautiously.

His shoulder still aching and bleeding, Stryker tensed, expecting her to attack him again. Reaching up, she sank her hand into his hair and pulled his lips down to hers so that she could give him a kiss so feral and hot it set fire to his blood. His body roared to life as he returned it with every part of himself that had missed her.

Growling, she pulled back and glared at him before she shoved him away. "That is only to remind you what you gave up. My heart is dead except for Medea. She alone keeps that last piece of me."

"Then I will release her."

She snorted contemptuously. "Your tricks won't work on me."

"No trick. You gave me your word and I'm giving you my faith. I trust you to abide by our terms and so I release her back into your custody."

Zephyra narrowed her eyes on him, not trusting him for a moment. He was smarter than any man she'd ever known. Cunning. He knew how to manipulate people to get what he wanted. He always had.

Everyone except his worthless father.

More handsome than any of the gods, her Strykerius

had once made her body burn with insatiable lust. Now she only felt anger and hatred.

It was so strange to see him now with those eerie swirling eyes. As a mortal, his eyes had been the clearest blue. She'd wanted to bear sons and daughters with those eyes to remind her of how much she loved him.

Medea's eyes had been green like hers, and while they'd been mortal she'd been grateful to the gods for that small mercy. Until the night Apollo had cursed every member of her race because a group of Atlantean soldiers had slaughtered his Greek mistress and bastard son.

It had been on Medea's sixth birthday, and there while they celebrated Zephyra had watched her daughter's eyes turn black. Unaware at that time of what had caused the curse, Zephyra had held her daughter as she had vomited food and started craving blood.

Once Zephyra understood what had been done to them—what they'd been cursed to—she'd hated everything to do with Stryker and his father, Apollo.

"Tell me. Do you still worship your father?"

Bitter disgust flared deep in his eyes. "I hate him with every breath I take."

"Then we do have one thing in common."

"We also have a daughter."

She curled her lip at his audacity. "No. *I* have a daughter. I won't let you claim Medea when you were never there for her. She is mine."

Stryker shook his head. "Children are willful. No matter how much you love them and no matter how hard you try, they will have their own way. Parents be damned."

"But that wasn't true of you, was it?"

He winced at the truth. "I was only a boy, Zephyra. My

father would have killed me and you had I denied him his plan. Or at the very least he would have cursed us."

"He cursed us anyway, didn't he?"

"He did and I watched as every child and grandchild I had decayed into nothing before my eyes. I held my daughter while she screamed for a mercy that was hours in coming. I should have killed her and saved her that, but I was young and kept hoping she'd turn Daimon like her brothers. But she refused until she finally turned to dust. One by one, every member of my family perished and suffered. I have nothing now. No one."

Zephyra wanted to insult him for his womanish maudlin. But the truth was it touched a part of her that she'd reserved only for her daughter. She actually wanted to comfort him for his losses. Her worst fear had been to watch her daughter age and die.

Luckily, Medea was stronger than that.

"Does Medea have any children?"

Zephyra steeled herself against the pain that innocent question evoked. The bitter memories that burned deep inside her. "She had a son." More beautiful than any baby ever born. Praxis had been precious and sweet. Always laughing. Always hugging.

"Where is he now?"

She forced all emotion out of her voice. "Dead."

Stryker's eyes darkened at her monosyllabic answer. "Her husband?"

"Ironic really. Against my wishes, she and her husband were members of the Cult of Pollux." Those were Apollites who believed in doing nothing to circumvent Apollo's curse. They lived peacefully among the humans, waiting to die horribly on their birthdays. Each member of the cult took a vow to harm no human or any other life-form.

"Her husband was killed by the same angry humans who feared his fangs. He tried to distract the humans so that she and their child could get to safety. They beat him down and ripped his heart out of his chest, then they captured her and tortured her for days. They tore her son out of her arms and killed him before her eyes." Indignant rage burned deep inside her. "He was only five years old. And they would have killed her, too, had I not found her in time. It's what made her the warrior she is. She hates all humans for their cruelty, just as I do. They are all animals fit for nothing but slaughter, and I enjoy wholeheartedly playing the butcher."

Stryker understood those sentiments. He'd seen their cruelty firsthand against his people and his children. It was why he had no sympathy for mankind. Why he had no mercy on them. Why should they live in peace while his own people had no future?

But her words confused him as he looked around the stone temple where the walls were decorated with peaceful scenes of women dancing with deer. This was where Artemis's human worshipers still paid tribute to her. "Yet you live here with them?"

"Only a small group. Servants to Artemis who gave us shelter when we needed it. They have watched over us for centuries, and so we let them live."

He scowled. "Why would the goddess do that?"

"Artemis has always been good to us. And in return for her shelter, I do a few odd jobs for her."

"Such as?"

"Killing you."

Humor flickered in his eyes as he drew near her. "Back to that, are we?"

"We will always come back to that."

"Fair enough." He sighed. "Come, Phyra, let's find our daughter." He held his hand out to her.

She curled her lip in repugnance. "You can keep *that*"—she sneered at his proffered hand—"to yourself."

He tsked at her. "There was a time when you would have kissed my palm with loving tenderness. But in all honesty, I have to say that I'm surprised at you. A clever enemy would kiss my hand, then stab at my back while I was distracted."

She scoffed as she shoved his hand to the side. "A coward's action. Truly. Don't insult either one of us with such a suggestion. I don't believe in petty juvenile attacks. I go after what I want, and when it's the life of an enemy I don't want there to be any mistaking my intention. If you're worth my hatred, then you're worth my letting you know that I'm coming for you."

Stryker smiled at her angry words, grateful to hear them from her. "A true warrior's code." He respected her all the more for it. "Take my hand, Zephyra."

She spat at it.

Unamused, Stryker grabbed her and pulled her close. He wanted to strangle her for her obstinacy. Most of all he wanted to kiss her.

"I'm going to gut you," she warned.

He wiped her spittle off on her shirt even while she slapped at his hand. "So long as you do it naked, you'll have no complaints from me."

"You're a faithless pig." She moved to slap him.

He captured her hand in his and met her challenging

glare. "And you are a beautiful shrew. One who should be grateful that I'm nostalgic enough to not do to her what I would to anyone else who spat on me."

Zephyra held her breath as she saw the raw fury in his eyes. He was one step away from hitting her, and though a part of her wanted him to, his restraint surprised her. In the world where they'd been born, a man had a right to beat a woman. Yet he'd refrained from striking her with his hand even in their fight.

Even in the year when they'd been married in ancient Greece, he'd never harmed her. Never lifted a finger against her while he was merciless to others. It was what she'd loved most about him.

He'd made her feel safe. Protected. If anyone had so much as glanced askance at her, Stryker gutted them.

She missed that stupid little boy whose eyes had glowed with love every time he looked at her.

The man before her was formidable. This wasn't a callow youth trying to please her. He was an accomplished warrior with eleven thousand years of survival training behind him. Of commanding an army of the damned that waged war against mankind and the immortal Dark-Hunters who protected them.

Though she'd wanted to kill Stryker many times over the centuries, she'd never been able to get to him until now. All these years, he'd been holed up in Kalosis and the only way in was an invitation from either Stryker or Apollymi.

So long as she served Artemis, Apollymi would have nothing to do with her. And asking him for it would have ruined her surprise attack.

However, his reputation among their people was legendary. The Apollites worshiped him and his band of elite Spathi warriors. Even she respected him for his battles.

But it didn't change what he'd done to her and Medea. To this day, Zephyra could see him turning around and slinking out of their cottage to be with the woman his father had wanted him to marry. However, she'd given him her word to stay her fight and be damned if she'd break it. She was better than that.

"I hate your hair black," she snarled before she took his hand.

Stryker laughed at her capitulation and barb. She wasn't giving in and she didn't hesitate to let him know it. Closing his hand around hers, he took her into Kalosis, where he ruled.

As soon as they were safely in the hell realm, she snatched her hand away as she turned around in the dark room where he held court over all the Daimons who called this place home. "Rather glum, isn't it?"

"It works for me."

She didn't comment as she returned to face him. "Where's Medea?"

"In my chambers. Come and I'll take you to her."

War paused as he materialized in the back hallway of a mansion that reminded him of an old Greek villa. The dark gray shutters were drawn tight against an unforgiving sun that spilled through the slats to highlight the breezy distance. White walls held old photos of a young boy and a very attractive woman with blond hair and laughing blue eyes.

A strange sound of foreign music drifted through the

walls, along with laughter and cars from outside. But there was no laughter inside. All was silent and still.

Closing his eyes, War searched the house with his powers until he found the one he'd been sent to kill.

Nick Gautier.

But he wasn't alone. There was a woman lying in bed with him. Both naked. Both sweaty from sex.

Centuries ago, War would have slaughtered the woman without hesitation.

No doubt he still should. . . .

Lowering his head, he walked through the walls until he came to the room where a large four-poster bed housed the two of them. They were entwined in black silk sheets. A tray holding a bottle of half-empty wine was on the nightstand, where red roses were strewn as if they'd been tossed down.

The man, Nick, lay atop the woman, nibbling at her ribs while she drew circles over his back. Shoulder-length brown hair obscured the man's face. The woman, however, was beautiful. Long black hair spilled across the pillows as she arched her back and kept her eyes tightly closed.

War paused at the sight of her naked, sculpted body. He hadn't tasted a woman in centuries. Hadn't felt a kind caress since . . .

The mere thought of that bitch threw his temper into overdrive. Wanting blood, he closed the distance between them. He grabbed Nick by his throat and threw him into the wall.

"Get out," he ordered the woman, who drew back with a scream.

"Go, Jennifer. Now!"

She didn't hesitate. Wrapping the sheet around her, she

scrambled from the large plantation bed and ran for the door.

Gautier straightened up to glare at him. He had three days' growth of beard on his face, which was marked by a double bow and arrow mark. The sign of Artemis.

War frowned at its presence. And its significance.

Not that it mattered. He'd been born to piss off the gods.

"Who the fuck are you?" Nick asked. Throwing his arms out, he manifested clothes on his body.

War laughed. "Call me Death."

"No offense, I'd rather call you pathetic." He slung his hand out.

War tsked as he saw the shurikens headed for him. "Talk about pathetic." He flashed himself across the room and grabbed Gautier by his throat as the shurikens planted themselves harmlessly into the bedposts. War lifted him up from the floor and held him against the wall.

Nick choked as he tried to break the man's hold on him. "What are you?"

"I told you. I'm Death. Now be a good little boy and die."

Nick's breathing intensified.

War slammed him back against the wall three times, trying to crush his windpipe. The plaster of the wall cracked into a spiderweb pattern. War's actions split Nick's lips and the knuckles of the hand he held him by, causing their blood to mix. He tightened his grip, waiting for the light to fade from the man's eyes as he died.

It didn't. Instead, red laced itself through Nick's dark pupils, turning them the color of blood before the red spread through the swirling silver of his irises.

Before War could move, Gautier slammed his hand against his arm, breaking his hold.

Shocked, War stumbled back.

Nick's skin darkened three shades. Panting, he looked at War. "What's happening to me? What'd you do?"

War attacked.

Gautier blocked his punch with his arm, then head-butted War hard. He staggered back as he realized the impossible.

He was about to seriously get his ass kicked.

Stryker had only taken two steps toward his room with Zephyra to release Medea when a bright light illuminated the hallway. No one should be able to breach the sanctity of this hall without his invitation. . . .

Frowning, he turned to find War, who looked extremely pissed as the spirit appeared before them.

"Is something wrong?" he asked War.

"Is something wrong?" he repeated. "Surely you're not that stupid, are you?"

"Apparently I am, because unless Acheron and Nick are dead, I can think of no reason for your presence here."

War walked slowly toward him, nostrils flaring. "Dead? You fool, are you really so stupid?"

Stryker narrowed his eyes as his anger ignited. "At least I'm not the one wasting time with repetitive insults. Either explain yourself or get out."

"Fine. Let me try this in a manner that even an imbecile can comprehend. When you summoned me, you forgot to tell me a couple of extremely important facts. Acheron isn't just a god. He's Chthonian, protected by another Chthonian and a Charonte army."

Folding his arms over his chest, Stryker let out an agitated breath. Why would that matter to something like War? It was why Stryker had gone to him to begin with. If Acheron wasn't so damned hard to kill, he'd have done it himself centuries ago. "You were created to kill the Chthonians. That shouldn't be a problem for you."

"You should have warned me."

As if that would matter? "Trivial details. I thought you could handle it."

"I can kill him. It will just take more time."

"And?"

"You neglected to tell me about Nick Gautier."

"What about him? He's a Dark-Hunter. A worthless human who sold his soul to Artemis to serve in her army. Surely the great War isn't afraid of the likes of him."

War scoffed. "Dark-Hunter, my ass. Gautier is a Malachai, you stupid son of a bitch."

Stryker bristled under the insult. "A what?"

"Malachai," Zephyra repeated, her tone reverent. "Are you sure?"

War turned his dark gaze on her and nodded. "In all the universe a Malachai is the only thing that can kill *me*."

Stryker made a sound of disgust deep in his throat. "You've got to be kidding me. I thought you were the most powerful of beings. Even the gods fear you."

"We all have predators," War growled. "The entire universe exists in a system of checks and balances. I just met my zero balance."

Stryker cursed. "Are you honestly telling me that the most powerful creature on this planet is a pathetic Cajun guttersnipe who offed himself because one of my men killed his mommy?"

His sarcasm was equally matched by War's. "Unless

you happen to have a Sephiroth just lying around here someplace sunning himself, yeah."

"What the hell's a Sephiroth?"

Zephyra laughed as she came up behind him to place her hand on his shoulder. "Stryker, you poor baby, you have been living in this hole for far too long."

"What do you mean?"

"What I mean, dear man, is if you want Gautier dead, then come talk to Mama. It seems your negotiating power over me just ended. Oooo, baby, this is going to get good now."

5

Nick lay on the floor, trembling and in a cold sweat as he tried to focus. It was no use. Everything swam before his eyes. His body felt like it was black asphalt at three o'clock on a late August afternoon in the French Quarter.

What was happening to him?

"Shh . . ." A tender hand brushed his sweaty hair back from his face.

Looking up, he found Menyara there. Tiny and beautiful, her Creole skin was the perfect café au lait color. Her green eyes watched him with concern. "It's all right, *mon petit ang*," she said in a deep voice that had always reminded him of Eartha Kitt's.

"What are you doing here?" he asked, his voice thick and scratchy.

"I felt your powers unlock and came as soon as I could."

He frowned in confusion. "What?"

Menyara shook her head as she gathered him into her arms and held him like she'd done when he'd been a scared little boy afraid of the neighborhood bullies. "My poor Ambrosius. You've been through so much already. Now there's something I'd hoped I'd never have to tell you . . ."

* * *

"I don't understand." Stryker shook his head, trying to make sense of what Zephyra and War had told him. "How can Nick Gautier be this supremely powerful creature? He's a worthless gnat."

War took a deep breath before he spoke in an impatient tone. "When the Primus Bellum was fought, the darkest power—the Mavromino—created the Malachai to bring down the Sephirii. Guardians and consorts of the first order of gods, the Sephirii were soldiers who enforced the original laws of the universe. When the Mavromino turned against the Source and thought to end all creation, the Sephirii were unleashed to kill him. Most of them flew into traps. But enough Sephirii survived to declare war on the Malachai, and they would have destroyed them had they not been betrayed by one of their own."

"There's always one, isn't there?" Stryker asked rhetorically. In every house, there was always one malcontent jealous prick out to destroy everyone else just for spite. The entire history of the earth was written in the blood of those betrayed by the very people they'd foolishly trusted.

He looked at War. "So how many Malachai are there now?"

"There should be none. When the truce finally came, both sides agreed to execute their own soldiers. All of the Malachai and Sephirii were then put down."

"Except for one," Zephyra said, stepping forward. "The Betrayer who'd helped Mavromino was to live on to suffer and to see what he'd done. His powers were bound and he was to be forever shamed and enslaved."

War nodded. "Checks and balances. Apparently when

they allowed the one Sephiroth to live, the primal order allowed a Malachai to escape as well. And today, I met the last of their breed."

Fucking figured. Stryker should have known it wouldn't be so easy to kill off the two men who aggravated him most. But then, on the bright side, it made him feel better that War was having as hard a time bringing them down as he had. At least it wasn't a question of his lacking skill.

The universe just basically sucked and blew.

"Where is this Sephiroth?" Stryker asked Zephyra.

"In Greece. In the last functioning temple of Artemis."

Stryker snorted as realization stung him. He knew instantly who the Sephiroth was and why he'd been so abused. "Jared."

She inclined her head in a sarcastic gesture. "Jared."

Which begged one extremely important question. "And just how did you happen to come into possession of him?"

She refused to answer. "All that matters is that I own him and he will do whatever I say without question."

Yeah, right. She seemed a little too optimistic for his mental health. "He didn't seem so compliant when I met him."

"Perhaps not, but he will do as we want. Trust me."

Stryker was less than convinced. Still, he noted her peculiar choice of pronoun. "We?"

"You want Gautier dead. I want you dead. Personally I don't care if this Gautier lives or dies, but if he is a threat to my Sephiroth, I want him terminated, too. Best to catch him before he learns to use his powers."

Stryker smiled. "A woman after my own heart."

For once her look was seductive and it made him hard just to see it. "You're absolutely right about that. Nothing would please me more than ripping that organ out of you and feasting on it."

War arched a brow at her open hostility. "Mmm, a woman I can relate to. Please tell me you're unattached."

"She's my wife," Stryker snapped.

"Was," Zephyra corrected quickly. "You seem to have forgotten an important verb tense." She looked up at War. "He divorced me."

War lifted her hand to his lips and placed a tender kiss on her knuckles. "Pleased to meet you, my lady. What name do I apply to one so fair and vicious?"

"Zephyra."

"Like the wind. Soft and gentle."

She gave him a sly smile. "And capable of utter destruction when riled."

He sucked in his breath in sharp appreciation. "I commend you, Stryker. You have excellent taste in women. Too bad you weren't man enough to hold on to her."

Against his better sense, Stryker shoved him away from her. "Zephyra is mine. You'd do well to remember that."

War looked less than intimidated as he turned to address Zephyra. "After you kill him, give me a call and I'll show you what a real man is capable of. In the meantime, if we're going to kill the Malachai, and I definitely am in for that, we need to get started. Every second we delay, his powers grow."

"Then back to Greece to release my Sephiroth." She looked at Stryker. "Return me to my temple."

Jared sighed as his bloodied and raw wrists throbbed in utter agony. How he wished he could die. But this was his fate for all eternity.

It's what you deserve, traitor.

Perhaps it was. But at the time he'd done it, he'd made the only decision he'd been able to.

Leverage. Life was all about leverage and the balance of power had never been with him. All creatures were victims of their births and families. With all the power he commanded, not even he had been immune. Disgusted by that, he tensed as he felt a foreign ripple through the air around him. He knew that sensation . . .

An instant later, clarity came as the door opened to admit his bane Zephyra and two men. One was the Daimon demigod again. The other . . .

Polemus. War.

Bravo that. They needed the spirit of war awakened like he needed a hot poker shoved up his ass. *Keep that idea to yourself, boy. You don't need to give Zephyra any more suggestions on how to make you suffer.*

True enough. She lived to make him beg her for mercy.

Jared met Zephyra's hostile glare and knew instantly why they were there. "It never fails to amaze me what people will do to have their way. I won't kill him for you. You know better than to ask that of me."

Zephyra tsked as she pulled a dagger out of her boot. "Why do we have to play this game, Jared? You know my thoughts. I know you're already in my head reading them. Now be a good boy and do what I say."

He was so tired of following orders. Of having no will of his own. It was time he stopped serving and took control of his miserable life. "I don't care what you do to me."

She ran a deceptively tender hand down his grizzled cheek, making him ache for a real caress. One that wouldn't turn vicious on him. "I know you don't. But we both know you don't feel that way about your little friend. Him you would die to protect."

He tensed at the mention of his demon companion. "Nim's not here. He left."

"Of course he did." Her tone was mocking.

"Nim?" Stryker asked.

Zephyra glanced at him over her shoulder. "An inutile slug demon Jared adopted."

"I did no such thing." Nim had adopted him, and he'd been trying ever since to get rid of him. The demon was a liability he didn't want or need to carry. Honestly, he was sick of Nim hanging around and complicating his worthless life even more. All the demon did was get him into trouble. And worse, Nim got him tortured.

She dragged the dagger's tip down the divine markings on his left arm. At one time he'd worn them with pride. Now they only reminded him of his humiliation. They marked him as a slave. The last of his kind.

"Is he here?" she asked.

He hissed as she laid open the length of the tattoo. His blood beaded under the line, trickling down his flesh. Stryker turned away as if the sight sickened him.

Zephyra wasn't so kind. "Looks like I guessed wrongly."

Jared met her gaze without flinching as his anger snapped. "I told you he left."

"Really?" She trailed the dagger over his collar bone. "I'll bet he's hiding on your back."

Jared gasped as she plunged the dagger deep into his shoulder, through the tattoo that was there. Pain seared him.

"Zephyra, stop!" Stryker snapped. "There's no need for this."

"Trust me, it's the only way to get his compliance. But don't feel bad for him, Stryker. He slit the throats of his own people, didn't you, Jared? Those he didn't kill, he led to the slaughter."

Pain and fury mixed inside him. "Shut up!"

"Why? It's the truth. You've never cared about anyone but yourself. So give us the demon and let me end your suffering where he's concerned."

Against his will, he jerked as she trailed the knife over the tattoo that wasn't branded into his skin. It merged with the others, but it wasn't his . . .

"Aha, found the little bugger, did I?" She clenched the dagger tight, pressing it into his skin where Nim was resting.

Jared ground his teeth. If she stabbed Nim while he slept on his body, it would kill the demon.

"Shall I liberate you from your annoyance?" She pressed the tip in, drawing blood.

Jared tried to pull away, but he couldn't. The chains held him tight and gave him no choice. "Stop!" he growled. "Don't hurt him."

"Kill Gautier and I'll let your demon live."

"And if I can't kill him?"

She jerked his hair hard, slamming his head back into the wall. "You don't want to find out. Trust me." Snapping her fingers, she used her powers to open his shackles.

Jared fell back against the wall and slid to the floor, his entire body aching. He couldn't remember the last time he'd been freed. From the sensation of his stiff muscles, it felt like centuries and it probably was.

Zephyra stood over him, looking down. "Clean yourself, dog. Bring me the head of the Malachai and I'll give you two days to wench and drink before I call you back. Betray me and you will think these past centuries were paradise."

Jared laughed bitterly. "Your mercy is beyond reproach, my lady."

"Sarcasm . . . such sweet music to me." She kicked him hard in the ribs. "Now go and carry out your orders."

Stryker met Jared's searing gaze. Hatred burned bright, but something told him the hatred was directed more inwardly than out. The poor creature. It would be kindest to kill him.

"Are you sure he can do this?" Stryker asked Zephyra as she sheathed the dagger back into her boot.

She led him out of the room and into the hallway. War pulled up their rear. "Don't let his sniveling fool you. He was created to kill."

"So was the Malachai."

"Yes, but the Malachai is half human and new to his powers. Jared should make easy work of him." Pausing in the hallway, she looked past Stryker to War. "Keep an eye on Jared. Make sure his little demon doesn't go free. That stupid slug is the only way I have to really control him."

Stryker watched as War inclined his head to her before he returned to the room where Jared had been left. "How do you know he's not going to rebel and kill War?"

She snorted. "So what if he does? Are you two friends?"

"Hardly, but if War is gone, Jared could come after you."

"So long as he wears that collar, Jared is my property. He can't kill me anymore than I can kill him. I can make him bleed and suffer, but the collar won't allow him to attack his owner in any manner. In fact, if I'm under attack, he has no choice except to defend me whether he wants to or not."

That had to be one of the cruelest things he'd ever heard of. He couldn't imagine a worse punishment than being forced to protect someone he hated. Someone who tortured him.

And it made him take a hard look at the woman in front of him. She was so familiar and at the same time so foreign. What had happened to the woman he'd married? "I remember this beautiful girl who wouldn't even allow me to have a cat in the house because she didn't want it to hurt the mice. A woman who made me carry any insect outside to set it free rather than kill it."

Her black eyes met his, and there inside he saw a hatred so potent, it stole his breath. "And I remember the sounds of my grandson screaming for mercy as he was viciously killed for being different and I was powerless to help him. I'm not that little girl you left behind, Stryker. I'm a vengeful woman at war with the world that did her wrong."

"Then you understand me. I didn't ask for this existence and I want the blood of everyone who took part in damning me to it. My father, Apollymi, Acheron, and Nick Gautier."

"What of Artemis?"

"I have no love for her. But there's no real hatred for her either. So long as she stays out of my way, I don't care what happens where she's concerned."

Zephyra looked up at him. His black hair contrasted sharply with his swirling silver eyes. He looked nothing like the boy who'd stolen her heart. The boy she'd wanted to grow old with. In those days, she'd expected to spend forty years with him, if they were lucky, before death separated them.

Eleven thousand years later, here they stood. Toe to toe. Enemy to enemy.

It was ironic really. At fourteen, she would have sold her soul to spend eternity with him. Now she only wanted to see him die miserably.

How the world changed . . .

"Now, are you going to fulfill your word and release Medea?"

Stryker wondered at her sudden change of subject. "Absolutely." He held his hand out toward her again, expecting her to slap it away.

She narrowed her gaze on it as if the thought was in her mind. Just when he was sure she'd knock it away, she reached out and took it gently in hers.

Stryker didn't know why that made his heartbeat increase, but it did. Her skin was so soft. Her hand dainty and small. He could crush every bone in it and yet this one hand had once held enough power to bring him to his knees. "I'd forgotten how small you are."

She'd always seemed larger than life. But with her near, he remembered just how good she'd felt snuggled up to him at night.

"I'm big enough to kick your ass."

He lifted her hand so that he could place a kiss on her palm. "I look forward to it."

Her eyes darkened. "Are you delaying me on purpose?"

"No." He placed her hand in the crook of his elbow and flashed them back to the receiving room in Kalosis. "I will keep my promises to you. Always."

"I might buy that had you not already broken the most

significant promise a man can make to a woman. At the first test of your father, you fled. Call me jaded."

"There's no need to be jaded, my love." He led her to his chambers where an extremely irate Medea was waiting for them.

As soon as he opened the door, Zephyra left him to make sure no harm had come to their daughter.

Medea glared hatefully at him. "You're right, Mum. He is a prick."

Zephyra laughed. "Eleven thousand years and you still don't listen to my wisdom."

"You're only fourteen years older than I. It doesn't really give you much of an advantage now, does it?" Medea looked past her mother. "Why's he still breathing?"

"We've made a warrior's pact, he and I. For the next two weeks we have to suffer him and then I can cut his throat."

Stryker let out a deep breath at their rancorous reunion. "You two do realize that I'm still present?"

Zephyra gave him a haughty stare. "We know. We just don't care."

"Oh. Well, as long as we're straight on that . . ." He rolled his eyes. "Why don't I have one of my servants show Medea to her own set of rooms?"

"What about me?" Zephyra asked.

A slow smile spread across his face. "You'll stay here. With me."

Zephyra folded her arms over her chest. Stryker was being just a hair overconfident where she was concerned. While she had to admit he was a handsome man, it didn't change the fact that she hated him. "You're awfully sure of your charms."

"I've had time to hone them."

Medea curled her lip. "Gag reflex on the daughter, parents. Please respect the fact that vomiting up blood is disgusting and unless you two want to be hosed down with it, I'll take those rooms now, please."

"Davyn!" Stryker called.

His Daimon appeared instantly. "My lord?"

"Show my daughter to Satara's rooms. Make sure she has everything she needs."

Davyn inclined his head to him. "Is she free to come and go?"

He looked to Zephyra. "Are you going to send her to kill me?"

"No. I gave you my word, and unlike you, I stand by it. You're safe, coward. I would never send a little girl in to do her mother's work."

He didn't respond to her insults. "Give her access to the boltholes."

"Yes, my lord."

"Medea?" Stryker waited until she'd looked back at him before he spoke again. "Don't worry. Satara's rooms are far enough away that you won't be subjected to the sounds of our wild monkey sex."

Zephyra gaped.

Medea looked much less than pleased. "You were right, Mum. I should have allowed you to cut his throat." She faced Davyn. "Get me out of here as quickly as possible."

Davyn's eyes danced with humor as he shut the doors behind them.

As soon as they were alone, Zephyra shook her head. "That was a cruel thing to do to her."

"I couldn't resist. Besides, you should have taught her to never let anyone know her weaknesses."

"We're her parents. We're supposed to love her and not slash at her weaknesses."

"And yet here we sit plotting the death of *my* father and aunt."

"*You're* plotting their deaths. I'm only waiting to kill you."

"True, but the point is . . . family today, enemies tomorrow."

"And that has always been your problem, Stryker. I believe in family forever. As they say, blood is thicker than water, and in the case of Apollites, it's even more true."

If only he could believe in that. But it had never been proven true in his experience. All family did was provide an inroad for enemies. "When has my family ever stood by me?"

"I think the real question is when have you ever stood by them? I would have been there for you. Forever. But you never gave me the chance."

In spite of the hurt and betrayals of his past, he was piqued by her words. He wanted so much to have someone he could trust beside him. Just once. Only Urian had been there for him, and it was why he'd been so angry when he'd learned that Urian had kept secrets from him. That his son had gone behind his back . . .

Did he dare trust Zephyra?

"I'm giving you that chance now."

Zephyra stepped away. "It's too late. Too many *centuries* have passed. There was a time when I lived only to hear a kind word from your lips. But that ship sank under an assault of bitterness that no amount of charm or guile will recover."

Stryker dipped his head down to where their lips were

almost touching. "The fierce rhythm of your heart tells me that you're lying. You still want me."

"Don't mistake my wrath for lust. It's your blood I want, not your body."

He didn't believe that. Not for a minute. "Tell me honestly that you're not thinking even a little bit about what I look like naked. That you're not remembering the way we made love to each other."

She reached down to carefully cup his erection in her hand. "You're a man, Stryker. I know that's what you think about." She clenched her hand tightly, making him gasp and double over as pain ripped through his groin. She sank her nails into his scrotum. "But I'm a woman, and as the great poet so cleverly wrote, hell hath no fury as a woman scorned. Consider me your personal hell." With one hard jerk, she stepped away.

Stryker wanted to blast her, but his body hurt so much that all he could do was glare at her as she turned and left him alone in his room.

"This isn't over, love," he growled painfully. He was going to reclaim her and make her beg for his forgiveness. No matter what it took, he would have her.

Then he would kill her himself.

6

"How's he doing?"

Tory looked up from where Ash was lying on the bed, resting, to meet Savitar's lavender gaze. Strange, she could have sworn his eyes were green earlier. . . .

He was out of his wet suit and dressed in a pair of white linen pants with an open beach shirt that showed off his sculpted torso. His long brown hair was swept back from his handsome face.

"War tore him up pretty badly, but—"

"I'll live," Ash said, rolling over to look at them. He propped himself up on the pillows and then brushed his black hair back with his fingers. "Believe me, I've had worse beatings. Just not recently."

Tory gave him a chiding stare. "I don't know, you did get run over by a car not that long ago. . . ."

Ash snorted as he laced his fingers with hers. "In my defense, I was preoccupied by a certain"—he gave her a meaningful glare—"human having a near-death experience. That doesn't count."

Savitar ignored his jibe. "Well, the good news is we routed him. The bad news is—"

Ash finished the sentence for him. "He'll be back."

Savitar nodded.

Tory swallowed as fear seized her. "Should we start making preparations here?"

Savitar looked completely offended by her question. "Punk-ass won't come to *my* island. He knows better. You don't tap on the Devil's shoulder unless you're willing to dance to his tune."

Ash cleared his throat and gave Savitar a droll stare. "Actually, Tory, there's a reason the island moves all the time. Sav is a bit paranoid, so the island is heavily shielded from paranormal types. You can't get to Neratiti without a special invitation from our host, which is why Alexion brought you here. We knew it would be the only place War couldn't get to. Me and mine have a standing invitation that doesn't extend to the rest of the known universe."

Savitar bristled. "And even if he could find it, he wouldn't dare bring his loserness here. I'd kick it back to the Stone Age," Savitar said with humor dancing in his eyes. "And don't knock my paranoia, grom. It's what saved your hide, now isn't it?"

"Yes, and thank you."

Savitar inclined his head to him. "You're welcome. But don't get into trouble again. Your mother has turned nagging for pain into an Olympic sport and she's been making my head ache over you. I'd tell you to go let her sit on you until you hatch, but I don't want the world to end. Suck ass though it is. However, if the nagging persists, I might change my mind and take you to her myself."

Ash laughed. "I'll keep that in mind. So any leads on who woke up our new friend and told him to come play with me?"

Tory gave them a sullen look. "My money's on Artemis."

Savitar made a buzzer sound. "I'll take that bet, because you lose. Word from Artipou herself. She didn't do this, which is more good news for you two since it seems she's acclimating to the idea of not being Ash's girl anymore. Not happy about it, but she's not issuing death warrants on you two, either. Small victory, true. But better than none at all."

Tory frowned. "Then who—"

"Our boy Stryker unleashed him."

Ash cursed. "Figures. Where is War now?"

"Off the grid, which means he's probably back in Kalosis to report his spectacular failure to Stryker."

Ash's eyes narrowed with concern. "Is my mother safe?"

"Judging by the noise in my head over you, that's a definite affirmative. But don't worry. I had the Charonte rally around her. She's not happy about it, but for once she's being reasonable. Her main concern is your safety. And she said for you to do what you have to to keep yourself healthy. Her life be damned."

Ash snorted. "I'm not going to kill Stryker and then bury my mother. Why the hell did she tie their life forces together?"

Savitar shrugged. "She lacks our ability to see the future. Her powers are destruction, not prophecy. I'm sure had she known he would one day threaten you, she'd have killed him herself. And now you know why I take pity on no one. All compassion does is come back and bite the fat of your arse."

Ash pulled the covers back from the bed and started to rise.

Tory caught him and pushed him back toward the pillows. "You should rest."

He kissed her hand. "I can't. There's a lunatic on the loose and probably hiding in my mother's home." Closing his eyes, he manifested clothes on his body. "We have to prepare. Find a place where we can face War without a high bystander body count."

Savitar rolled his eyes. "Little brother, I don't mean to be a downer, but we're talking about War here. There's no way to mitigate damages. He won't let us. I was there with twenty-five Chthonians to fight him and he spanked our hides like we were Lemurian slave women. Two of us had our hearts ripped out and shoved down our throats while he laughed, then he licked the blood clean from his fingers and came at the rest of us. *I* barely survived and it took me two decades of human time to recuperate from those wounds. Don't think I fear the bastard, I don't. I just want you to fully understand what it is we're dealing with."

Ash frowned at his words, but his resolve was set. They had to defeat War one way or another. "How did you trap him last time?"

"Ishtar, Eirene, Bia, and the Gigantes came to our rescue. Out of that list, the goddess Eirene is the only one left alive. And we're down to only eight surviving Chthonians. That number includes you."

Even so, Ash refused to believe it was hopeless. "There's always an off-switch. We have to find it."

"We will try. In the meantime, you should know that your boy Urian got word from the other side. Stryker is pulling in Daimons from all over the world, amassing numbers that would make Cecil B. DeMille proud."

"Why?"

"Stryker's planning to rain hell on the humans come Christmas day. Of course Urian said you could probably offset that by offering yourself up as a sacrifice. Stryker might be willing to call the attack off if you surrender yourself to War and die a painful death."

Tory's gaze narrowed angrily on Ash. "Don't you dare. I swear, Acheron Parthenopaeus, if you even think about it, I'll beat you down until you beg me for mercy."

Ash tightened his grip on her hand. "Don't worry. Even if I turned myself in, he'd still go after the humans. It's his nature, and I'm not stupid enough to think he'd ever show mercy. What is it you're always saying? It's not the hand you're dealt that matters. It's how you play the cards you hold." He rose from the bed. "Sav, I need you to take up residence with my mother."

He choked at the suggestion. "Are you insane? That woman hates my guts. No, she doesn't hate me. Hatred for her would be a step up toward possibly liking me someday."

Which was something Ash had never understood, but it didn't change the fact that he couldn't leave her alone with Stryker and War. "Take Alexion and Danger with you and stand by her side to make sure they don't hurt her." She'd tolerate them around her a lot easier than she would Savitar. "Otherwise I'll have to do it, and since the point of this is to avoid the apocalypse, my presence in her home would be extremely counterproductive."

If Ash were to ever step foot in Kalosis, his mother would destroy the earth even faster than Stryker and War. "You're the only one I trust to keep her safe from Stryker, War, and Kessar. Even though my mother and I don't always get along and we're on opposite sides of this war, she is my mother and I don't want her hurt."

Savitar looked like he'd rather be gutted. Not that Ash

blamed him. His mother could be extremely . . . temperamental and difficult to deal with . . . and she loved *him*. Savitar she barely tolerated.

"All right," Savitar relented. "I'll go. But you owe me. Major owe, so if I ever need something, no matter what it is, I own you."

Ash snorted. "She's not that bad."

"How you figure that, grom? Your mother's the Destroyer. It's a title she not only earned, but one she relishes. And you're sending me in with only a few Charonte as backup. What did I ever do to you?"

He laughed. "Man up, Sav. You're whining like a little girl."

"If your mother has her way, she'll turn me into one, and I look like shit in pink. Thanks, kid."

Ash shook his head as he watched the Chthonian vanish. As Ash started across the room, he found Tory firmly planted in his way. She stood like a military commander ready for war—which boded bad for him. "What?"

"Where are you going?"

"To see Nick."

She scoffed. "Do you really think that will be productive? The man hates your guts more than Stryker does. You'll be lucky if he doesn't pull your spine out through your nostrils."

"Nice to have Miss Merry Sunshine back again. Any other Eeyore outlooks you'd like to share?"

"Just one. If you leave here, War can find you again. What are you going to do if that happens?"

"Leave bloodstains on his best shirt."

Her eyes darkened. "You're not funny, Ash. You said it yourself. This island is the only place safe from War."

"And I'm not a wimp, baby. I'm a god. I'm not going to

hide out here because I'm afraid of getting hurt. I have to warn Nick that he has an enemy after him. I owe him that much."

She folded her arms over her chest and gave him a determined glare. "Then I'm coming with you."

Like hell. He'd tie her down before he allowed that. While she had some of his mother's powers, she didn't have them all, and unlike him she wasn't used to battling for her life. "I'll take Xirena with me. But you will stay here and not argue with me."

She growled at him. "You stubborn man."

He gave her a charming smile he hoped would melt some of her ire. "I learned from the best."

"Yeah, I know. I've met your mother."

Leaving the demon xirena outside to keep her safe should a fight break out, Ash paused inside Nick's house as he felt for the Cajun's presence. There was no heartbeat to be heard.

But there was an undeniable power here. Ancient and cold, it set off every warning in Ash's body.

Ready to battle, he flashed himself upstairs to Nick's bedroom, where it felt the strongest. As soon as Ash manifested, a tall, lean redheaded man turned toward him. Eerie yellow eyes were filled with torment and power, and set in a face so delicately chiseled it bordered on pretty. His shoulder-length red hair framed his face perfectly. Dressed in black Goth, like Ash, the man was someone he hadn't seen in centuries.

"Jared?"

The Sephiroth inclined his head respectfully. "Long time no see, Atlantean."

"Why are you here?"

Jared sighed before he set one of Nick's Voodoo dolls back on his dresser. "Probably the same thing that you're doing here. Looking for Nick Gautier. I suppose my only question to you is if he's your friend or foe."

"Does it matter?"

His face steeled. "Not really. I just want to know how angry you're going to be when I kill him."

"Very."

Jared sighed. "Damn shame, that. But it changes nothing." He walked around the room, absorbing Nick's essence so that he could track him.

Ash used his powers to shield Nick so that Jared couldn't get an accurate reading. "Why are you so interested in Nick?"

Jared flicked at the black leather containment collar around his throat with his thumb. "Not my place to question why. I'm merely here to obey like the mindless supplicant they've forced me to become."

Ash flinched at the reminder of slavery. A common bond they shared and one he wouldn't wish on his worst enemy. He would give anything to free the being before him, but Jared's kind of slavery was never-ending.

"Can I ask a favor of you?" Jared said in a tone that told him how much he hated to ask for anything.

Even so, Ash was cautious. Favors seldom turned out well for anyone. "Depends on the favor."

Jared gave him a tight smile as he pulled his black leather coat off and exposed the dragon tattoo on his forearm. "Nim. Human form. Now."

Ash watched as the dark shadow twisted up from Jared's arm to manifest into a young man before him. No taller than five-eight, the demon was dressed like a steampunk, complete with large goggles that rested on his mop of black dreadlocks and a small goatee. His fingernails were painted as black as his eyes and clothes. The only color on his body came from a small pink stuffed bunny that he had chained to his hip.

Nim's black eyes fastened on Acheron and widened. He darted behind Jared's back to hide. "Friend or foe?"

Jared let out an aggravated breath. "Friend. And a good one at that."

Nim peeked around like an unsure child. "He reeks of Charonte demon."

"I know and I want you to go with him."

"No!" the small demon barked. "Nim stays with Jared. Always."

Jared cursed. "Could you help a brother out, Acheron? I need you to take custody of Nim and keep him safe for me."

"No!" Nim snapped, even more determined than before.

Jared growled in response. "Damn it, Nimrod. For once in your life, do what I ask and go with Acheron."

The demon clutched the small pink bunny to his chest and frantically shook his head no. "Nim stays with Jared. Those are the laws."

A muscle twitched in Jared's jaw. "I should have never saved your life."

Ash felt his pain and understood what Jared was doing. Since Ash had a demon of his own, he knew what a weakness they could be. And what a responsibility. Even though the demon appeared to be around the human age of twenty, his actions said he was even younger than Ash's Simi. "Nothing worse than adolescent demons."

"You have no idea."

"Actually, I do." Ash approached Nim slowly, like he would a small toddler. "Nim, you can come with me and I promise nothing will hurt you."

Nim gave him a mean, sullen stare. "I don't know you."

Jared tried to push him toward Ash. "He's a good man."

Nim bared his fangs at both of them in a vicious hiss. "He's been with the Charonte and they hate me. They hurt Nim and make him bleed. I want to stay with Jared." Nim immediately returned to sleep as a small dragon tattoo on Jared's neck.

Jared let out a long, aggravated breath. "Is there any way to get him off me like this?"

"No."

"Figures." His eyes shimmered with gold flecks that flipped until his eyes were a solid golden amber. "One day my master is going to kill him if I don't find him a new home."

"I think you need to tell him that."

"He says he'd rather be dead than leave me. According to him, we're family. I guess that makes me the psycho uncle no one wants to talk to. And he's the kid with only imaginary friends for company. Normal Rockwell, here we come."

Ash smiled at his twist on the painter's name. Honestly, Ash felt for Jared, but there was nothing either of them could do. "Then it's his decision."

Jared gave him a harsh stare. "Would you feel that way if it were Simi?"

"You know the answer."

"And you know why I have to get him off me."

True enough. There was nothing worse than having an exposed weakness that those around you preyed on. One they used to control your actions and subjugate you.

Ash knew that better than anyone. And he felt sorry for Jared's situation.

Sighing, Ash changed the subject to something he could perhaps control. "So why were you ordered to kill Nick?"

Jared shrugged his coat back on. "He's the last of the Malachai bloodline."

Ash laughed at the absurdity of that idea. "Nick Gautier is a Malachai? C'mon, Jared. Lay off the crack."

"I'm not joking. He's the last of their breed."

Stunned, Ash actually gaped. Nick Gautier? And yet as ludicrous as that seemed, it strangely made sense. Nick's unfounded powers. Ash's inability to control him . . .

Shit.

How could he have missed it?

You weren't looking for it. Who would have? They were an extinct breed.

"Don't feel so bad," Jared said softly. "His powers were bound and hidden much the way yours were when you were human. It wasn't until War attacked him that they kicked in."

"Does Nick know what he is?"

Jared shook his head. "My job is to kill him before he learns it."

"I can't let you do that."

"You have no choice and neither do I." He vanished before Ash could even draw breath to speak.

"Jared!"

The Sephiroth ignored him completely. "Damn it!" If Jared found Nick before he did, the boy was deader than five o'clock roadkill.

* * *

"You're looking entirely too smug with yourself."

Stryker glanced over his shoulder to see Zephyra eyeing him. "I have you here. Why shouldn't I be pleased?"

"I can think of a million reasons, starting with the fact that I want to kill you more than I want to breathe. As for the others, would you prefer them in order of importance or alphabetically?"

He laughed. "Tell me honestly . . . didn't you ever miss me?"

"No."

Those words struck him hard. "Not once?"

She folded her arms over her chest. "You know what I remember about you, Stryker? It was the last words you said to me. 'There's no reason for me to stay.' Then you walked out of my house and never looked back. No reason for you to stay, you said. None." She narrowed her eyes dangerously at him. "You severed my heart with those few words. I'd have rather you hit me."

Stryker paused as he saw that night so clearly in his mind. She'd stood before him with tears in her eyes. Not a single one had fallen. A tribute to her strength. He'd wanted nothing more than to pull her into his arms and tell her that he didn't give a damn about his father. That she was the only one he loved and that he'd die to protect her.

Had he stayed with her, his father would have killed her, no doubt. And if Apollo hadn't, he would have sent Artemis in to do the honor as Zephyra birthed his child and then he would have lost them both. Apollo was grotesquely vindictive that way. Stryker had tried to explain it to Zephyra, but she'd refused to listen.

"Then I will die loving you." That had been her answer to his arguments.

It'd been a sacrifice he hadn't been willing to make. He thought it best that she hate him and live rather than she love him and die.

If only he'd known then what was waiting for them in the future.

"I didn't mean those words."

She scoffed. "Of course not. You were thoughtless, et cetera, et cetera. I really don't care anymore."

"If you really didn't care, you wouldn't remember them."

"Don't flatter yourself. I wrote you off the same way you wrote me off. Unlike Medea, I don't need closure. I just need you dead."

"So we're back to that."

"We will always come back to that."

Stryker would curse and rail, but honestly, it was what he deserved. She was right. He'd walked out and never looked back.

No, that wasn't true. He had looked back. Often. He'd remembered their time together. Remembered the way she looked first thing in the morning when she'd been snuggled up beside him. The way she'd shyly glance at him as if she could eat him alive.

He'd hated himself for giving that up. For giving *her* up.

Sighing, he moved toward the door. "I have duties to attend. Should you need anything, call for Davyn." Without another word, he was gone.

Zephyra watched as he left her alone in his room. The look of hurt in his silver eyes had made her ache, and she hated herself for that weakness. Why did she still want to hold him after what he'd done to her?

Yes, she wanted to claw out his eyes and stab him until he was dead.

But underneath that anger and hurt was the part of her that still loved him. The part of her that she tried so hard to bury and ignore. He was a beast and a coward.

He's the father of your daughter.

So what? A biological donor who'd left them. That didn't make him a father. It made him an asshole. Her fury renewed, she glanced about the room that he slept in. It was rather plain. Burgundy coverings on the bed. No windows. A small chest of drawers and nothing hanging on the walls.

"You live like a bear in a cave."

There wasn't even a book on the nightstand. Which begged the question of why he had one. Then again, the top drawer was slightly cracked open. Perhaps there was one inside. Curious, she walked over to it and opened it.

Her breath caught in her throat.

In the bottom of that drawer was the last thing she had ever expected to see again. It was the hand-painted tile that he'd commissioned of her as a wedding present. Memories slammed into her as she stared at the faded image of her in ancient Greek clothing, her blond hair bound up as curls fell around her face. Large green eyes were set in the countenance of utter innocence. She'd forgotten all about this tile's existence.

But Stryker hadn't. In spite of everything, he'd kept it. And underneath it was another tile and pictures of men who bore a striking resemblance to him. One picture in particular caught her attention. It was three men, similar in face and form, dressed in clothes from the 1930s. They had their arms slung over each other's shoulders as they smiled happily.

His sons.

Over and over, she found pictures of them.

The only other tile in the drawer was that of a girl who looked almost identical to Medea. A chill went down her spine as she ran her finger over the faded writing in the lower right-hand corner. *Tannis*. She must have been his daughter, too.

She flipped it aside to find the most recent photo in the drawer. From the looks of the quality of the picture and the black clothing, she would guess it was no more than ten years old. It was of a young man with white-blond hair that was pulled back into a ponytail—the middle of the same three brothers from the 1930s. Even though his features were masculine, they were so close to Medea's as to be eerie. And as Zephyra tilted the photo in the light she realized something.

The stains on it were from tears.

"No," she breathed, unable to imagine Stryker crying over anything. He'd always been rigidly unsentimental. She'd seen him brutally wounded in sword practice and his eyes hadn't even misted.

The only time she'd known them to cloud was . . .

The night he'd left her.

And yet as she ran her hand over the stains, she knew nothing else would have caused them. Who, other than him, would have held this photograph in his room and cried? No one. They were his and he'd kept all of this in a place where he thought no one would find it.

"Dear gods." The bastard had a heart. Who knew?

"I will love you forever, Phyra. Never doubt that or me."

Her throat tightened as she looked down at the tile of herself that she'd put on the tabletop. Had he really missed her? Pined for her?

Don't be ridiculous. He probably planned this for you to find.

Planned it? He'd thought her dead. Why would he hang on to her image all these centuries unless she meant something to him? She certainly had kept nothing of his.

"Don't you dare weaken," she snarled at herself. "He's nothing." Determined to stay hard, she put the pictures back, then froze as she saw something she'd missed earlier. It was a small green frayed ribbon.

The same ribbon she'd worn twined through her hair on the tile. And there, tied in the middle of it, was the wedding ring she'd thrown in his face when he'd told her he was leaving.

Her eyes teared as she saw the ancient carving on the band. *S'agapo.* "I love you" in Greek.

"Damn you," she growled as she weakened even more in the face of his obvious love. He had cared about her. Through all these centuries, he'd kept her as close to him as he could.

Unable to stand it, she left his room and went in search of his study. She hadn't gone far when Davyn appeared.

"Can I help you?"

"I want to see Stryker. Now."

"He doesn't like to be disturbed when he's in his study."

"I really don't care." She stepped past him.

Davyn sighed heavily before he passed her and then led her to the correct destination. He knocked on the door. "My lord?"

"What!" Stryker barked.

Zephyra stepped around Davyn and threw open the door to find Stryker sitting at his desk, looking into a small round ball. No, not just looking, he was fixated by it.

"What are you doing?" she asked, her voice rife with

her agitation that she used to cover the tender feelings inside her.

He glanced up. "Trying to find Gautier. What are you doing here?"

Truthfully, she wasn't sure. She didn't want to be here and yet . . . "I wanted to see you."

"Leave," he ordered Davyn, who obeyed instantly. As soon as they were alone, he looked back at her. "I thought you'd seen more than your fair share of me."

She had and . . .

He'd kept a tile of her. How could something so insipidly stupid weaken her? She'd always thought herself above such petty sentimentality.

Apparently she was wrong.

Before she could stop herself, she moved to his side. "Why didn't you go after Gautier yourself?"

"I tried. The little bastard is fast and extremely resourceful. Not to mention his powers aren't anything to laugh at. I stupidly thought he received most of that from our blood exchange. Now that I know what he is, it makes even more sense why I was having such a hard time controlling him. I should have been feeding from him and taking *his* powers."

"You couldn't tell?"

"No. Whoever bound his powers did one hell of a job. Case in point, I can't find him anywhere. Even though we're supposed to share sight, he's off my radar completely."

"That's impossible."

He gave her a dry "duh" stare. "I know that. Yet here I am, completely blind to him."

She stepped around his desk to look into the sfora. "When was the last time you had a visual?"

He looked aghast at her. "Are you helping me?"

She refused to give him the satisfaction. "Shut up and answer my question."

A slow smile spread over his face and the teasing gleam in his eyes set her ire off. "You *are* helping me."

"Don't get used to it. I'm a woman of my word, and since I can't kill you it's not in my nature to crochet and do nothing. Why are we going to kill this man anyway?"

"He murdered my sister."

That was a good reason. "Bastard scum."

Stryker nodded in approval. "I had him in my sights a couple of hours ago before War went after him."

"Then he's probably in hiding."

"My thoughts exactly. But where?"

"The best place to hide is in plain sight. The bugger is there. We just have to figure it out."

Nick raked his hands through his hair as he stared at the tiny African-American woman before him. She was a woman he'd thought he'd known his entire life and here in the last few minutes he'd learned that he had never really known her at all.

"I don't understand this. My father was a psychotic criminal who beat the hell out of my mom whenever she was dumb enough to let him into our apartment between his unfortunate incarcerations."

Menyara shook her head. "Your father was a demon who preferred prison because it was the last place the people who would kill him would think to look for him. Not to mention it allowed him to feed off their evil energy. He drew power from all their negativity."

Nick refused to believe it. It just wasn't possible. "You're wrong. My father was human." A corrupt, mean, and vicious man, but human through and through.

She shook her head again. "Listen to me, Ambrosius. I was there when you were born. I'm the one who delivered you and used my powers to keep you hidden from the rest of the worlds—those seen and those unknown. I knew the power you would one day wield and it terrified me even then. Why do you think I've watched over you so closely all these years?"

"I thought it was because you loved me and my mother."

"I do love you and I did love Cherise. She was a good woman with the heart of an angel. Never did she harm or think ill of a single person. It was why Adarian was able to seduce her. Why he was so attracted to her even when he shouldn't have been. He chose her for the sacred honor of being the mother to his legacy. What he never counted on was me and the degree to which your mother's purity would affect you."

"You're so full of shit, Menyara, you ought to be a cow pasture."

She angled one bony finger at him. "You better check that tone, boy. You're not so big I can't spank you like I did when you were young."

"I'm all-powerful. Isn't that what you told me?"

"And I bound your powers once. Don't think I can't do it again. Believe me, you're not the most powerful creature in this universe. There are many who can take you down."

Nick pulled back. Attacking her was pointless and it made him feel like his father—something he'd always despised. She was right. She'd been there all of his life, like a second mother to him. "I'm sorry, Mennie. I'm just having a hard time with all this. No offense, but it's a little hard to swallow."

She placed her hand against the bow and arrow mark of Artemis on his cheek. "You tried to sell your soul to a goddess for vengeance. How ludicrous is that?"

"Point taken, and I might add it turned out really bad. I just wish I understood more about all of this."

She dropped her hand to his shoulder. "What do you remember of your father?"

"Only the back of his hand as it fell across my face. He had 'hate' tattooed on the fingers of his right hand and 'kill' on those of his left. I don't even really remember what he looked like. All I see is a mountain of a man with eyes filled with hatred."

She sighed gently. "The Malachai. Corrupt. Angry. Bitter. Demons all. They were created from the worst of the universe to fight against those who were pure and caring. In spite of his flaws, your father survived longer than any Malachai before him. But he knew his time was growing short, which is why he fathered you. Each Malachai is allowed only one single son to carry on his legacy. You are it."

"And I killed myself, so it's all over."

She shook her head. "You have a means to return from the dead. You can reclaim your soul and be reborn."

"To what purpose?"

She smiled at him. "Only you can answer that question. Only we, ourselves, can define our purpose in this world. Your father's was to hurt and punish. Mine has been to protect you. Your goal . . . ?"

"To kill Acheron Parthenopaeus."

"And will that truly fill the bitter hole you've placed in your heart?"

Nick snarled at her, "I didn't put that hole there. *He* did."

"Look at me," she barked. "You tell Menyara the truth, boy."

Nick ground his teeth as bitter emotions swelled inside him. "Ash killed my mother."

"A Daimon killed your mother because you came late to her job to walk her home. You know the truth, Ambrosius. Admit it to yourself. Ash would have never allowed her to die had he been able to get there. He was under brutal attack that night. Even though he was angry at you, he would have given his life to protect hers. To this day, he visits her grave to honor her even more than you do."

Tears stung his eyes as pain tore through him. He wanted his mother back. To see her one more time. To feel her hand on his cheek as she smiled at him with pride in her kind eyes. He wanted to go back in time and save her from the vicious murder. She'd been the best mother anyone could have and she'd died brutally in the hands of his enemies.

She hadn't deserved that.

And she hadn't deserved a son like him, who'd been unable to protect her from harm.

Still Menyara goaded him. "You're the one who put her in danger. Not Acheron. It was you who failed her. You who killed yourself."

Nick roared as fury flowed through his veins. Throwing his head back, he let out the pain in what shook the room like a sonic boom. His vision changed. . . . No longer could he see colors. Rather he saw the universe for what it was. Heard the fabric of life that surrounded and bound every living creature.

He'd never known such power. Such rage and hatred. He could taste it on his tongue.

Menyara looked at him without fear or trepidation. "You now have the power to kill Acheron. Will you?"

He bared his fangs at Menyara as fire emanated from his hands and ran up the length of both his arms. "Hell yes."

At long last, Acheron Parthenopaeus was about to die.

7

Stryker sucked his breath in sharply as Zephyra leaned down to look into the sfora. She smelled so good, it literally made his mouth water. She traced the clouds with one long fingernail. Chills rose on his body as he imagined her running it over his skin. He was so hard and needy that it was all he could do not to grab her and pull her close.

She would kill him if he tried. Not to mention he'd never once rough-handled her. Men he would gut without hesitation, even many women, but when it came to her . . . he wasn't sure if he could ever hurt the woman he'd loved so much.

Zephyra froze as she became aware of the sudden bulge in Stryker's pants. The subtle changes to his breathing. She couldn't remember the last time she'd taken a lover. But the experience had been poor enough that she'd decided she'd rather take matters into her own hands than be disappointed again.

Stryker had never once disappointed her. He'd been more than just a skilled lover. He'd been a considerate one.

Swallowing, she pulled back. At least until her gaze fell to his lips.

"I've missed you, too," she breathed before she could stop herself.

Stryker froze. Those simple words seared him as he saw the way her eyes darkened. Unable to stand it, he pulled her toward him so that he could kiss her. The moment her lips touched his and her tongue swept across his teeth, he was blinded by need. Blinded by memories so sweet and precious that he'd never thought to experience them again.

Pulling her into his lap, he growled at how good she felt there. She was so tiny that she weighed next to nothing. The scent of her skin intoxicated him.

Zephyra groaned at how good he tasted. At how strong he felt and how hard his lean body was. She hated how much she'd missed this.

How much she'd missed him. But there was no denying it.

Eleven thousand years later, the man still set her senses on fire.

Needing him with a fury she didn't want to understand, she straddled his lap and leaned back long enough to jerk his shirt over his head.

One corner of his mouth quirked up into a teasing smile.

She placed her fingertip over his lips. "One single word and I swear I'll rip your tongue out."

"So I haven't won you over?"

She dropped his shirt to the floor. "This isn't about winning anything. It's about lust. I want you completely out of my system."

"You think this will do it?"

"As soon as I realize how bad you suck in bed, I'll never want to touch you again."

He laughed as he rose up with her wrapped around him, then leaned her back against his desk. "Oh, baby, I've never in my life sucked in bed."

She scoffed even though she knew from experience that he'd never disappointed her. Hopefully, though, his streak would end and he'd have gotten worse with age . . .

He dipped his head down to hers to kiss her again as he ran his hand over her body. She shivered in pleasure, especially as she felt the size of his bulge between her legs. She wanted him desperately.

Stryker reached for the button on her top at the same moment something struck his door. Frowning, he looked up to see the doors clatter open. Davyn hit the floor in a bloody heap before a group of twenty demons came through the threshold.

"Knock, knock," Kessar snarled. "Looks like there's a new power in town and it ain't you."

Stryker stepped back and pulled Zephyra from the desk. Returning his shirt to his body with his powers, he placed himself between Zephyra and the demon. "What the hell's going on?"

"Natural selection." Kessar blasted him.

Stryker hissed as pain flooded his body. But he wasn't a callow youth unused to battle. Summoning his black body armor, he upturned his desk and blasted it toward the demon. Kessar ducked before he sent another blast at Stryker, who returned it with one of his own. Their powers tangled in an arc of sizzling color. But every heartbeat he blasted cost him physically. He could feel his strength draining, and given the number of demons coming in, a depleted Daimon was a dead one.

"Run, Phyra," he ordered her over his shoulder.

"Not without you." Before he could stop her, she added

her own blast to the demons', driving them back. "We need to get out of here. Now," she said.

Stryker looked to where Davyn was still unconscious on the floor. "We have to get Davyn out."

"Let him die."

"I don't leave my men behind." At least not the ones who were actually loyal to him. The ones like Desiderius who had questionable loyalty he was more than quick to sacrifice. But Davyn had never given him any reason to doubt his service, and for those men Stryker would die to protect them.

She growled at him, "Get him and hurry."

The moment he moved toward Davyn, Kessar attacked. He caught Stryker about the waist and threw him to the ground. He cursed, kicking Kessar back. "You snide halitosis-breathing worthless shit sack. Get off me."

One of the other demons came at him. Stryker ducked and caught sight of Zephyra pinning one to the ground. "Don't let them bite you. You'll become one of them if they do."

She laughed evilly as her eyes changed to a bright yellow laced with red. "You're a little late with your warning." She caught the demon closest to her and twisted his arm off. He dropped to the ground screaming before she stabbed him between his eyes and killed him. "Been there, done that, and am craving their blood more than they're craving mine."

Kessar and the others pulled back as they realized they were dealing with something more than just a regular Daimon.

"Got your buddy?" Her snide tone irritated Stryker.

Stryker lifted Davyn up from the floor and slung him over his shoulder. "I don't run from crackheads like this."

He started after Kessar, then paused as he realized the hallway was littered with the bodies of his Daimon army. "What the hell is going on?"

"They're converting your Daimons to demons. If you want to live, you better get out of here."

"I don't retreat."

She grabbed him and forced him to face her. "Everyone retreats sometimes. Open the portal and get us out of here. Now!"

Stryker growled before he obeyed her. Until they knew better what was going on, he would listen to her even though he didn't want to.

She pulled him out of Kalosis back to her temple, where Medea was. They appeared in Medea's room, where their daughter was sitting at her computer.

"Put him on the bed," Zephyra ordered Stryker.

"Excuse me?" Medea looked horrified by the prospect as she rose to her feet. "I don't want an unknown man in my bed."

"Those words do a father proud. Thank you for raising her right." He flipped Davyn onto the pink coverlet and left him there.

Zephyra scoffed. "Don't start on me. I might rethink tossing you back in with the demons."

Stryker straightened to look at her. "Which brings me to the question of the hour. What exactly are you now?"

She let out a long breath before she answered. "Well, besides pissed, I'm part demon."

Those words chilled him. She seemed so normal and yet . . . with demon blood in her, there was a lot she could be capable of. "How?"

She shrugged. "I was bitten by a gallu—the same one

who owned Jared. He thought to make me his mindless sycophant, and what he learned is that I'm a lot stronger than I look. I killed the bastard."

Medea sighed. "Why don't you tell him the truth, Mum?"

"Truth?" Stryker asked with a frown.

Zephyra cursed as she glared at her daughter. Her eyes snapping fire, she turned toward Stryker. "Fine. I traded my humanity so that Medea would live longer than her twenty-seventh birthday."

"What are you talking about?"

"Unlike you," Zephyra sneered, "I didn't have an Atlantean goddess willing to show me how to take human souls to live. I asked Artemis to intervene on Medea's behalf and she refused. She told me she wouldn't countermand her brother's curse even for her own niece. After I'd already lost my grandson and son-in-law to the humans, I wasn't about to let my own baby die because of Apollo. So I conjured one of the brokers and promised him my soul if he'd protect her."

It sounded easy enough, but there was one problem. Demon brokers didn't respond to Daimon requests. "You can't do that. Only a demon can."

She gave him a highly sarcastic look of appreciation. "You're such a brainiac, baby. And to think, I thought I married you for those amazing abs. Who knew all that brainpower was buried under those bulging biceps?"

Medea made a choking sound before she spoke again. "She allowed a demon to feed on her and convert her so that she could summon a broker."

The look of sarcasm mixed with annoyance was transferred to Medea.

Disregarding Zephyra's prickliness, Stryker was

amazed by her capacity to love. It touched him profoundly that she'd make so great a sacrifice to protect their child. It was that deep ability to care for her loved ones that had made him fall in love with her in ancient Greece.

"After I was converted, I turned on the demon and killed him. The beauty of the gallu. If you kill the one who bites you, you regain your self-control and keep the powers of the gallu to boot. It's beautiful really, except for the annoying blood craving that was added to the one I already had due to Apollo. But life is nothing if not a series of trade-offs, eh?"

Perhaps. But it still left one unanswered question. "And Jared?"

"He was offered to me to keep me from killing the gallu demon. I took custody of him and then nailed the demon to the wall of his own home. No one threatens me or my child. Ever. And I'll *never* be someone's slave. No one controls me."

He could respect all of that. He'd done worse things to the ones who'd killed his sons.

Except for Urian.

Unwilling to think about that, he narrowed his gaze on Zephyra. "That explains your advanced age." Demons, even if they were only half bloods or converts, were excluded from Apollo's curse. "But what of hers?" He indicated Medea with a jerk of his chin.

Zephyra crossed her arms over her chest. "I had to trade my soul for her life, which is now tied to mine. Strange how the gods love to do that. Sadistic and cold, really. But no matter. Unlike us, she doesn't have to feed on humans to live longer—she's still an Apollite technically. She could even have more children if she could ever find a man who wasn't worthless."

"I did find one," Medea said, her voice breaking. "The humans butchered him."

Zephyra touched her lightly on the arm. "I know, baby. I didn't mean to be so callous. I loved him, too." She looked back at Stryker. "It's why I made sure I slaughtered every descendent of the families who took his life and why I relished each and every kill."

Stryker gave her a formal ancient military salute. "And that's why I admire you so. A warrior's code to the end." Blood for blood. Tit for tat. Life for life.

It was the one thing they'd always seen eye to eye on.

Davyn groaned from the bed as he finally came to. Lifting his head, he focused on Stryker. "How many of our men did they kill?"

"I don't know. What happened?"

"War." His voice was weak and strained, as if pain had just ripped through him. He brushed his hair back from his face before he pushed himself into a sitting position. "He told the demons that they shouldn't be subservient to you anymore. That they should rise up and kill us all to take over Kalosis. He said it would be the perfect demon haven, once all the Daimons were dead or converted."

Stryker growled low in the back of his throat. "Treacherous bastard."

Zephyra scoffed. "You're the one who unleashed him."

"To kill Nick and Ash," he said defensively.

She arched one taunting brow. "What did you think he'd do after that?"

"I assumed he'd kill me, not my people."

Zephyra laughed sarcastically. "The man's name is War. Did that not clue you in about his personality? This would be tantamount to meeting Peone and expecting the goddess of retaliation to forgive you and blithely walk away to let you live a happy life."

Medea frowned. "I thought that was Nemesis."

Zephyra gave her a droll stare. "Keep to your Atlantean gods, sweetie. Peone is retribution for murder. Nemesis is a goddess of balance. She punishes those who have too much happiness or who get away with screwing people over. Big difference between the two."

"Oh. Never mind." Medea stepped back.

Stryker inclined his head to Zephyra. "I'm impressed you still remember the old gods. But it doesn't change the fact that I need to get back to Kalosis and kick those assholes out."

"Why are you so suicidal?"

"I'm not suicidal. Those are my people down there and I'm not going to leave them to die without my leadership." He vanished.

Zephyra stiffened at his abrupt departure. "Did he just go back?" she asked Davyn.

He nodded. "My lord plays games, but not when it comes to invaders. He brought the demons in and no doubt feels responsible."

She tried to flash herself to Kalosis, but since she didn't have a standing invitation, she couldn't. "Davyn, can you open a bolt hole?"

He closed his eyes, then shook his head. "Stryker must have locked me out."

"Damn him. Jared!" she shouted, calling him back from his quest to find and kill Nick.

He appeared before her instantly. "Akra?" he asked, using the Atlantean word for owner and mistress.

"I need you to go to Kalosis and keep Stryker from dying. Help him drive the demons out."

"Your will is mine," he said in the most sarcastic of tones. She was actually amazed he was willing to obey without argument. But an instant later, he was gone.

Medea scowled in confusion. "I thought your intent was to kill Stryker?"

"Oh, honey, after all that man has put me through, I alone deserve the honor. Be damned if some demon by-blow is going to rob me of that pleasure."

Stryker used a fire blast to sear the demons closest to him as he joined his men and women who were holding them off. "Where's Apollymi?"

"Behind you."

He turned to see her there with her eyes blazing red. "We need to get you to safety," he told her, not wanting either of them to die until he took care of this.

She arched a brow at that. "Since when does my safety concern you? I thought you wanted me dead."

It was true, he had. But not right now. "I want to renew my lease on life. At least for two more weeks."

"In that case . . ." She slung her arms out and formed a whirlwind around the demons. They shrieked and screamed as it enveloped them and lifted them from the ground.

A hole appeared in the room, sucking them into the center of it. An instant later, they were all gone.

Now that was one seriously handy skill. "And that, my friends, is the difference between a full-fledged goddess and a demigod," he said under his breath.

Her expression unamused, she turned to Stryker. "And *that*, unfortunately, won't last because someone"—she pinned him with an angry glare—"gave them access to my realm. Perhaps I should feed you to them after all."

"Give me a couple of hours before you do. Right now, I need to take inventory of the damage done to my men."

"Since when do you care what happens to them?"

He didn't answer. It was true he liked to pretend he had no feelings whatsoever. That he was above anything as petty as emotions. But he knew the truth.

He ached and he cared even when he didn't want to. No matter how hard he tried, he was still a man.

"My men need me." He walked past an angry Savitar, who was heading toward Apollymi.

"Why didn't you stay put?" Savitar snarled at her.

She gave him a cold, haughty stare. "I'm the goddess of destruction. Did you really think I'd stay put while they ate their way through my home?" She curled her lip. "I need you to get Sin after them. He's a Sumerian god, he should police the creation of his own pantheon and clean up their mess."

Savitar snorted. "You know if I do that, your granddaughter will be fighting right along beside him, don't you? The last time she fought the gallu, they almost converted her into one of them."

She hissed at him, "Why did she marry that no-account Sumerian god? Fine. Don't tell them." She looked around the debris. "Strykerius, I expect you and your men to clean this mess up."

Stryker started to snap at her, then caught himself. Pissing her off wouldn't accomplish anything and they had a lot to do. "You know this isn't over. War will be back."

"Yes, I do know that. Thank you for reminding me. In

the meantime, we should make some preparations. Anyone know a good exterminator?"

No sooner had those words left her lips than Jared, looking much better than he had last time they'd met, appeared beside Stryker. Dressed in a black leather jacket, black button-down shirt, and black jeans, Jared's eyes were covered with a pair of opaque sunglasses. His auburn hair had been pulled back into a sleek ponytail.

The Sephiroth glanced around with a frown. "Looks like I missed a party. Good. I wasn't really in the mood to off demons this evening. Haven't had my coffee yet."

Savitar grimaced. "You drink coffee?"

His face was stoic. "No, but it was my pathetic attempt at humor."

"What are you doing here?" Apollymi asked him. It was obvious from her tone that she didn't appreciate an uninvited creature popping into her domain.

"I was ordered to protect him." He jerked his chin toward Stryker.

Apollymi folded her arms over her chest. "Well, I asked for an exterminator and look who appears. Want to take out War for us?"

"I can't."

She looked less than pleased by his response. "Why not?"

"Primal Source," Savitar said drily. "Jared was created to protect those powers. No one can make him kill them."

Jared nodded. "Exactly. Not even my owner can command that."

Apollymi frowned. "I don't understand. You can kill the Malachai. Weren't they born of the same powers?"

Jared sighed. "The Malachai declared enmity on the

Source, thereby severing those ties. Because they threatened the Source, the Sepherii were able to attack and kill them. Until War makes a like threat against the primal powers, I can't touch him."

One corner of Savitar's mouth quirked up. "Well, don't you suck?"

Jared's features softened. "Oh, believe me, I couldn't agree more. Just be grateful it's not contagious."

Stryker ignored them as he considered what he'd inadvertently set into motion by wanting revenge. How simple it'd all seemed. War killed Ash and Nick, then him. Now there was a lot more going on here. "We have to find some way to contain War."

Savitar gave him a droll glare. "You're the one who unleashed him."

"Yeah, well, let's move on from the blame game. I was having suicidal thoughts and it seemed like a good idea at the time. In retrospect, not so much."

"Most major mistakes do," Apollymi said quietly. "Not many people carry out thoughts they know going into it are stupid . . . morons not included."

Savitar laughed. "Then that leaves you out, huh, Stryker."

He glared at Savitar. "For the record, we're not friends."

"For the record, I don't care."

"Enough, children," Apollymi said between clenched teeth. "In case you haven't noticed, we have a major situation playing out. We have to find and stop War, corral the gallu, protect Apostolos, and get Savitar out of here."

"Why the latter?" Jared asked.

"Because I hate his guts."

Savitar shook his head. "I hate you, too, precious."

She sneered at him. "Put on some real clothes. What is that you're wearing and does it come in adult sizes?"

He looked highly offended by her attack on his wardrobe. "Cargo pants and a Hawaiian shirt are real clothes."

"Not in my realm they're not, and button that shirt."

"Hey!" he snapped as the shirt closed itself. "You know there are women who would pay to see me naked."

"I'm sure there are women *you* pay to see you naked. Perish the thought, but I'm not one of either group. Now hush while I think."

Stryker was amused by their bantering. He'd never seen Apollymi quite so animated. Or Savitar flustered. Any other time, he'd goad them into continuing, but they had too much to do for him to play Loki.

Jared stepped back. "While you plan and plot, I have a Malachai to kill." He vanished.

Savitar sighed. "I really don't think Acheron is going to approve of that action."

"No," Apollymi agreed. "I would send you after him, but I don't want Apostolos angry at me."

Savitar let out an elongated breath. "You know we have to stay on guard. War's modus operandi is to divide and conquer. He turns all friends into enemies."

Stryker rolled his eyes. "Well, since the three of us hate each other, there's not much more he can do."

Apollymi gave him a hard stare. "I don't hate you, Stryker. I would have never brought you into my realm if I had." She vanished.

Stunned and uncertain about those uncharacteristic words, Stryker followed her. The one thing he'd learned over the centuries was that Apollymi was even less sentimental than he was.

Then again, there was another side to him in private

that no one else saw, and it made him wonder what secrets she held.

She'd adjourned to her secluded garden that was walled in by marble. Black roses bloomed all around in memory and in mourning of the son she could never see. Her two Charonte bodyguards stood on the side like statues. But for an occasional blink, it would be easy to think them dead.

"What are you saying?" he asked her as she took a perch on the edge of the pool that flowed backward, up the wall.

"I'm tired, Strykerius." She got up to leave.

He did what he'd never done before. He pulled her to a stop. "I want an answer from you."

She shrugged his touch away. "How dense you are, child. In all your hatred have you never once thought through our relationship?"

"Believe me, these last few years I've done nothing but. You used me and then you cast me off."

She shook her head. "I adopted you, Strykerius. When your children died, I wept with you."

"The hell you did."

She pulled back the sleeve of her gown to show him her wrist. There were eleven black teardrops tattooed into her skin. It was the Atlantean custom to remember loved ones who'd died. "The one at the top is for my son. The rest are for your children."

He touched her arm, unable to believe her. "What about Urian? You told me to kill him."

"I told you your son had a secret that you should investigate. That he was keeping things from you. I never intended for you to kill him. You did that on your own."

"I don't believe you."

"You don't have to. I really don't care anymore. I would end both our lives at this point, but until I know for a fact that War is contained and my son is safe, I'm stuck here."

"With me."

Her silver eyes flashed in the dim light. But he saw the pain that she hid so elegantly. "I didn't say that."

"Your tone did."

She let out an aggravated breath. "You are so blind. Everything is black or white. I either hate you or love you. But that's not how it goes. Life is never that clear-cut. Emotions aren't that clear-cut." She touched him softly on the cheek. "Think, Strykerius. You and I were an allied force for thousands of years. Us against your father and Artemis. Against her army of Dark-Hunters and the humans we both hate. The only one I ever forbade you to touch was Apostolos, and now you know why. He is my son. But even so, I sheltered you and yours. I brought you in and taught you how to steal the humans' souls."

"So that you could hurt my father for killing Acheron."

She inclined her head respectfully. "That is true. Originally, I couldn't see anything more than my own revenge. But I watched as your children grew . . . as you grew, and I watched as they died. Do you really think me so cold that never once did I care?"

"Yes, I do. You killed your own family. All of them."

Her face turned to stone. It betrayed no emotion or passion. "I held the same anger then that you held the night you cut Urian's throat. No, I held even more. Their betrayal against me was far greater than what your son did to you. What Urian did he did out of love for a woman. He wasn't trying to hurt you. He was only trying to find happiness for the two of them and he meant you no slight. What my family did to me was out of selfish fear. They united against me to imprison me and kill my son. *That* is unforgivable."

She paused as the pain in her eyes flared bright and he saw how much she still ached over what had happened. "But just like you, after they were all gone and I was alone, I grieved for what I'd done. I missed that family, sorry though it was, and I wanted to see them again."

She looked over her shoulder to where her demons were still standing at attention. "While I cherish my Charonte army, it wasn't the same as my family." She turned her attention to him and her gaze softened. "And then this golden-haired youth called out to me as he begged the powers that be for some way to save his small children from an unfair fate. He reminded me of my own son and so I offered to him what I'd never offered to another." The tenderness vanished under the cold countenance that was so familiar. "I bound my life to you in order to save you. The only time you and I were ever at odds was when I ordered you to leave Apostolos alone and you refused to do so."

"You failed to tell me he was your son."

"Because I knew it would hurt you," she said between clenched teeth. "Why else would I have kept that a secret?"

"You were trying to control me."

"I never," she snarled. "I turned you loose to wreak revenge against your father. I opened my entire realm to your kind and allowed you to take refuge here. Every Dark-Hunter you killed, every human life you destroyed, I took pride in it as any mother would."

Still, he refused to believe her. She'd been using him . . .

And yet he remembered the way they'd been over the

centuries. She'd always welcomed him into her private chambers. Always welcomed his company.

He missed that more than he wanted to admit to himself.

"Why haven't you told me this before now?"

She sighed. "Because I would rather you hate me for Urian's death than hate yourself. No parent should ever know such grief."

"I don't believe you."

"Then don't. We both know compassion isn't my strong suit. I barely understand it." She raked him with a cool glance. "I barely understand you." She gathered the skirts of her black gown and walked past him.

Stryker watched her as her words echoed in his ears. She might not understand compassion, but she did know how to love. Her uncompromising protection and sacrifice for Acheron was beyond reproach. It was what had set Stryker's jealousy off and made him turn against her.

He'd wanted her to love him like that.

Stryker winced at the undeniable truth. He'd been taken out of his mother's womb before he was born and given over to Apollo's priestesses to raise. While they'd never been cruel where he was concerned, they'd all been afraid of him. He'd never known a real mother.

Not until Apollymi.

Even so, he wasn't sure if he could trust her. Did he dare? But for all her malice, he'd never known her to lie. She might omit things, but she didn't come straight out and lie. . . .

Closing his eyes, he ground his teeth as pain assailed him. It was hard to be responsible for so many and to have no one he could fully trust.

Gods, how tired he was of being alone in the universe. Of standing strong all the time.

Not wanting to dwell on that, he left the garden to return to where his men were still tending to the wounded and killing those who were converting.

"Are we at war, my lord?"

He looked at Ann, a small, beautiful blond Daimon female, and nodded. "The demons are no longer welcomed here. We extended our hands in friendship and they repaid us in bloodshed." Little surprise really, a demon was a demon. He should have known better than to think they could ever combine forces with the gallu. "But that's all right. What we lack in numbers we make up for with vicious and cunning. We are Daimon and we are Spathi. Now let us show those bastards what we can do."

His men shouted in approval.

Savitar laughed behind him.

Stryker cast him an angry glare. "You find something funny, Chthonian?"

"Yeah, I do. I find it hysterical that your new lease on life is named War."

He gave Savitar a look to let him know what he thought of him—not much. "At least I have a lease."

"True, but you do know what the problem with a lease is?"

"What?"

"They usually run out sooner than later. And if you're not paying close attention to the fine print, you always get burned."

"You're not scaring me."

"Don't want to scare you. But if I were you, I wouldn't leave my women out in the open too long while I trifle down here. War has a nasty way of spilling over into peaceful areas, if you catch my meaning."

A bad feeling went through Stryker. Surely War wouldn't . . .

Of course he would.

His heart hammering, Stryker knew he had to get to Medea and Zephyra before it was too late.

8

Zephyra looked up from her desk at the sound of a light tapping on her door. "Come in, love," she said, knowing by the sound of it that it would be Medea.

Sure enough, she pushed the door open to peer into the room. "Am I disturbing you?"

"No, baby. I was just straightening up a bit."

Medea arched one brow at that. Zephyra couldn't blame her. She was, after all, horrifyingly tidy on her worst day. But it was a nervous habit she had. Whenever things were confusing, she had a compulsive need to clean what she could.

"How's our guest?" she asked, trying to distract her daughter from that bold scrutiny.

"Eyeing a couple of the priestesses for dinner. I've already warned him that they're off the menu even though he thinks they'd be quite tasty."

"Good. I don't want to fight Artemis on that."

Medea entered the room and closed the door. "You still love him, don't you?"

"Love who?" she asked, trying to make light of the question. "Davyn? I don't even know him. The only thing I love about him is his absence."

"My father."

She hated how pointed Medea could be at times. "I don't love him, either," she said dismissively. "I can barely stand his presence."

"And yet you light up every time he looks at you."

Zephyra put a stack of papers into the garbage can. "Don't be ridiculous."

Medea stopped her as she started for her desk again. "I know you, Matera. You've always been very calculated and cold. For centuries I've worried that my stupidity had killed something inside you."

She frowned at her daughter. "What stupidity?"

"Living with the humans. Being naive enough to think that so long as we didn't harm them, they wouldn't harm us. I still remember what you said to me a few weeks before they attacked us. 'You can't tame a wolf and expect it to lie before your hearth in harmony. Sooner or later, the nature of the beast sets in and it does what its instincts tell it—it kills.' I thought then that you were talking about us, but you weren't. And after we were attacked—after you were almost killed trying to save me—something inside you died. That piece of sympathy for others. The ability to have mercy."

It was true. Any belief she'd had in the world, in kindness or so-called humanity, had died alongside her grandson. *Kill the monster. Rip out his heart so he doesn't kill us.*

Five years old . . . no monster. Just a child, screaming for his parents to save him. For his grandmother to make them stop hurting him. She'd done her best to protect them all and the sad truth was her best hadn't been good enough. They'd dragged him down and clubbed him to death.

Her baby's baby.

She *had* died that night, and it was a sad, hollow core that was now her heart.

"Life is hard," she said with a calmness she didn't really feel. She'd known it even before then. As the daughter of a fisherman, she'd been raised with hunger and poverty gnawing at her belly and dignity while her father had tried to eke out a living from the sea. His failure to do so had caused him to turn on his own family. It'd turned him into a bitter drunk who blamed them for his own failings. Blamed them for the fact that he'd had them and that they depended on him for their support. He'd hated them all and he'd never failed to show them that.

In all her life, she'd never known respect or kindness until a lean, handsome boy had stopped her on the docks.

Even now she could see the sun highlighted in his blond hair. See the admiration in those beautiful blue eyes as he'd looked at her. He'd been wrapped in the purple chiton of a nobleman that set off his young warrior's body that was already showing the promise of the man he'd grow into.

Thinking he intended to accost her as many others had before him, including her own drunken father, she'd kneed him in the groin and run.

He'd chased her down only to apologize for scaring her.

Apologize. The son of a god to a common fishmonger dressed in rags. It'd been love at first sentence. Then when he'd taken his own cloak off to shield her from the stern sea breeze, she'd melted on the spot.

There for the briefest of times, she'd felt loved and cherished. She'd felt worth something more than dirt beneath other people's feet.

Until Apollo had come in condemning their relationship on the grounds that she was garbage, unworthy of a demigod, and Stryker had sheepishly obeyed his father's orders to leave her.

Anger tore through her from the memory.

"I don't believe in fairy tales," Zephyra told her daughter.

"Yet you raised me on those stories."

Because she'd wanted her child to be a better person than she was. She hadn't wanted to kill Medea's innocence the way her own had been slaughtered.

"I love you, child," she whispered. "In all my life, you are the only thing that has brought me unending joy. You are the only one I would die to protect. I don't love your father. I'm not capable of it anymore."

Medea inclined her head to her. "As you say, Mum. But I still see the light that comes on the moment he enters the room." She started to leave, then paused. "For the record, if by some miracle I could have Evander back in my life, I wouldn't push him away. I'd hold him close for the rest of eternity."

"He didn't abandon you when you were a fourteen-year-old girl pregnant with his child."

"True, but Evander wasn't a fourteen-year-old boy whose father had the power to kill us both with a single thought."

Zephyra didn't speak as Medea left her alone. It was true. Stryker had only been a boy himself and he had left her quite a bit of money to care for herself and the baby, but the shattered pieces of her heart refused to rationalize his behavior.

He should have fought for what he loved.

That was what she couldn't forgive. Ever. No, what she couldn't forgive was the way he'd made her feel like an insignificant worm unworthy of his love. She'd have rather he let his father kill her than to be that demoralized again. Everyone deserved dignity.

Everyone.

Except for Jared, and as she stood there she realized why she took so much joy in torturing him. He'd betrayed his own family, too. His fellow soldiers. When they had needed to band together, to fight for their survival, he'd been the one to hand them over to their enemies for slaughter.

She would forever hate him for that. Just as she would hate Stryker for his abandonment.

Sighing, she turned to reorganize the desk that she'd just organized a few minutes ago. She'd only taken a step when a light flashed.

It was Stryker.

Damn if Medea wasn't right. Her heartbeat picked up at the way he looked standing there. One lock of his black hair fell into his eyes. His features were steeled and perfect, and dusted by just the tiniest bit of whiskers. Nothing would give her more satisfaction than running her tongue down the line of his jaw and letting that shadow prick at her skin.

Anger ripped through her at the thought and the way her body betrayed the hatred she wanted to feel toward him. "What do you want?"

Stryker barely caught himself before the word "you" popped out of his mouth. It was what he wanted. *All* he needed. And right now, what he wanted most was to unbraid her blond hair and let it fall over his bare chest while she rode him the way she used to.

His cock hardened painfully. That was the most

difficult part about being around her. All he had to do was smell the slightest whiff of her lavender and valerian scent and he was rife with need.

Forcing himself to move on, he cleared his throat. "I need you and Medea to return with me to Kalosis."

"Do you really think that's safer than here?"

"Since there's an army of Charonte down there and a pissed-off goddess wanting blood, yes. Unless you know something about Artemis's buried maternal instincts that I don't. But honestly, I can't see her rising to your defense any more than she'd rise to mine."

She glared at him. "I want you to know that I'm only agreeing to this to keep Medea safe. Otherwise I'd tell you to stick it where the sun doesn't shine."

He gave her a wry grin. "Sweetie, I'm sticking you both where the sun doesn't shine. Unlike here, there's no daylight in Kalosis. Ever."

"You're not funny."

"Really? I find myself quite entertaining."

"You would."

Stryker didn't comment anymore as she stepped around him to gather a few items, including makeup and lotion. A foreign tug went through him as he remembered the way she used to meticulously apply both in the morning. He'd lie in bed while she smeared the lotion on her face, then used kohl to line her eyes and a balm of henna on her lips.

There'd been nothing more pleasing to watch. It was so womanly and sweet.

So Zephyra.

"What are you staring at?" she snapped at him.

"Nothing." His voice was more curt than he meant for it to be, but he had no intention of letting her know just how tender his emotions were where she was concerned. It would give her a power over him that she didn't need to know about.

Once she had her things gathered, he took them from her. At first she started to snatch them back. Then, without a word, she relented.

"I'll get Medea."

"Is Davyn still in her room?"

She headed for the door. "He was walking around the grounds earlier, so I'm not sure."

He followed her down the hallway to Medea's room and then froze as he found the two of them playing chess at her table that was set next to the window. Davyn's face was bruised and swollen from his attack, but otherwise he appeared to be back in business.

Zephyra put her hands on her hips. "Should I be concerned that the two of you appear so cozy in here?"

Medea studied the board. "Relax, Mum. He's actually nice for a Daimon."

Zephyra cast an arch stare at Stryker. "I think you should have a word with your man."

"Why?"

"He's alone in your daughter's bedroom with her."

"Playing chess."

"For now . . ."

Stryker laughed. "Relax, Phyra. I'd be more concerned if he were in here with my son than with my daughter. The biggest threat he poses is he might want to borrow her shoes."

Her lips formed a silent *oh*.

Davyn laughed as he moved his bishop. "You don't have to worry about that, either, since she has the tiniest feet I've ever seen on a woman. Besides, just because I prefer men doesn't mean I want to be a woman. Trust me."

Zephyra clapped her hands together commandingly. "All right, I need the two of you up. Medea, gather your things. We're going to stay with your father for a bit."

She was aghast at Zephyra's declaration. "Why?" she asked Stryker.

He bristled under her tone. "I'm your father. You don't question me."

She shot to her feet.

Zephyra sighed aloud. "Medea, stop your anger and do as he says." She turned to face Stryker with an evil glare. "And you need to remember that she's the daughter you've never met. Not one of your soldiers to be ordered about."

Davyn rose more slowly. "If it makes you feel better, Medea, his tone was much nicer when he barked at you than when he barks at us."

Stryker cut a murderous look in his direction. "You need to stay out of this."

"Yes, my lord."

Medea paused by her mother's side. "I don't see why we have to run from demons."

"Not demons, love. War. And we're not running. We're strategically taking the high ground so that we can hold him off until we find his weakness. Now get your things."

Nick jumped as he walked past a mirror and caught sight of himself. "Holy shit," he breathed. His skin was bloodred and covered with ancient black symbols. But it was his face that held him paralyzed.

His hair was black, streaked with red that came down

into his face. Black lines cut across both his eyes and down his cheeks. His ebony eyes flashed red.

Stunned, he looked down to see his arms and hands were also red marked by black.

"What the hell is going on?"

"It's your true form."

He turned to see Menyara, only he didn't see the older woman who'd raised him. Now she was taller than him and looked to be in her early twenties. She was dressed in a black halter top with tight black pants, her long hair swept up into a stylized ponytail.

"Who are you? Really?"

Menyara tossed him one of the two staves she held. "I've been known by many names over the centuries. But you would know me best by Ma'at."

Nick's heart skipped as he remembered the Egyptian goddess. She was the one who upheld the order of the universe. Goddess of justice and truth. Menyara had given him a statue of her on his seventh birthday.

"She will protect you from harm, Nicholas. Put her by your bed and no one will ever harm you while you sleep. She will watch over you. Always." He could still remember her telling him that.

Bitter anger swept though him. "For a goddess of truth, you've lied your ass off to me."

Menyara smiled. "Not lied, sweetie. I merely withheld a few facts from you and your mother. If it makes you feel better, I'm the reason Cherise was never suspicious of your Dark-Hunters. I kept her carefully shielded from all the paranormal events in her life. Just as I tried to do with you. But fate is a bitch who won't be denied. You were meant to ascend to your powers and not even mine could keep you sheltered forever."

"I would say thanks for keeping my mother blind to my extracurricular activities, but that's part of what got her killed." He tested the weight of the staff. "What am I supposed to do with this?"

She brought hers down across his face, forcing him to block the stroke with his staff. "You have to learn to fight."

"I was born fighting." This time, he barely countered her move before she hit his head.

"People, but not the powers who will come for you now." She swung at him again.

Nick blocked and twisted the staff from her grip. He smiled proudly as he disarmed her. "Told you. I'm the best there ever was."

She snorted at his arrogance. "And I'm a goddess of truth, not of war. Beating me shows you can defeat an old woman. Nothing more. Don't get cocky."

Nick curled his lip. "You know, if you were going to shield me and my mother, you should have shielded us from poverty." Pain ripped through him as he remembered the defeated look on his mother's face every time she brushed her hand through his hair, then took the stage to strip her clothes off so that she could feed him. She'd once told him that the only reason she took him to work with her was to remind her why she had to do what she did. Otherwise she would have run for the door.

Guilt ate at him. It always had. He'd ruined his mother's life, and then his own stupidity had ended it.

Menyara held her hand up and snatched the staff from his tight grip. She shoved him back into the wall with one end of it. He grimaced in pain as she dug the tip into his chest.

"That poverty is what made you human, boy. Without it or your mother, you would be exactly as your father."

"Bullshit!"

She opened her mouth to speak, then froze.

An instant later, a blinding light flashed through the room. Nick hissed as it cut across him, burning his skin.

Something ferocious slammed into him, lifting him up from the floor and pinning him to the ceiling. He tried to push himself away, but he felt like a roach under someone's foot as they pressed it against the floor.

Suddenly he hit the ground.

Menyara ran to him as he groaned in pain. His ears buzzing, he tried to focus. Every part of him hurt.

Until he looked up.

There across the room was Acheron, and he was fighting a man who bore the same stylized patterns on his skin that Nick had. Only where Nick's were red this man's symbols were black and where his were black the man's were red.

"Stay out of this, Atlantean," the demon thing snarled.

Acheron caught the blast sent toward him with his hand. "Menyara, get Nick out of here. Now!"

Before Nick could protest, she wrapped herself around him and everything went black.

Jared cursed as they vanished. "What are you doing?"

"I told you. I am honor-bound to keep him safe and so I will protect him with my life."

"Are you insane?"

Ash took a step back as the Sephiroth stopped fighting him. "I'm an Atlantean god, Jared. I swore to his mother that no one would ever harm him. You know what that means."

Jared stepped back, too, as he calmed. His skin immediately returned to its human appearance. "So when I kill him, you die, too. Are you out of your freakin' mind? Why would you do that?"

"Because I thought he was human and I owed his mother that promise."

"And now you know the truth. You are a Chthonian, charged with maintaining the balance of the universe. The Malachai must die."

Ash shook his head. "The order of the universe is for him to live so long as you do."

Jared laughed. "You don't get it, do you? I want to die, Acheron. If I kill him, I will go with him." He shoved Ash back, then disappeared.

Ash cursed as he realized he had no way to track him. *Damn.* "Jared!" he snarled, shooting his voice out into the ether so that the Sephiroth would hear it. "You don't get it. If I die, the world dies with me. You can't kill Nick Gautier."

Jared didn't respond.

Ash let out an aggravated breath. Jared was right, Ash was charged with keeping the order of the universe. And no one was going to stop him from carrying out his duties.

"Savitar?" he whispered, summoning him.

Savitar appeared as an apparition beside him. "What, grom?"

"You knew about Nick, didn't you?"

Savitar averted his gaze, affirming Ash's suspicion.

"Why didn't you tell me?" Ash asked.

"I won't tamper with fate. You know that. But, yeah, when you asked me to train Nick and I saw him for the first time, I knew what he was. It's why I didn't train him. Had I started, it would have unlocked his powers. His shield was solid so long as he wasn't struck by those of us who draw our powers from the Source."

Ash frowned at the news. "Then why didn't his powers unlock the night I fought him?"

"I don't know. Probably had something to do with the fact that your powers are mixed. Or it could be something as simple as you two were close friends, and even though you fought, you wouldn't have really killed him. Even at your angriest, you were never a real threat to him. He didn't need his powers to protect himself from you."

"And yet I'm the reason he died."

"No, Nick is the reason he died. He pulled the trigger."

How simple Savitar made it sound, but it didn't change the one single truth of that night. "Because I cursed him to it."

Savitar gave him a droll stare. "Be glad I'm not physically there or I'd slap you upside the head. You know how free will works, so stop the whining and get off the cross. Someone needs the wood."

Ash wasn't amused and he wasn't a martyr crying over inconsequential crap. There was no denying that he'd been the one to set all of this into motion. But past regrets weren't solving the current problem. "How do I stop Jared?"

"You can't. Only his master can rein him in."

"And if she won't?"

"We're all screwed."

Stryker hated how much he loved seeing Zephyra's belongings mixed in with his. Her hairbrush, her lotions.

Her perfume. He picked the latter up so that he could smell it.

"What are you doing?"

He put the small glass container down immediately. "Nothing."

"It wasn't nothing. You were mooning over my things, weren't you?"

He arched one brow at her choice of words. "'Mooning'? What kind of archaic term is that?"

She returned his stare with one of her own. "You're not going to distract me that easily. You were pining for me just now."

He took a step toward her and eyed her suspiciously, yet she showed no emotion whatsoever. If only he could train his men to be this effective . . . "Is that what you want me to say? You already know how much I missed you."

She narrowed her eyes. "But I want to hear you say it."

"Why?"

She leaned against him and gave him a glance that was part malice, part joy, and part teasing. "Because I want to see how much my absence has tortured you."

He started to leave, but he couldn't make his body obey him. He couldn't. Instead, he found the one simple truth leaving his lips. "I've missed you."

Zephyra wanted to slap him for those words. She wanted to beat him until the hurt inside her stopped aching. But she knew the truth. There wasn't enough abuse in the world to erase the damage he'd wrought. "Do you think that fixes anything?"

"It fixes nothing." His tone was brittle. "But while you stand there, hating me, think of it from my point of view. I'm the one who fucked up, and that's the reality and knowledge I've had to live with every single day of my life. You were my one true heart. My other half and *I* walked out on you. Have you any idea how much that knowledge has eaten at me?"

She sank her hand in his hair and wrenched it until he grimaced. Unable to cope with all the tangled emotions roiling through her, she jerked him close and kissed him fiercely.

Stryker breathed her in as her tongue danced with his and he tasted her fully. In all his life, she was the only thing that he'd ever really craved. Needing to be as close to her as possible, he scooped her up in his arms and carried her to the bed.

She only broke from his kiss long enough to pull his shirt over his head. Unable to bear another second without her, he used his powers to strip their clothes off completely.

She pulled back with arched brows. "That's a handy power you have there," she breathed against his lips.

Before he could respond, she rolled him over on the mattress, nipping at his chin with her fangs. Stryker growled at how good she felt. Holding her, he traveled back to the days when he'd been nothing more than a young prince. The world had been new and fresh. There had been no hatred in his heart. No loneliness.

In her arms, he'd always been able to see into forever.

Now she attacked him with the same fervor he felt looking at her. Closing his eyes, he savored her naked skin against his. Her hands clutching his body tight. Even though he was damned and lost, this was heaven and she was his angel.

Zephyra pressed her cheek against his as she tugged at his earlobe with her teeth. His whiskers scraped her skin, raising chills on her body. He smelled of male and spicy aftershave that blended well with her own scent. For years after he'd left, she'd kept his tunic and held it in the wee hours of the night, aching for his return.

In a fit of anger over Apollo's curse, she'd burned it. But now that she was with Stryker again, she wanted to forgive him everything. To go back in time and keep him by her side.

If only she could.

"I need you inside me," she whispered. Their play could come later. Right now she wanted to be as close to him as was possible.

He answered her with one low groan as he slid himself into her body to accommodate her request.

She cried out in pleasure as she ground herself against his hips, needing to be a part of him. She'd forgotten just how good it felt to be with a man, especially one so skilled. His every thrust, every lick, set her on fire until she wanted to scream in bliss.

Stryker rolled with her, planting her in the center of the bed as he moved even faster and harder against her. His silvery gaze locked with hers, and there in the dim light the exposed vulnerability inside him made her breath catch. The arrogance of his youth was gone, and the pain inside the man tore her apart. So much had happened to both of them since that day in Agapa's temple when they'd bound themselves as husband and wife.

Once again, she saw the tall, uncertain youth who'd laid the dagger's blade to his hand as he cut himself. "With my blood, my heart, my soul, I swear to dedicate my life to yours. Wherever I am, you shall be with me in my thoughts forever. This I vow before your gods and mine. We are now united and only death will divide us." Then he'd leaned forward and whispered in her ear, "Even then I shall find a way to be by your side. You and me, Phyra. For all eternity."

A tear slid from the corner of her eye as that memory burned her. She'd believed in him.

"Phyra?"

She swallowed as he stopped moving and looked down at her.

"Am I hurting you?"

A sob caught in her throat. "You tore my heart out, you bastard. You made me believe in you when I believed in no one except me."

Stryker sucked his breath in at those words that shredded his soul. "All I ever wanted to be was the man you saw me as. I wish to the gods that I could undo what I did. That I'd stayed and died by your side as I should have. But I can't undo the past. I can't undo the hurt. I know it's no consolation, but I promise you it was no easier on me." His gaze seared her. "I've never in my life apologized for anything. I've never begged anyone for anything. But I am sorry for what I did and I would gladly go down on my knees if you could forgive me for it."

She pushed him away, then rolled to sit up. "I don't know how to forgive anymore."

Stryker winced as those words tore through him. He deserved nothing more than her scorn. But he couldn't let it go at that. His heart broken, he moved so that he could gently unbraid her hair. The silken strands teased at his flesh as he remembered her brushing it every night before she'd joined him in bed.

Zephyra clutched her fists into the cover as his tenderness touched her deeply. She didn't want to forgive him, but his words and sincerity weakened her. Looking at him over her shoulder, she melted even more. This was a man renowned for his cruelty and savagery. He hesitated at nothing.

Yet he brushed his hand through her hair as if afraid of hurting her.

How could she hate someone who loved her so much? Hate the man who'd given her the most precious thing in her life?

"This doesn't mean I like you," she growled before she pushed him back and straddled his hips.

Stryker smiled as Zephyra leaned over him and sank her fangs into his neck to feed. He would gladly let her bleed him dry if it meant he could hold her like this as he died. His head swam with the scent of her, the sensation of her breasts pressing against his chest while the small hairs at the juncture of her thighs rubbed against his hip.

Leaning his head down, he inhaled the valerian even as she nipped him painfully. This was paradise.

He brushed his hand down her arm until he laced his fingers with hers. Lifting her hand, he placed a kiss on her palm before he sank his fangs into her wrist.

She jerked ever so slightly, but she didn't pull away. Stryker growled at the sweet taste of her. And as he drank, he felt her powers merging with his. Until now, he'd had no idea just how much demonic energy she held.

I should never have been able to defeat her. . . .

He tensed at that realization. She'd let him win. A slow smile curled his lips, but he didn't speak. He didn't want to anger her again. Not when they were like this.

She pulled back to stare down at him. He released her hand as her hair teased his chest. Truly there was no more beautiful sight than her rising above him while her bare breasts brushed against him.

Zephyra was caught by the handsomeness of Stryker. The power of him. Now she knew the truth. He had restrained himself in their fight. He could have seriously hurt her and yet he hadn't.

If only she could trust him again.

Did she dare?

He lifted himself up so that he could gently suckle her breast. Cupping his head against her, she shivered at the sensation of his hot tongue sweeping over her. He lifted her effortlessly and set her down on him. She sucked her breath in sharply at the sensation of his body inside hers.

She lifted his chin up so that she could taste his lips again while she moved ever so slowly against him. How she delighted in the way he felt. In the sensation of his breath mingling with hers.

Stryker couldn't even think straight as his body cried out in pleasure. It took every piece of his control not to come from the sheer joy of being with her. He dug his nails into his palm in an effort to keep himself in check. But it was hard.

This was the only woman he'd ever loved.

A whisper of a smile curved his lips as he fingered her ear. There was one spot. . . .

Dipping his head, he swept his tongue behind her ear, down to the lobe.

She sucked her breath in sharply as chills spread over her, drawing her nipples tight.

"You're still so sensitive."

She gave him a heated look. "And what about you?"

"I've never been sensitive."

"Uh-huh." She swept her hands under his arms and down his ribs, making him jump. She groaned as it caused him to go even deeper inside her.

Laughing, Stryker pushed her back against the bed. Zephyra arched her back, bringing him in even deeper. He quickened his strokes until she couldn't stand it anymore. She came in a bright flash of sensations that exploded through her. Crying out, she wrapped herself around him and held him close as her body pulsed.

Stryker growled as he joined her in release. He held her close as his body shook and his toes curled.

She was delicious and he wanted to spend the rest of his life entwined with her naked in his bed.

He pulled back with an arrogant taunt. "So tell me, love . . . are you disappointed?"

She crinkled her nose. "Hmm, well, all things considered, I suppose there is a term for it."

"And that is?"

"'Poor play.'"

He snorted at her bad pun. "The night is still young. I have many more hours left to savor you, and I assure you when I'm done 'poor' is the last word that will come to your mind."

She put on a haughty front, unwilling to let him know exactly how pleased she was with him. "Well, if you wish to embarrass yourself again, who am I to stop you?"

He tsked at her. "You're so evil." He reached around her to pull back the covers so that he could tuck her into his bed.

"You were serious about continuing?" she asked.

"Absolutely. I have a few centuries to make up for."

She started to respond, but before she could there was a knock on his door.

He made sure she was covered completely, then he barked, "Come in."

It was Davyn. He took one step into the room, then

paused as he saw Stryker naked while she was beside him. He quickly averted his gaze. "My lord, I wanted to report that we're having another bit of a problem."

"And that is?"

"We can't feed."

Stryker exchanged a frown with her before he addressed Davyn. "What do you mean?"

"War and the demons have us locked in. If any Daimon leaves here to feed, they either kill him or convert him. We're trapped."

Stryker let out a foul curse. "How long until you need to feed again?"

"I fed last night, so I'm good for a few weeks. And you, sir?"

He glanced at Zephyra.

She went cold as she understood that look. "I've taken blood from you twice. . . ."

He nodded. "I'll be good for a couple of days."

She swallowed in fear of his dry tone as a sense of dread went through her. "How many?"

"Maybe two."

And then he'd be dead.

9

Zephyra didn't speak again until Davyn had left them alone. Stryker turned toward her on the bed and her gaze dropped to where she'd stabbed him earlier. He followed the line of her eyes. Though the wound was healing, it was still a nasty reminder of her temper.

And deadly aim.

"Looks like you'll be getting your wish sooner rather than later, huh?" he said flippantly.

She clutched the sheet to her chest. "There has to be a way out of here."

"Yes, but they have one advantage. The demons aren't nocturnal. They can box us in day and night. We can only feed after dark."

"Can you bring humans here?"

In theory, yes. But things were seldom so simple. "Only if they stumble into a bolt hole. Something much easier said than done. We usually only get kids with those traps, and a large number of Daimons, including myself, have trouble swallowing the soul of a child. Even if they are human cattle."

Her gaze darkened with fury. "They've killed our children without flinching."

Again, not so simple. "Their parents kill our children,

not them. They're innocent in this fight. My father forced me to be a monster when he cursed me to this life, but I refuse to lose all sense of myself to his lunacy."

She shook her head. "You're a warrior. Are you telling me that you've never slaughtered a child in battle?"

"I trained for war as a mortal, but I never battled until after I became a Daimon. So no, I've never taken the life of a child. Having been a father, I don't know if I ever could." He narrowed his eyes on her. "And that doesn't make me a coward."

Zephyra held her hands up in surrender at his hostile tone. She'd inadvertently struck a nerve when she hadn't meant to. "It never crossed my mind." At least not over his inability to harm a child. Other things he'd done . . .

That was another story.

As he got up from the bed, she saw the tattoo on his right shoulder blade that had escaped her attention while she'd been focused on their earlier play. It made her do a double take as the tattoo fully registered in her mind.

No, it couldn't be. . . .

"Stop," she said, pulling him back to examine it.

It was a broken heart with thorny vines twisted through it and a sword that plunged down its carmine center. But it was the ribbon and the name it contained that covered the tattoo that made her breath catch in her throat.

Zephyra.

Beneath it were eighteen small black teardrops that formed an intricate pattern. She traced them with her fingertip. "Who are these for?"

"One for each of my children and grandchildren. And one for each of my wives."

But it was her name he'd put inside the ribbon. Hers alone that marked his broken heart.

She glanced up to meet his gaze as he looked at her over his shoulder. Memories of their past together and conflicted emotions ripped through her. He was so familiar and so alien.

"Who are you, Strykerius?"

"I'm a lost soul," he breathed quietly. "I had a purpose at one time, but I stumbled on the path of it."

"And now?"

His gaze narrowed dangerously. Seductively. "I see what I want again, but for the first time in my life, I'm not sure if I can claim it. I should have never left you and I know it."

She laid her hand against the stubble of his cheek. "I'm a servant of Artemis. I owe her for taking me in when no one else would."

"Haven't you paid that debt a thousandfold?"

Zephyra paused. Had she? Artemis could be so fickle and cold. Over the centuries, Zephyra had executed countless humans for Artemis and others who'd defamed or offended the goddess. Strange how she'd never really thought about leaving Artemis's service before this. She'd been content to stay in the shelter of the goddess's temple and merely exist. Her only goal in all these centuries had been to protect her daughter.

How could she not have had a goal other than that? Because her last goal had been to grow old and love a man who'd walked out the door and broken her heart. Her spirit. Her life.

After that, she'd vowed to never set herself up again for so much pain. Once had definitely been enough for her.

Stryker turned around on the bed to face her with a look so intense and raw it raised chills on her body. "Join me again, Phyra. Stand by my side and I will lay the world of man at your feet. We will find a way to break my father's curse and take our place in the sunlight."

"I haven't touched daylight in over eleven thousand years. Not since the night we were warned of the curse."

"I would give that to you."

She shook her head in denial. "You promised me the world once before and then you threw it in my face."

"I'm different now, Phyra. I'm not a scared child living in his father's shadow. I've learned from my mistake and I swear that I will never again leave you."

She wanted to believe that but didn't know if she could. Promises were so easy to make and so hard to keep. It was a rare person who could carry through their execution. "And yet you'll die in two days if we don't feed you."

"Even in death, I shall find a way to be by your side."

Those words set her anger on fire as he reminded her of the vow he'd taken at their wedding. "How dare you!" she snarled, shoving him back.

"I don't understand."

"You mock me with those words."

His expression was true bafflement. How could he not know? "How so?"

"You promised me love and you left less than a year later. How can I trust you now?"

"I never married again after my wife died. Not in all these centuries and not because of how I felt about her. It was the memory of you that kept me single. No woman has ever captivated me the way you did."

And no other man had ever claimed her heart. None. Only Stryker had been able to break the shield she'd erected around herself.

It was why she hated him so much.

"Matera!"

She looked at the door at the same time Medea slung it open. For once Medea didn't react to seeing them naked in bed together. That alone told Zephyra how dire the news was.

"Kessar has sent an emissary to speak with Father. He needs to come immediately."

Stryker's clothes appeared on his body as he left the bed. Zephyra was just about to reach for hers when he dressed her, too. She scooted out of bed to meet Medea in the doorway.

Stryker took the lead.

Medea lifted one curious brow as she drew even to Zephyra, but said nothing as they followed Stryker down the hallway to the receiving hall. There in the dim light, the Daimons were gathered around a tall, lithe gallu female. Her long black hair was loose around her shoulders as she curled her lips in repugnance at the gathered Daimons.

Stryker didn't speak as he walked past her to the dais where his black skeletal throne waited. It shimmered in the dim light and looked as menacing and lethal as the man who occupied it. Zephyra followed him up, expecting him to protest. He didn't. With the presence of a god, he took a seat nonchalantly and stared at the gallu as if she were an insect on his floor he was about to step on. Zephyra took position on the right-hand side of his throne. She braced one hand on the top spindle that was carved into the image of a spine.

"You have word from Kessar?" Stryker asked the gallu.

"He offers you a chance to surrender."

Stryker laughed aloud at her stupidity. At Kessar's

audacity. If they thought to make him blink, they were sadly mistaken. "I told him to quit sucking the blood of idiots. It's now infected his own intellect."

The female gallu snapped her fingers.

Two more gallu came forward with a Daimon in chains. It was Illyria, one of his Spathi commanders. Her pale blond hair was a stark contrast to her black clothing. True to her nature and station, she didn't beg as they brutally forced her to her knees.

But she was weak. Her skin held that ashen, iridescent cast that came from waiting too long to feed. Her body was starting to age and decay. Already she looked older than twenty-seven. In a matter of minutes, she'd become middle-aged.

"Give them nothing, my lord," Illyria spat, trying to fight the two gallu who held her.

"She will die if you don't surrender."

Stryker shrugged. "We all die, gallu. You should be more concerned about your own fate."

She raked him with a cold glare. "Your skin shows that you need to feed, too." She cupped Illyria's chin in her hand. "Look at her aging. Her bones are becoming brittle. She won't last out the hour. Even if you feed from one another, you will only die that much sooner."

Stryker maintained his air of nonchalance. "I'm not Sisyphus trying to restrain death. Illyria is a soldier. If it's her time, it's her time. I'm not at war with Atropos. It's her will to take us whenever she likes. My only goal is to die with dignity."

Zephyra was impressed by Stryker's demeanor and levelheaded negotiation. He wasn't the same as the boy she'd known. The man before her was fierce and not willing to be intimidated.

She could appreciate that. Just as she saw the aggravation in the eyes of the gallu. The demon was about to slip up.

And as Zephyra glared at the gallu, an idea came to her. It was bold but illuminating. She placed her hand on Stryker's shoulder and leaned forward to whisper into his ear. "Drink from the gallu. . . ."

Stryker went still at her words. Gallu blood was infectious. It could convert anyone who came into contact with it into one of them and make that person a mindless zombie for them to control. Did Zephyra hate him so much that she wished that fate on him?

He met her gaze. She was beautiful there, by his side. It was where she should have always been. Yet he didn't know if he could trust her. What she proposed . . .

It was suicide.

"Trust me," she breathed in his ear, sending chills down his body.

Did he dare? She'd said it herself, women were vengeful to the end.

Her dark eyes seared him and told him nothing about her intent. She could be setting him up to live.

Or die.

"Take the gallu's soul," she said in a tone so low he wasn't even sure he heard it. "Kill the bitch and she can't control you."

Losing patience, the gallu cleared her throat. "You are completely cut off. We will take all of you down. Your only hope is to surrender and beg mercy from Kessar and the rest of us."

The universe would shatter to pieces before he begged anyone for anything.

Stryker rose slowly to his feet. Zephyra still gave him

no clue as to her mood or intent. If she was being honest. Or setting him up.

No matter, he wasn't one to be bullied ever. Descending his dais, he walked toward the gallu. The two holding Illyria tightened their grips, ready to kill her should he move on them.

"Sriana ey froya," he said in Atlantean to Illyria. *Succor them and destroy them.* He glanced at Illyria and felt his eyes change. No longer silver, he knew they were now glowing red. He was calling forth the god powers inside him. Turning back to the gallu, he locked gazes with her.

She stiffened instantly as her will was negated by the one blessing Apollo had forgotten to take from the Apollites when he'd cursed them.

They could control anyone with a weak will. It was that gift that allowed them to take human souls into their bodies. But the hard part was finding humans whose love of life was strong, but their minds were weak. In the case of the gallu, the two were synonymous.

Stryker held his hand out to her. "Come to me, gallu."

She didn't hesitate to obey.

A slow smile curled his lips as he pulled her close and then sank his fangs into her throat. She cried out as he drank and she bled.

Illyria followed suit on the gallu to her left while Davyn grabbed the one on her right.

Stryker's head swam at the taste of power inside the gallu blood. At least until his stomach began to cramp and ache. Instinctively he started to pull away, only to find Zephyra there.

"Don't stop," she said, holding his head to the gallu's throat. "Not until she's dead."

He pulled back enough so that he could speak. "I think I'm converting. I don't feel right."

"You will. Trust me."

She kept saying that, but he still wasn't sure if he should believe her. Honestly, he felt ill from the blood. As if he would vomit at any moment. But he kept his fangs in the gallu's throat and continued to drain her until Zephyra pierced her between her eyes to kill her.

Then he felt it. That moment when the last gasp of life left and the body went limp in his arms. He held the demon's chest against his heart—the center of his being—and waited for her soul to merge with his. Normally the absorption was a small shock that was followed by a sense of profound invigoration.

This time it struck him like a lightning bolt and caused him to drop the body and stagger back. He cried out as it ripped through him, blackening his skin. He struggled to breathe, but it was impossible. Over and over he saw lights flashing around him and heard the sound of his blood pumping through his veins. It was like staring at the fabric of the universe. The power coalesced inside him, heating his body and making his senses swirl.

He cast his gaze around the room and noted the way his men shrank back. Suddenly Zephyra was there.

She took his face in her hands. "Look at me, Strykerius. Focus."

He did and as their gazes locked his heart slowed down. His vision and hearing cleared.

A slow smile curved her lips an instant before she ripped his shirt open. He frowned as she placed her hand over his heart, where there was no longer a black mark denoting where the soul exchange took place. Stryker stared at the unblemished skin in confusion. The moment an Apollite took a human soul into their body to elongate their life, a black mark appeared over their heart where the souls merged.

His was gone.

"I don't understand."

"When a Daimon merges with a demon, you have the strength of both species. They are immortal. Now so are you."

He was aghast. "How is this possible?"

She smiled evilly. "Gallu blood is potent. Whatever it is that makes it infectious merges with our DNA and strengthens us. You're free from having to take souls in."

He turned to look at Davyn and Illyria, who were now standing over the bodies of the gallu they'd killed. "We're not gallu slaves?"

Zephyra shook her head. "Not once your master is killed. It's a new world, Stryker. A new dawn."

And Zephyra had given it to him. Nothing could have meant more.

"The only thing that will kill you now is decapitation."

He wanted to shout out in joy. "How many Daimons can we convert with one gallu? If we feed the blood to several and then kill the demon, will it convert all and then free them when we kill it?"

She shrugged. "There's only one way to find out. Try it and see."

Stryker laughed as he looked around at the Spathi who'd gathered. "You heard the lady. Let's hold an experiment and see what happens. If it works, we feed from and then kill them and we no longer have to take human souls to live. I think it's time we had open season on the gallu." He laughed again at the very idea of turning the tables on Kessar and his people. "Who's hungry?"

A roar went up.

Stryker turned toward Davyn. "Open a bolt hole and let's grab us one more gallu to test my lady's theory."

Davyn bowed his head and saluted him. "As you wish, my lord." He motioned for Illyria and two more Spathi to join him.

Stryker returned to his throne, where he sat with a whole new outlook on the future of his people. The dawn of the Daimon was just beginning, and he intended to rain hell on the humans before all was said and done.

Gazing down, he curled his lip at the three gallu bodies on the floor. They were as repugnant to him as his father. "Could someone clean up the mess? Take those outside and burn them."

A small group came forward to obey him as Zephyra ascended his dais.

Ignoring his people who watched, he took her hand into his and kissed her knuckles. "Thank you, Phyra. You could have kept that bit to yourself and allowed me and my people to die."

She cast her gaze to the room. "Regardless of how I feel about you personally, I am Atlantean and an Apollite." She swept her hand out to indicate his soldiers. "We are the last warriors of our kind. Be damned if I'm going to stand by and watch the gallu prey on us. They're inferior maggots. We are the children of the gods. We bow to no one."

Stryker smiled at the confusion on the faces of his people. "It just occurred to me that no one knows who you are, my love." Standing up, he turned her to face the crowd. "Daimons. My brothers and sisters, allow me to introduce Zephyra. My queen."

Zephyra tensed at his proclamation. "Aren't you being presumptuous?" she asked under her breath.

He leaned forward to whisper in her ear. "If you kill me, my people will need a leader. After this I trust you will do what's best for them. Whether married to me or not, you are my queen and my equal. There is no one else I would trust to lead and protect my people."

She inclined her head to him.

Stryker held his hand out toward Medea. "And this is my daughter. I trust you will all show Medea and Zephyra the respect and deference they deserve." He quirked a wry grin. "If not, I'm sure they'll painfully make you regret any slight you give them."

Medea looked less than pleased by the cheers that rang out around her. But Zephyra didn't seem to mind their adulation.

As Stryker took a step toward his daughter, Davyn returned with a gallu. He threw the demon toward the two Daimons who'd accompanied him. They set on the gallu with a fervor born of desperation and were joined by three more Daimons who helped in the feeding. The demon did his best to fight, but he was no match for the Daimons who held him down and preyed on him.

Stryker watched with a morbid fascination as the Daimons started converting. Would this work? Or would they have to put his men down?

The answer came as Davyn killed the gallu. The demon gave one last scream of pain and then died on the floor below. The first Daimon, Laeta, grabbed the soul and took it in. Her eyes glowed red as she leaned her head back and cried out.

An instant later, she rose to her feet and lifted her shirt. Her Daimon's mark was gone.

And so were the marks from the others who'd fed on the gallu.

Stryker wanted to shout out in joy as he realized they'd found the key to their survival. The key to their salvation.

Overcome by happiness, he snatched Zephyra up and twirled around with her. "You are brilliant!" he said, laughing.

Zephyra couldn't breathe as she saw the boy she'd loved inside the man she loathed. This was the same Strykerius who'd stolen her heart. Closing her eyes, she savored the feel of him holding her. It felt so good to be held again. To feel like she was a part of something and not just going through the motions of life. For so long she'd been numb.

But right here, right now, she felt whole. Like she'd given something to the world that mattered. And to the Daimons who no longer had to scrounge for souls she had.

She'd given them life.

And now they, like Stryker, cheered her name. It was the headiest of combinations.

Smiling, she looked down into his silver eyes that shimmered with a life force equal to her own. Part of her wanted to hold on to him forever and the other wanted to beat him for not being there for her when she needed him. For not holding her hand while she struggled to bring their baby into the world. Not teaching Medea how to walk and talk.

He'd missed everything.

The war inside her was harsh and it was painful. How could he make her feel so torn?

And while he held her, all she could remember was how safe she felt in his arms. She was strong, stronger than she ever needed to be, and yet he made her weak in the knees and the heart. Made her want to lean on him even though she was more than capable of surviving alone.

Surviving. That's exactly what she did without him. She survived.

But with him, she lived.

In this moment, she surrendered herself to that sensation. To the sound of his laughter in her ears and the feel of his arms holding her close to that hard, perfect body. Growling with the ferocity of her need, she kissed him.

Stryker felt as if he could fly. He didn't know what it was about this woman, but she set fire to his soul. She always had.

"Didn't you two just get through doing that?" Medea asked in a surly tone.

Stryker pulled back with a laugh. "Are you going blind again, Daughter?"

"Scarred for life, thank you very much. I'm definitely going to need counseling."

Stryker traced the shape of Zephyra's lips before he gave her one more quick kiss. Then he looked back at his people. "Now that we know what we can do, let's tear those bastards apart. Davyn, open the bolt holes."

War stepped back and laughed as he watched the Daimons and the gallu tear into each other. It was absolutely beautiful.

"You are positively evil." Ker draped one long, graceful arm over his shoulder as she watched with him. "I love it."

It was so good to have her and Mache with him again.

"We still have the Malachai to deal with."

She sighed nonchalantly. "We will find him. Ma'at protects him, but she can't stand alone. I've been wanting a piece of her for quite some time. Have no fear. We'll both be appeased."

He watched as she split into ten beings.

"We'll find him," they said, their voices echoing. Then they took flight, leaving him alone with their source.

He sucked his breath in sharply at her ability to do that. It'd always made him hot. But there would be time for sex later. Right now they had to secure their freedom.

"Our fellow Greek gods are pulling together from other pantheons to come after us."

"Mache will handle them. He's already back with Eris, stirring them up against each other."

Eris . . . the goddess of discord. War had spent many a night in her bed, too. Though not an official member of his band, she'd been useful to him from time to time.

He stiffened as an idea struck him. "Get Eris. I have a job for her."

"And that is?"

"We need her to feed the Greek paranoia where Ma'at is concerned."

Ker frowned. "I don't understand."

"We convince the Greeks that she's going to use the Malachai to destroy them. As much as they hate anyone with ties to the Egyptians, they'll turn on her in a minute." He laughed again. "Think about it. Why else would she protect a Malachai unless her goal was to destroy the rest of the pantheons?"

"Because he's the balance."

War rolled his eyes. "You know that and I know that. But Eris can stir them up to where they won't think of it. Now go and feed their frenzy."

She vanished and left him to savor the scent of the bloodbath going on as the Daimons and gallu continued to clash.

This was what he'd been bred for.

It was a new world he was creating and it would just be a matter of time before he would have all of them dancing to his whims.

Now he just had one more thing to deal with and then the world would be his.

10

Zephyra sat on Stryker's throne while he and his Daimons were off fighting the gallu. She'd sent Medea with her father, then stayed behind to sort through everything that had happened in the last few hours.

She needed time alone to think and to absorb all the complications that had blindsided her. It was all coming at her too quickly, and she was overwhelmed by her emotions and by the sheer magnitude of Stryker's presence. And his passion. But as she sat here alone in the darkness, for the first time in centuries she could see a better future.

Stryker standing at her side while they fought to reclaim their place in the world that had been so hostile to them.

Closing her eyes, she imagined what it would be like to sit here with him while they commanded his army. Now that they had the power of the gallu inside them, they could come out of hiding and live again in the world of man.

No, not the world of man.

The world of the Daimon.

A slow smile curled her lips as she saw that so clearly in her mind. With Medea's powers, they could rout out whatever gallu were still around and corral other demons to see what powers they could strip from them and use, too. There was no limit to what they might be capable of doing.

They could even become a new breed of gods.

Why had she never thought of this before?

Because she'd been a shell of a person for far too long. She'd forgotten what it was like to have this fire inside her that wanted more. This fire that lived and breathed and consumed. The fire that wouldn't be denied and that craved a better existence than the one she'd known.

For the first time in centuries, she was whole and she saw a future for herself and her daughter. One of power . . .

Of destruction. . . .

"You don't need Stryker for that."

She opened her eyes to find War standing in front of her. More handsome than a god of destruction should be, he stood with his weight on one leg and an arrogant countenance that would have been devastating had she not known the truth of his lethal capriciousness. To him they were all nothing but pawns to be commanded and destroyed at his whims.

But she could never be so stupid. Rage simmered in her blood as she rose to her feet to let him know that she wasn't afraid of him or his powers. "What are you doing here?"

"I came to see Stryker, but instead, I see the most beautiful woman ever born. Truly you are exceptional."

She scoffed. "I don't flatter easily."

Before she could blink, he was beside her. His eyes were dark as he looked down at her with a hunger that was flattering, hot, and terrifying. A hint of a smile played at the edge of his lips. "And I don't give it as a rule. But you . . ." He sucked his breath in sharply as he gave her an appreciative once-over. "You are enough to drive even a god mad with desire."

She stiffened at his insinuation and at his underestimation of her resolve. "You're boring me."

His smile spread over his face and turned instantly charming . . . as if that could disguise the fact that he was a jackal waiting for a chance to leap at her throat. "I would never want to do that, love. In fact, what I want is to see you come into your own. Imagine a world where *you* alone rule. A world that is laid at your feet with servants and every desire you have ever had fulfilled."

Zephyra saw it clearly before her. Even with her eyes open, she could picture the very things he described. "And what price would I have to pay?"

He brushed a lock of her hair off her shoulder, his fingers lingering on her neck as he leaned close to inhale her scent. Strange how that failed to elicit the chills that appeared whenever Stryker touched her like that. Instead, she was cold and guarded. "No price. I only wanted to point out that Stryker has designated you and your daughter as his heirs. Should he die, all of this would be yours in his place."

She frowned at what he was implying.

"Think about it," he said seductively. "A world without serving Artemis. Thousands of warriors at your fingertips who are willing to die for your pleasure. Bolt holes that can take you anywhere on earth. You would be a power to reckon with and all you have to do is complete the mission Artemis gave you . . . the mission you owe her. Kill Stryker." He smiled at her as his tone turned deep and husky. "I know you want to, and deep inside so do you. Stryker left you once and you know that if given a chance, he'd do it again."

She tensed with the truth and doubt that lingered in her mind.

She knew she could trust herself. But could she honestly trust him?

"The gallu are in retreat."

Zephyra looked up as Stryker entered the bedroom, his eyes bright and cheeks flushed. He reminded her of a boy back from a thrill ride who was proud of himself for completing it.

It also reminded her of the boy who'd walked out and left her alone to fend for herself and her daughter. The boy who'd never once inquired about their welfare.

"Kill Stryker." War's words rang in her ears.

Strange how easy that assignment had seemed when Artemis had given it to her. It wasn't so simple now. Especially not when he flopped on the bed, by her side, and all the anger she wanted to feel toward him dissipated.

He was sex walking on two legs, and those legs were so long, they hung off the edge of the bed by at least ten inches. Even worse, the denim cupped his butt in a way that ought to be obscene and it made her want to sink her teeth into him. Or more to the point, wrap him around her until they were both sweaty and spent.

Kill him.

Ignoring her inner voice, she looked at him. "So you've routed them. Now what?"

He wiped at a smear of blood on his cheek and let out a tired sigh. His hair was damp and his cheeks mottled from the exertion of fighting. It made his silver eyes glow even more. "It's dawn, so we're pulling back. At dusk, we'll be back on their asses like Velcro." He let out another deep breath. "Kessar got away, which would have ruined my night had I not come home to find the most beautiful woman in the world lying on my bed." He lifted her hand up to nibble her fingertips. Chills spread up her arm, over her body, as his eyes seduced her even more. "It would have been better had she been naked, but warm and inviting either way."

She watched the way he savored her touch as he rubbed his bristled chin against her palm. The tickle made her instantly hot and aching. Until today, she'd never realized just how lonely she'd been. How much she wanted to be held by someone.

No, not someone. Him.

A hint of a smile curled his lips as he moved closer to her to place the faintest, softest kiss on her lips. His fangs scraped her bottom lip ever so gently. The mark of a true predator. When they'd been married, they'd had no fangs. No craving for blood . . .

They'd just been two kids in love.

Stryker moved from her lips to her neck, where he slowly laved her skin, making her wet and needy. "Stay with me, Phyra," he breathed in her ear.

"I'm not the one who left."

Stryker gathered her into his arms and savored the softness of her body against his as guilt shredded him. He'd made so many mistakes in his past. Mistakes that kept him awake long past dawn when he should have been sleeping. But with her here, he felt as if he had another chance to undo some of what tore at his conscience.

"I know." He wanted to make her forget the past. To earn her trust again. When he thought of all the years they'd been apart that they could have been together, it killed him. Because of his own stupidity, he'd missed everything.

His daughter's first step. First crush. Her marriage and the birth and death of the grandchild he'd never known. He should have been there to protect them.

It was what he'd promised.

Perhaps this was his punishment for making a vow before the gods that he hadn't kept. To see them now and lose them for eternity.

But he had to have hope. He couldn't just walk away without trying to salvage what they'd once shared. "Tell me what to say or do to earn your forgiveness."

Her eyes were as tormented as his soul. "I don't know, Stryker. Time has hardened me."

He snorted. "You? You're not the one who killed your own child over a simple act." Anger and grief ripped at his conscience as he saw Urian's face in his mind. But that was nothing compared to the guilt of what he'd done. "You talk about the humans killing your son-in-law when I'm the one who killed Urian's wife. I took from my child the one thing he loved more than the world. What kind of bastard am I?"

He had become his own father, and that he hated most of all. If only he could go back and undo that as well.

Zephyra brushed the hair back from his eyes. "Why?"

That was as complicated as the universe, and he was still trying to unravel all the reasons for what had spurred him to become the very monster he'd tried so hard not to be.

"She was part of Apollo's bastard Atlantean line. The descendant of my Apollite half sisters. For centuries, I'd been hunting them, killing them off in an effort to kill my father. So long as they live, he lives. He made the same bargain with their lineage as he made with mine . . . that our lives were conjoined—and unlike me and my descendants, they never went Daimon, so while my tie to him was severed, theirs never was. And after what he'd done to me over you, I wanted him dead."

He ground his teeth as raw emotions swelled and he craved the taste of his father's blood over everything. "All I remember from my childhood was the way my father doted on my sisters, especially the eldest, and how many times he said she should have been his legacy instead of me. No matter how hard I tried, I was never good enough for him. In retrospect, I don't know now why I even tried to please him, but since I had no mother to love me, I'd hoped that he might. It was why Satara and I were . . . well, as close as two vipers can be. Because her mother was human and not Apollite, she was never good enough for him, either. She was the only person he ever treated worse than me." It was also why he hated Apollymi so much. In the end, he hadn't been good enough for her any more than he'd been for his father.

She still preferred Acheron to him even though Acheron fought against her wishes and protected the very people she wanted to destroy. Meanwhile, he served her faithfully.

Just once in his existence, he wanted to be good enough for someone. To have one person who was willing to sacrifice for him.

But it wasn't meant to be.

"When Urian went behind my back to marry one of them and I found out about it, my temper exploded. I didn't see the repercussions past my need to strike out and hurt the very person I should have protected." He shook his head. "I'm such a bastard."

She didn't comment on that. Instead, she took his hand into hers and gave him a gimlet stare. "Why didn't you tell me this when we were married?"

He glanced down at their entwined hands and felt a surge of strength over the fact that she wasn't shoving him away in disgust. He'd never been this open with another soul and he wondered why he was so open now.

But then he knew. She was his heart and he'd missed having that vital organ. "I was ashamed. You were so impressed with my lineage that I didn't want you to know the truth of what my father thought of me. I didn't want anyone to ever learn it. I wanted to pretend that I was his beloved son who was destined to carry out his exalted plans."

He looked away, unable to bear her scrutiny as he laid bare the sorest part of his soul—it was a weapon he'd never laid into the hands of another being. "You know what the world was like then. I was the only Apollite son and my father used to tell me that my eldest sister was more of a man than I was." His gaze burned as he stared at the floor and he remembered his father putting him into a dress once. He'd barely stepped foot into his father's temple when Apollo had changed his clothes in the blink of an eye. *Now you look the part of your true nature. Perhaps I should geld you, too . . . if only I didn't need you to breed. I can only hope your sons have more testosterone than you do.* Those words and the humiliation he'd felt were still branded inside his soul. His father's derision had hardened him to the point he had nothing left for anyone else. "Have you any idea how painful that is to admit even now?"

Her gaze softened as she took his hand and held it against her heart. "Is that why you loved me? Because you didn't think you could do better?"

His anger snapped at such a question. "I loved you because of the way you made me feel whenever we were together. Like I mattered to you. In your eyes, I was the man I'd hoped to be even while my father told me the only thing I'd ever be was a disappointment to him. And I haven't felt that way since the night I walked out the door and left you. You say you died that night. I've died *every* night since then. Every one."

Her nails dug into the flesh of his hand. "I hate you, Stryker."

Honestly, he didn't expect anything more from her. It was all he seemed to elicit out of everyone. His heart aching, he started away from her side.

She caught him and pulled him back until he was lying in her arms.

Startled, he locked gazes with her.

"You're still as stupid now as you were then."

His temper flared at her angry words, but before he could tell her to fuck off, she pulled his head to hers and kissed him with a passion so furious it made his senses swirl.

Cupping her head in his hand, he breathed her in and let the feel of her lips chase away all the bad memories that haunted him. It was amazing the lies a person could hide. The shame that they never wanted exposed. It was so much easier to pretend that his father had loved him, that it had been an oversight that caused Apollo to curse him along with the rest of the Apollite race.

But the harsh, bare truth . . . it was something Stryker

had never wanted to face. His father hadn't cared. And that was hurtful. Angry. Debilitating.

He closed his eyes as Zephyra nipped his chin and took away the pain of his reality. Dissolving their clothes, he rolled until she was on top of him. She was the only one he'd ever given power over him to. He belonged to her and he knew it. She'd branded herself into his soul eleven thousand years ago that day on the dock when she'd run from him. And if he had to die, he wanted it to be by her hand. By the hand of someone who had at least loved him for a little while.

Reaching up, he cupped her face in his hands while he savored the sight of her naked body on top of his. He trailed his hands from her face down to her breasts. Lush and full, they, too, had haunted his nights and left him aching for the loss of her and for moments like this one.

"When are you ever going to learn me, Stryker?" she asked.

"How so?"

She traced the lines of his lips with one long finger-nail. "I say things in anger that I never mean. When I told you to leave, all I wanted was for you to stay. I wanted to hurt you the way you'd crushed me."

"You told me I was worthless."

"That I did mean. But only because you were packing your things to obey your father and to leave me. That made me feel worthless too and so I struck out at you."

And those words had ruined him. His anger surged anew. "And you'd made me feel like my father did. Like I was less than a man. His criticisms had always hurt, but yours cut me all the way to the bone. They left scars on me that still haven't healed."

She slapped at his chest. Not painfully, but forcefully enough to get her point across that she was still angry at him. "What do you think you did to me? Have you any idea how many times in my life I was called a whore? Before I went to Artemis, I went back to my father. He took the money you'd left with me and then threw me out to the streets. He told me that if I couldn't hold on to my husband I should go spread my legs for another who might find some use for me."

He winced and then glared, wishing he'd known about it. "I would have killed your father had I known."

"But you didn't and that's why I hated you even more. You knew what kind of hell I'd lived in before you married me. That my father was abusive and harsh. What did you think I was going to do on my own in a world where a woman couldn't even shop unless a man was with her?"

He pulled her down, over him. So close that he could feel her breath fall against his face. "All I could think of was my father killing you because of me and then making me live, knowing what I'd done to you, what I'd forced him to do. He would never have given me the peace of death. And I knew that was the one thing I wasn't strong enough to bear . . . living on after your death that I caused."

Zephyra wanted to forgive him. She did. But she'd been hurt so badly. Those early years with Medea had been so difficult, and while Artemis had given them shelter, she'd never been kind to either of them.

She'd changed so much since the night he'd left.

But then he'd changed, too. He wasn't the same little boy who was afraid of angering his father. The fact that he'd stalked and killed his father's lineage proved that.

Kill him.

It was what War wanted her to do. What Artemis wanted.

But what of her desires?

His silver eyes burned into her as the tormented pain in them reached far into her heart. "Forgive me, Zephyra, and I swear not to the gods but on my honor and soul that I won't ever disappoint you again. Let me do what I should have done all those centuries ago."

"And that is?"

"Give you my heart, my loyalty, and my service. No one will ever divide us again. I swear it on all that I am."

Zephyra raked her nails lightly over his chest. "The only one who ever divided us was you."

"And your angry stubbornness. I left, but you wounded me deep on my way out the door. You brutalized my dignity and my manhood. Had you not gone on the attack, I might have stood up to my father. But it was hard to rationalize staying with you when you said the very things to me that he did."

She frowned as she tried to remember their fight. His words still rang in her mind, but hers . . . those were hazy or missing. "What did I say?"

His features were shocked. "Don't you remember?"

"Not really."

Stryker reached up and placed his fingers against her temples. With his god's powers, he replayed that night for her. It was something he'd never done. He preferred to remember her holding him in her arms. But it was time she remembered exactly what she'd done to him.

He and his father were alone in the cottage that Stryker had called home with Zephyra.

Almost fifteen years old, he was gangly and lean. Not quite at home in his body, he'd been clumsy. Apollo had grabbed him by the hair, his face contorted by rage. "Do you really think I would tolerate you and that whore to breed? You will do as you're told, boy, or I'll rain down the wrath of the gods in a way that will make all past punishments look like paradise."

He'd tried to fight, but his powers were nothing in comparison to his father's. "She's all I've ever wanted, Father. Please don't ask me to do this."

Apollo had yanked harshly on his hair before he released him. "I'm not asking you anything. I'm telling you. If you're not gone from here by dawn, I will have her raped and beaten until you can't even recognize her."

Stryker had been horrified by the threat. "She carries your grandchild."

Apollo had seized him by the throat and shoved him back against the wall. "You test me again, boy, and I'll have you womanized and serving in Artemis's temple alongside Satara and the rest of her pasty maids." He'd flung Stryker into the opposite wall. "Come dawn if you're still here, you will watch her brutalized until she dies."

Tears had filled his eyes as he looked up at his father, his heart breaking. "Why would you do this to me?"

"You are my legacy. Through you, I will overthrow Zeus and rule this putrid world. It's time you grew up and were the man you were supposed to be. Disappoint me in this and, so help me, I really will turn you into a woman, and you can share in your little wife's fate if you disobey me again."

Apollo vanished.

Stryker slid to the floor as he looked around the room where, for the briefest of times, he'd been truly happy. It was the only time in his life that he'd felt loved or wanted. Not as someone else's destiny, but for himself.

He sobbed like he'd never done before. He knew he had no choice but to obey. How could anyone run from a god? Apollo wouldn't be denied, and he would take pleasure in making them suffer for defying him.

"I won't let them hurt you, Phyra," Stryker whispered as he forced himself to stand. His heart breaking, he gathered a few items. The green hair ribbon she'd worn at their wedding. The tile of her in her wedding dress and a small vial of her perfume. He paused at her vanity table where she sat every night and morning, preparing herself for bed and for the day.

All he'd wanted was to put his head in her lap and have her brush her fingers through his hair and tell him everything would be all right. That she would be safe.

But it wasn't meant to be.

Tonight he was going to ruin her and he knew it.

Wanting to die over it, he placed his items in a small purse that he secured to his belt. *I should leave before she returns.*

No, he couldn't do that to her. In spite of what his father thought, he wasn't a coward. He couldn't leave her without some explanation. Leave her to wonder why he hadn't come home or where he'd gone. To think him dead or worse, to watch for his return while he knew she'd never see him again. She deserved to hear the truth from him.

Drawing a ragged breath, he sat down and waited for her to return.

The moment she did, she took his breath away. Frail and petite, she was more beautiful than even Aphrodite. Her green eyes had flashed in the dim light while she moved to light more lamps.

Her smile bright, it had made him instantly sad at the

knowledge that he would never again see anything so spectacular. "Why are you sitting here in the darkness?"

He'd cleared his throat, but the hard lump in his stomach had merely drawn tighter. "I have something I need to speak to you about."

She set her parcels on the table. "As do I. I—"

"No, please, let me speak."

Frowning, she'd frozen in place. "I don't like your tone, Strykerius."

She'd never liked to hear sternness in his voice. It was why he'd tried so hard to never show her that side of himself. "I know, but what I have to say can't wait."

She'd flounced to stand by his side and smooth the scowl on his face with her delicate fingers. "You look so serious."

His tongue had felt so thick in his mouth that he feared it would choke him. All he wanted was to pull her into his arms and hold her forever.

Instead he was going to break both their hearts.

It has to be done. An image of her being attacked tore through him with a ferocity so raw it made him flinch. He had no doubt his father would carry out that threat.

Taking a deep breath for courage, he forced himself to speak. "I'm leaving."

"That's fine, *akribos*. When will you be back?"

He placed his hands on her upper arms to steady himself. "I won't be back. Ever."

The light had gone out of her eyes and struck him like a fist in his gullet. "What?"

"My father has a wedding for me planned tomorrow. If I don't leave and divorce you tonight, he'll kill you and the baby."

Rage had twisted her beautiful features into the mask of a gorgon. "What!" she roared. She shoved him away from her.

He'd reached out toward her. "I'm sorry, Phyra. I have no choice."

She'd slapped his touch away. "Yes, you do. We all have choices."

"No, we don't. I won't stay here and watch you die."

She sneered as she raked him with a repugnant curl of her lips. "You're a worthless coward."

That had set his own anger off. "No, I'm not."

She slapped him hard across the face. "You're right. Being a coward would be a step up for you."

Stryker had stood there, his cheek stinging as she railed against him. He couldn't even really hear all the insults. Only the words "pathetic," "worthless," and "coward" rang in his ears over and over again.

"I'm doing this to protect you and the baby. I'll make sure you're both taken care of."

"There is no baby," she spat at him. "I miscarried it."

He staggered back. "When?"

"This morning."

"Why didn't you tell me?"

"I just did. So don't worry about it. There's no baby in need of a coward for a father."

"I'm not a coward!"

She shoved him again. "Get out of my sight, you pathetic excuse for a man. I don't want you here. Gods, I can't believe I was stupid enough to let you into my bed. Stupid enough to trust you."

"I love you, Phyra."

She'd grabbed a bowl from the table and flung it at his

head. "Liar! You disgust me!" She'd literally beat him out of the door and then slammed it shut in his face. But not before she hurled her wedding ring at him.

Stryker had stood on the other side as he listened to her breaking and throwing things inside. He splayed his hand against the wood, wanting desperately to open the door. But why bother? She hated him now.

But not nearly as much as he hated himself.

"At least you'll be safe." He'd left her plenty of money. "And if you hate me, at least you won't miss me." He let his tears fall as he leaned his head against the door and clutched at the knob, desperate to open it and return to her.

If only he could.

He took her tile from his purse and looked at her face before he gave it one last kiss, then turned and walked away.

Zephyra gasped as Stryker pulled out of her mind and left her with the lasting image of him clutching her tile in his hand as he turned and left their cottage.

She narrowed her gaze on him. "Your father was going to have me raped?"

"It's what he said. I had no reason to think he was joking."

Her anger vanished under a wave of astonishment. "You were protecting me."

"It's what I've been trying to get through to you. Why else would I have left you when you were the very thing I lived for?"

Angry at the world, she kneed him in the side.

"Ow!" he snapped. "What was that for?"

"For being such an asshole. You ever keep a secret from me like that again and I swear I'll gut you over it."

"You were fourteen," he said defensively. "I thought if I told you what my father threatened, you'd be terrified."

He was right. Especially given the fact that she'd been attacked before him. That was why she'd loved him so much. He'd kept her safe, and it was why she'd hated him for leaving. Fear of being on her own, of not being able to protect herself or Medea . . .

That was also why she had merged with the gallu. She'd wanted the strength to protect her daughter. To make sure no man ever forced himself on her.

Still angry, she slapped at his chest. "I could beat you senseless."

One side of his mouth quirked up. "I told you to feel free so long as you did it naked. Like this, I'm at your mercy."

Zephyra's cheeks colored as she became aware of the fact that she was straddling him. How could she have forgotten that?

His gaze darkened. She took in his entire naked body. He was ripped and gorgeous. Absolute perfection.

And he'd proclaimed himself at her mercy. Leaning forward, she breathed in his ear, "You are insufferable."

Stryker sucked his breath in sharply as she tongued his lobe, sending chills over him. Her actions were so tender and loving while she continued to insult him. He couldn't help but laugh.

"You find me funny?"

"I find you delectable." He moved to suckle her breast. "Wonderful and delicious."

She sucked her breath in sharply. "You're a sick man to love a woman who hates you."

"If I am, then I want no cure."

She shook her head at his teasing tone. "What am I going to do with you?"

"Just hold me. Let me love you the way I should have all along."

She moaned as he drove himself deep inside her body with one full, hard thrust. Gods, how good he felt. In his arms, it was hard to remember why she was supposed to hate him.

Maybe because she didn't really hate him after all. As he'd said, they were soul mates. Partners. Without him, she'd been incomplete, and now that she had him back . . .

It was wonderful.

And as he slowly made love to her, she realized that she was standing at the same crossroads where he'd been the night his father had demanded he leave.

She knew where the one path led. It was desolate loneliness spent in bitterness over the past.

The other was even more terrifying. For that road meant that she'd have to trust in him again. That she'd have to allow him back into the place where only he could do her harm.

Dare she chance it?

Looking down at him as he took her hand into his and laid her palm against his cheek, she knew the answer.

She didn't want to live without him.

Her heart pounding, she locked herself around him and rolled over until he was on top of her.

Stryker frowned slightly as he sensed a change in her. A softening in her touch as she dragged her nails down his spine. That gentleness combined with the sight of her under him was enough to push him over the edge. He had to fight to restrain himself and wait for her.

But when she came, she screamed out his name, and in that one instant he knew he would kill or die for this woman. She alone held that power over him. Joining her release, he growled in satisfaction as his body spasmed.

Collapsing against her, he held her tight. "I love you, Phyra," he whispered in her ear.

Then, in the lowest of tones, he heard the words that meant the most to him. "I love you, too."

Menyara paused as she felt ultimate power behind her. It rippled in the air and made the hair on the back of her neck rise. "Why are you skulking about, Jared?"

He materialized before her. "I'm not skulking."

"Whatever you say, child. Whatever you say."

Stepping back, he narrowed his gaze on her. "Why are you protecting the Malachai?"

She ignored his question. There was no need to go there with him, not when she knew what was really on his mind. "I know the sorrow inside you and I know why it is you did what you did. But in spite of what you think, the death of the Malachai won't give you solace. It won't take away the torment or the guilt that weighs on your conscience."

He curled his lips at her. "Stop with the mojo bullshit. I'm not one of your neophyte disciples training for war. I'm a veteran of the apocalypse. I've been on both sides of hell and am sick of the shit. I want his life and I won't be denied. Surely to the Source I've earned some kind of respite after all these centuries of abuse."

She shook her head. "The Source isn't appeased even now. The only way to have the Malachai is through me."

Jared summoned his powers into a typhoon around

him. The force of them swirled, lifting his hair up to fan around him as his wings spread wide and his eyes glowed a bright gold. "Then I will have your life."

Menyara brought her hands up to catch the blast he sent toward her and return it with one of her own. "You're not a Chthonian and I'm not about to let you have him."

She heard a sharp laugh behind her.

"You can't destroy her, Sephiroth. But I have no such restrictions."

Turning, she saw War smirking at her. "What are you doing here?"

"Making a deal with the devil."

Menyara started to leave, but before she could, a loud boom echoed in her ears an instant before everything went black.

11

Stryker lay abed with Zephyra in his arms as he listened to her soft snore. Smiling to himself, he traced the outline of her features with his fingers. She was so beautiful. Delicate. He'd missed her so much. And it felt so good to hold her again. There was nothing in his life that he'd ever cherished more than these quiet hours alone with her like this.

He was just dozing off when a sharp knock startled him. "Enter."

Davyn came in with a look that told him something was seriously wrong.

"What?"

Davyn swallowed. "We were routing the gallu and . . ." He flinched and looked away as if terrified of continuing.

"And what?" Stryker growled from between clenched teeth.

Davyn swallowed hard. "War brought in reinforcements."

No shit. Why would that cause him to be so afraid? It was only to be expected. The surprise would have been for him to continue fighting alone. "We can get the—"

"They captured Medea."

Zephyra shot up in the bed, fully alert as a wave of rage singed him. "They *what*?"

"Took Medea," Davyn repeated, his voice hollow. He met Stryker's gaze and the shame in his eyes would have touched Stryker had he not been so angry at the man. "War wants you to surrender to him or he will kill her."

Stryker's curse matched Zephyra's. "Rally our men," Stryker ordered.

Zephyra caught his arm as he started to leave the bed. "We can't fight him. He'll kill her."

Davyn nodded. "She's right. War was clear. He wants you to come alone or her life is forfeit."

Stryker ground his teeth as he hated himself for putting his own daughter in harm's way. He met Zephyra's gaze and saw the fear that hid behind her anger. "I started this and I will finish it. I swear to the gods that I won't let him hurt her."

"You'd better both return. I don't like funerals." Her tone was a quiet whisper in the darkness.

Stryker pulled her close and kissed her forehead. No words had ever meant more to him. "Don't worry. I've buried bigger assholes than this and I intend to laugh on that bastard's grave."

Nick cocked his head as he felt a foreign sensation flutter over his skin—like a delicate butterfly's wings dancing against his flesh. He turned quickly to find a woman behind him. Tiny and lithe, she held a power to her that warned him she was as lethal as she was beautiful. "Who are you?"

An evil smile played at the edges of her lips. "Call me Ker. War sent me to tell you that we hold the goddess

Menyara. If you want her returned, you're to come un-armed and alone to the St. Louis Cemetery at midnight."

He scoffed at her. "Rather cliche, isn't it?"

"Not really." She vanished.

Nick sat down slowly as he watched the skin on his arm change to the now familiar red and black pattern. He was stronger than he'd ever been before. His power felt absolute . . . if he knew how to control it. But the problem was, the strength was followed by great weakness. He could feel it, he just couldn't really utilize it.

His heart heavy, he looked around the room of the tiny house Menyara had called home since the days of his childhood. Drawings and statues of ancient gods and goddesses were littered about and now he saw the writings of protection on the walls that had been invisible to his human sight. This was where she'd kept him safe . . . as a child and as the monster he'd become.

The humble shotgun shack was hardly fit for a goddess, yet this had been Menyara's abode of choice. And it was here she'd partially raised him alongside his mother.

Wincing, he saw his mother's lifeless body in his mind. Felt her cold flesh as he'd tried to revive her. Her blood had soaked him as his world shattered in one hollowed-out heartbeat. He didn't know if he'd ever be the same again. The anger. The hurt. The betrayal. It was all still fresh. Still biting.

"I miss you, Mom," he whispered as bitter agony washed through him. She'd died because of him and him alone. He knew that. He just didn't want to face that fact.

Now Menyara's life was in his hands.

He could either swallow his pride and save her or he could charge in and watch her die . . .

The choice was his alone to make.

*　*　*

Ash stood on the balcony of Savitar's walkway, which overlooked the great hall below. Hidden by shadows, he watched as Tory, Danger, and Simi laughed while they ate ice cream sundaes. Indescribable emotions tore through him. But the one thing he could name was the feeling of warmth he had every time he saw them. The feeling of family.

Not once in his life had he ever thought to have this sensation of peace and happiness. To know the gentle touch of a woman who truly loved him. A touch he could trust to never turn painful or brutal. Truly, it was a miracle.

Tory looked up as if she sensed him and smiled a smile that struck him like a hammer. He took a step forward, then froze as he felt the last presence he would have ever expected.

Nick.

Ash didn't move as he sensed Nick at his back and waited for him to attack.

He didn't. Instead, Nick let out a deep breath before he spoke in a low, lethal tone. "I trusted you, you bastard, and you let me down."

"I know," Ash said quietly as he tightened his grip on the banister. "I should have told you about Simi and I didn't. But then, I knew how you were around women."

"I would never have touched her had I known she was your daughter."

Ash turned to face him. "We both fucked up, Nick. We were both trying to protect ourselves from harm, and in doing so, we ruined the very things we wanted to shield. I should have trusted you more, but my past has never lent itself to such openness." He let out his own tired sigh. "So are you here to fight me?"

Nick's eyes sparkled red in the shadows. "Believe me, nothing would give me more pleasure than killing you. But I need a favor and I don't have anyone else to turn to."

Ash arched his brow at that. He knew the bitter pill Nick was swallowing and the last thing he would do was make it burn more. "What's happened?"

"War took Menyara. I need to know his weakness so that I can help her."

Ash let out a light laugh at the irony. "You are his weakness."

"At full strength. Maybe. But I can't stop him like this, can I?"

Ash shook his head.

"Can you?"

"Not alone."

Nick took one step closer to him. "Then tell me what I need to do."

"Ash!"

Ash stepped back to look down where Tory was calling him. If he'd thought Nick was a shock, it was nothing compared to what waited for him there. He had to blink twice just to make sure he wasn't hallucinating.

"Damn. Lucifer must be sitting on icicles today." Ash glanced back to Nick. "Stay here for a few."

"Ash—"

"Trust me, Nick. Stay hidden and I'll be right back." Ash flashed himself down to the table where Stryker was standing next to Tory.

The Daimon looked less than happy to be there, but that was nothing compared to Ash's feelings, especially since the Daimon stood practically on top of two of the six most important people in Ash's world.

Ash narrowed his gaze. "What are you doing here?"

"Savitar sent me to speak to you."

Ash arched a brow, but he knew Stryker wasn't lying. There was no other way for him to have gotten in here unchallenged. "So what's up?"

Stryker's features were completely blank. "War has taken my daughter and is holding her." There was a crack in his voice to let Ash know the man wasn't as ambivalent as he was trying to appear.

Ash shook his head. "There seems to be a lot of that going around suddenly."

"Has he taken Kat?"

Ash laughed at the very thought of War trying that award-winning act of stupidity on *his* daughter . . .

But that thought scattered as he realized how simple the solution to all their problems was.

Kat. There was a weapon War wouldn't see coming and by the time he realized it, he'd be defeated and back under their complete control.

Deadening his expression, Ash folded his arms over his chest as he met Tory's gaze and winked at her. She, Simi, and Danger were completely composed and silent as if waiting to see whether they should attack Stryker or let him live on in peace. "I assume you're here to beg a favor."

"I beg for nothing. I'm merely proposing a temporary truce."

Ash scoffed. "A truce to deal with the very thing you unleashed in an effort to kill me?"

Stryker shrugged nonchalantly. "Why bicker over split hairs?"

"True. After all, we have much larger grudges against each other than that."

Stryker's eyes turned dark, his expression deadly. "Then you refuse?"

"No. War has to be stopped, and it will take the whole of us to do it."

"The whole of who?"

Before Ash could answer, Nick appeared beside them. Curling his lip, Stryker stepped forward to attack him.

Ash forced Stryker back and put himself between the two. "Think of your daughter. You kill him, we're screwed and she's dead."

Stryker cursed. "Fine. But once War is put down, I'll be after the two of you again."

Grinning snidely, Ash let go of Stryker and stepped to the side of the two men. He held his hand out. "Works for me. For the ones we love, today we're allies. Tomorrow we resume our natural order of mortal enemies. Gentlemen, and I use that term loosely for all of us, have we an accord?"

Nick covered his hand with his own. "I'm in."

Stryker hesitated. "For Medea." He placed his hand over theirs.

Tory gave a light laugh. "What a freaky alliance this is. So what do we do now?"

Ash didn't hesitate with his answer. "You stay here."

She growled at him. "Acheron—"

"No arguments, Sota. I swear, it'll be fine."

"We've had this macho discussion before, and you normally lose."

It was true, he did have a hard time saying no to her, but for all that, she was more than reasonable, which was why he loved her. "And I know you're fully capable of holding your own. The gods know, I'm not strong enough to stand against you for long, but in this, I need a clear head which means I need you out of harm's way."

"Fine. But anything goes wrong and I'm coming in."

"Nothing's going to go wrong."

She looked at Nick and then Stryker before she returned her gaze to him. "You are such an optimist. My Spidey-sense is tingling all over the place."

He leaned forward and kissed her forehead. "That's from eating the ice cream. Relax."

Danger snorted. "Relax. Trust me. It'll be all right. Isn't that how I ended up dead?"

Ash grimaced at the reminder. "Stop feeding her anxiety."

Simi perked up at his comment. "Anxiety. The Simi's never eaten that before." She looked at Danger. "Is that tasty?"

"Not really."

"Oh. Maybe we should put barbecue sauce on it. Everything's better with barbecue."

Ash shook his head. "And on that note, we're going to plan our strategy."

Tory moved to his side. "That I can do."

Yes, she could. Taking her hand, Ash led her and the others to Savitar's office where they could outline their attack and share what each knew about War and his weaknesses.

Ker tsked as she watched the men and one woman adjourn to a paneled room where they sat plotting War's demise. "How quaint. The mice are herding together in an effort to take us down."

War laughed at Ker. "I expected no less. But they underestimate us. By morning, they'll all be dead, and with the blood of the Malachai, we'll be able to revive our brethren. While mankind prepares for their Christmas Day, we're going to celebrate with a feast of their souls. At midnight, the veil between the worlds is thin and Nick is going to open up a new era. Let the bloodbath begin."

Ker smiled brightly. "I can't wait."

Ash checked the blades in his boots to make sure they were working. He turned his head as he felt someone enter the room to his left. It was Urian.

"You're helping my father?" It was more an accusation than a question.

Ash made sure to keep all emotion out of his voice. "We have to stop War."

"Stryker murdered my wife," Urian snarled.

"I know."

Urian shook his head as his eyes flared with anger. "How could you help something like him?"

Ash had had enough with both the accusations and the self-pity. There was a lot more at stake here that just hurt feelings and past betrayals. "You helped him for centuries. Need I remind you of how many lives you took under his command? Lives who were related to you—you killed Phoebe's mother and her sister."

He flinched at the truth. "I loved my wife. I never meant to hurt her."

No, but it didn't change the fact that he had. Repeatedly. Urian had taken from his wife the very people she loved more than anything. It was hypocritical of him to hold that same action against his father. For too many centuries, Urian and his brothers had been a tool that Stryker had used more than effectively.

But times changed.

And it was time the man learned about Medea. "By the way, you have a sister."

Urian tensed. "What?"

Ash met his gaze levelly and kept his expression completely stoic. "It's the life of your sister we're going to protect. Not your father's."

He shook his head in denial. "My sister died eleven thousand years ago."

"Medea is a half-sister."

That wiped the disbelief from his face and returned anger to his cold eyes. "And I should care, why?"

Ash held his hands up in surrender. "You're right. You shouldn't care at all. She's nothing to you which is why I haven't invited you to join us." Ash started past him.

Urian pulled him to a stop. His eyes were harsh and biting. They accused him even more than Urian's words had. "How would you feel if my father had killed Tory?"

Ash answered honestly and without hesitation, "I would feel soulless. Lost and hurt beyond repair."

Urian looked away. "Then you understand me. And why I want him dead."

Ash pulled Urian's hand off his arm. "He knows that too. But have you ever considered that he might regret what he did to you?"

"My father? Get real. The bastard has never regretted a single thing in his entire life."

Even as corrupt as Stryker was, Ash had a hard time believing that. "We all have regrets, Urian. Nothing that lives is immune from that nasty emotion."

"So what? You want me to go kiss and make up?"

"Hardly. But I want you to set aside your own hurt and anger to see clearly for a minute. This isn't about you and your father anymore than it's about me and Nick hating each other over something we can't change. This is about saving the lives of a million innocent people. People like Phoebe who don't deserve to be hunted and killed. If I can stand at the side of my enemies for the greater good, so can you."

Urian scoffed. "Well, I guess I'm just not as special as you are."

"No one knows their true mettle until it's been tested. This is yours. Whether you pass or fail is entirely up to you. I can't tell you what to do, but I know where I'll be tonight . . ." He hesitated before he asked the most important question: "So what do you choose?"

"Gory death."

Ash shook his head. "You stubborn bastards. Take it from someone who knows firsthand, there's a lot to be said for forgiveness. Grudges seldom hurt anyone except the one bearing them."

"And there's a lot to be said for knocking enemies upside their heads and cracking their skulls open."

Ash felt a tic start in his jaw over the man's obdurate nature. "To everything there is a season, and tonight ours is to stand together or lose everything. I'm not fighting for Stryker or to save your sister. I'm fighting to protect the ones I love. The ones who will suffer most if War isn't stopped . . . children like Eric and—"

"I get it," he snapped at the mention of his nephew.

"Do you?"

Urian's gaze hardened. "I will be there, but once our enemies are put down—"

"We fight each other. Understood."

Urian nodded. He took a step back, then paused before he stepped even closer to Ash. "I want the honest truth about something. Could you really fight with someone who did as much damage to you as my father has done to me?"

Ash met his gaze without blinking. "I subjugated myself to the goddess who drugged me to the point I couldn't protect my sister and nephew the night they were brutally slaughtered, and they were the only two people in the universe who'd ever given two shits about me. Later that same day, she stood back and let her twin brother butcher me on the floor like an animal, yet within hours after that I sold myself to her to protect mankind. For the sake of the Dark-Hunters, I subjected myself to her cruel whims for eleven thousand years. So, yeah, Urian, I think I could manage to suck it up for an hour to protect the rest of the world."

Urian let out a slow breath. "You know you're the only man alive I'd ever follow after what I've been through. You're also the only one I respect."

"And you're one of the extremely few I trust."

Urian held his hand up to him. "Brothers?"

"Brothers to the end," Ash said, taking his hand and clutching it tight. "Now before we get all girly and cry, get your ass upstairs and prepare for what's coming."

Stryker stepped back as he adjusted the brace on his left arm. It wasn't often he wore the titanium-laced armor, but since they were about to be up against the gods only knew what, he wanted to be prepared.

He left his room to find Zephyra in his office, staring

into the sfora as she tried to locate Medea. It wasn't working. Wherever War was keeping her was off limits to them.

"I'll bring her back. I swear it."

Zephyra rose slowly as her gaze held his captive. "I wish you'd reconsider my offer."

"You won't be fighting with a level head, and you know it. We don't know what we're walking into, but I'm sure War isn't going to play by any rules. As Acheron said to his woman, I can't fight if my attention is partially on you. I'll need every advantage I can have."

Zephyra nodded in understanding. She reached up to brush a lock of coal-black hair back from his eyes. Her chest was tight with fear not just for Medea, but for him, too. How unfair to lose him now when she'd just found him again. "Will I be able to watch in the sfora?"

"You should."

"Then know that I'll be laughing at your ineptitude every time your enemies strike you, and if you fail to return with my daughter, I'll have your heart and your head for decorations."

Stryker narrowed his gaze on her and would have told her exactly what he thought of that had a small glint on her hand not caught his attention.

It was her wedding band. The one he'd kept all these centuries in his room. That one ring belied and translated her words.

She didn't want him harmed . . .

A slow smile curved his lips as he lifted her other hand to place a kiss on it. "Your words are noted, my most prickly rose. And I shall endeavor to keep your amusement at a bare minimum."

As he stepped away, she grabbed the buckles on the front of his armor and pulled him back to her lips so that she could kiss him.

Stryker growled at how good she tasted. "I want you here naked when I return."

"You return whole and I promise you a night you won't soon forget."

"I intend to hold you to that, my lady."

Zephyra nodded and let him go even though all she wanted to do was hold him closer to her. *Don't get killed.* The words hung in her throat as unimaginable pain ripped through her, but she wouldn't say those words. She wouldn't jinx him or let the Fates know how much he meant to her. If she did, they might kill him just for spite. So instead, she clenched her hands and watched him leave the room to join his enemies to fight for their daughter's life.

Come back to me, please.

Stryker paused at the door to take one last look at Zephyra. Calm and composed, she didn't appear to care in the least what happened to him. At least until he saw the way she clenched her fists. A small smile played at the edge of his lips as that warmed every part of his body. "I'll be back, Phyra."

"And you better have our daughter with you."

The smile broke at her use of "our." "I will." Inclining his head to her, he slipped out the door and went to their rendezvous spot in New Orleans. It was the quiet alley on Pere Antione outside of the Ethel Kidd realty offices. In the shadow of the Cathedral, his plan had originally been to unleash his men onto humanity from this very place— give or take a few feet. Now, here he was fighting not only to protect the ones he viewed as food, but to protect his own.

Yeah . . . Fate was ever a capricious viper.

A bright flash made him squint as Acheron appeared before him. Dressed in a long black leather duster, jeans, and a My Chemical Romance T-shirt, the Atlantean's eyes were covered by a pair of opaque sunglasses.

Nick Gautier flashed in a second later. His black clothing was much more reserved. A black button-down shirt and slacks. The only thing that made him stand out was the double bow and arrow mark of Artemis that was branded on his cheek.

Ash broke into an arrogant grin. "So are we going to continue glaring angrily at each other while we pose in our tough stances? Or use our time to work out a plan that hopefully doesn't end with our mutual deaths?"

"I vote for mutual death," Gautier grumbled. "But only after Menyara is safe."

"And Medea," Stryker added. "I want you both to swear that regardless of what happens to me, you won't allow her to die."

"I swear," Ash said.

They looked at Nick.

"She's done me no harm. I'll get her out of there if it's at all possible."

Stryker nodded even though he wanted to gut the man who'd killed his sister. Then again, Satara's plan had been to have Nick rape Ash's fiancée. Instead Nick had stabbed her and taken Ash's woman to safety. In all honesty, he could almost respect Gautier's actions. Had it not been his sister Gautier had killed, he might even have considered them noble.

Still Satara had been his ally for centuries. Even though she'd been crueler and colder than any creature he'd ever known, it didn't change the fact that Stryker had loved her in spite of her faults.

Turning his thoughts to Ash, he folded his arms over his chest. "What do you have planned?"

Before Ash could answer, Kat popped in. Stryker arched a brow at her appearance. Over six feet tall, she bore a striking resemblance to her mother, Artemis, right down to her bright green eyes. But she had Acheron's blond hair and, lucky for them all, his temperament.

Her presence surprised him. "You're bringing your daughter into this?"

Ash shrugged. "She has an interesting ability that I think will make War back down."

"And that is?"

Kat's grin was identical to the one Ash had worn earlier. "I can siphon powers out of the gods."

"Really?" Stryker took a step back from her.

Kat laughed evilly. "You never realized how close to the edge you treaded when you insulted me, did you?"

"Apparently not. So how does this siphon work?"

She wiggled one threatening finger in his direction. "I have to be touching the person . . . Good thing I find you so repulsive I never wanted to do that, eh?"

Stryker rolled his eyes before he turned his attention back to Acheron. "What if we can't get her close enough to War to touch him?"

"I'll take her home," the deeply accented voice came out of the darkness.

Stryker turned to find Kat's husband Sin behind him. Strange, he hadn't heard or felt the Sumerian god's appearance. That spoke volumes about Sin's powers that he could mask them so completely. And it made him feel more confident that they could surprise War and his entourage, too.

Stryker pulled his pocket watch out to check the time. It was fifteen till. "Showtime, folks. Are we ready?"

"We're ready."

Stryker scowled at Artemis's voice as she, Athena, Ares, and Hades joined them. "What are you doing here?"

Artemis looked at Kat. "You're not sending my baby into danger without me."

Ash choked. "Now you discover maternal instinct?"

She narrowed her gaze on him.

"She's always been protective of me," Kat said with a laugh. "In a very Artemis sort of way."

"Like a viper nursing eggs," Stryker added under his breath.

Artemis raked him with a cold, scathing glare. "Did you dare to say something to me?"

"Good to see you again, Grandma."

Artemis curled her lip as she stepped away.

Nick cleared his throat in order to gain their attention. "You know there's one slight problem with this."

"We were told to come alone," Ash answered.

Stryker shrugged. "They told the three of us to come alone at the same time which by nature would make us a group."

Ash gave a half-hearted laugh. "Yeah, but I think Nick's right. The three of us need to head in alone to see what's up and to keep them from being suspicious." He glanced to Kat. "Give us five minutes before you drop in."

"Will do."

"What about us?" Ares asked.

Kat threw her arm around him and smiled. "You'll be

hanging back with me. Hopefully I'm the one thing he won't see coming."

Athena stepped forward. "Good luck, gentlemen."

Ash inclined his head before he looked to Stryker and Nick. "You ready?"

Nick nodded.

"Always," Stryker said.

They took up positions with Acheron in the middle as they left the dark alley and headed down St. Ann toward the cemetery. Ash's long black coat fanned out slightly from his ankles as they walked like hungry predators toward a meeting Stryker was sure all of them could have done without. As if one beast outlined by moonlight, they moved in complete synchronization.

The only sounds they could hear were the music from Bourbon Street, the beating of their hearts, and the clicking of their boots on the pavement. The streets glistened from an earlier rain as dark clouds still hung above them and the street turned from commercial buildings into residential.

"How many times have you walked this street, Gautier?" Stryker asked.

"A thousand or better and I intend to be here for a thousand more."

Stryker nodded until they neared the cemetery, and he realized something. War did nothing without express intent. "Why do you think War chose this place to meet?"

Ash paused to look at him. "He wouldn't care about solitude."

Nick snorted. "Maybe he likes dead people."

A chill went down Stryker's spine at those words.

They'd barely left Nick's lips before he saw just how right that sarcastic comment was. There before him stood three women.

Nick's mother, Stryker's daughter, and Ash's sister.

12

Stryker couldn't breathe as he saw a face that had been relegated to his memories. Ethereal and pale, Tannis was as beautiful as her mother had been. White blond hair framed a face that was perfect and frail.

Unconsciously, he took a step toward her.

Ash caught his arm and pulled him to a stop. "It's a trick."

Nick shook his head as he started forward. "Mom?"

Ash let go of Stryker to grab at Nick. Furious, the man snapped around and moved to slug him hard. Ash ducked, then shoved him back. "Get a grip, Nick. War is playing on our emotions."

"Why did you let me die, Acheron?"

Ash went completely still as he heard Ryssa's voice speaking the flawless Greek of his childhood.

Her pale hair was caught up in blue ribbons that matched the ancient Greek gown she wore—the very dress she'd been wearing the night the Apollite soldiers had brutalized her and ended her life. "I called out for you to help me, *akribos,* but you didn't answer me. You never came."

Guilt shredded him. He tightened his grip on Nick's

shirt, needing the stability of his old friend to hold his resolve. "You're not real," he snarled.

She moved forward to touch him with a hand so warm it belied the paleness of her hollow form. "You're still the child catching sunbeams in his hand, aren't you? Come with me, Acheron. I can keep you safe from this world that wants no part of you."

Bitter ache and loss welled up inside him as every part of his being wanted to go to Ryssa and have her comfort him. No longer was he a god of infinite power. That one touch reduced him to the boy who'd only wanted to feel the comfort of a loving touch. The boy who'd worshiped his older sister . . .

"Nicky?"

Ash winced at the sound of Cherise's voice. Tears glistened in Nick's eyes, but to his credit, he kept them from falling.

Dressed in the same cream dress they'd buried her in, Cherise stood quietly in the darkness. Her face showed no signs of the violence that had ended her life. She looked just as real and whole as the last time Ash had seen her waiting for Nick to come walk her home from work. "Come to your mama, cher. It's been too long since I last held my baby boy."

"Papa? Is that you? I'm scared, Papa. I don't understand what's happening to me. Please help me."

Stryker shook his head to clear it as every paternal instinct he had demanded he comfort his child. This was the girl he'd held in his arms and rocked to sleep. The woman whose hand he'd held as she screamed for mercy the entire day her body had decayed into dust.

She ran at him. "Papa?"

Growling, he ducked and spun away from her. She stared at him in confusion.

"Are they real?" Stryker asked Acheron.

Ash was still holding Nick back. "I don't know."

Cherise touched Ash's shoulder. "Of course I'm real, cher. Don't be playing with me like this." She tsked at Ash. "You still too skinny, child. You need some of my hash browns to fatten you up."

"Mama?" Nick shoved Ash back so that he could wrap his arms around her. The moment he did, she screamed in agony and faded into the mist.

"*Akribos*?" Ryssa said as she approached Ash slowly. "Why does it hurt now?" Then she, too, screamed out.

Tannis's cries joined hers as she fell to her knees and covered her ears with her hands.

"What's happening?" Nick looked as bewildered as Stryker felt.

Without answering, Stryker ran to Tannis to help her, but she vanished before he could reach her.

Bitter laughter echoed around them. "You didn't think I just held Menyara and Medea, did you?"

Stryker curled his lip as War materialized in front of them. "What is this?"

"This is the butcher telling the sheep to lie down at his feet." He held his hand out and Ker appeared by his side with her wings spread wide as she smiled snidely at them. "I think you guys forgot that Ker is the goddess of cruel and violent death. Your women all died horribly—"

"And are subject to her." Ash cursed. "That's why we had to meet here. Ker's a Greek goddess and couldn't have touched them except in a cemetery where the doorway between this realm and their final resting places is an open channel." He looked at Nick. "She's pulled their souls out and is holding them."

Stryker resisted the urge to be an "I told you so." "What do you want?" he asked War.

A wry grin taunted them. "Simple, really. Your lives."

Stryker returned that look with one of his own. "And you'll release them."

"Of course."

All three of them shook their heads. They knew better. Stryker met Ash's gaze, then Nick's. He saw the same determination in their eyes that he was sure he had in his. As painful as it was, they weren't here to fight for the dead.

They were here to fight for the living.

Inclining his head to Ash, Stryker held his hands up and blasted War with his powers. Ash joined him.

"Kat!" Ash shouted, summoning the others.

They appeared instantly.

War laughed as Ker multiplied and a bright flash lit the entire cemetery. The ground below them shook, knocking all of them off their feet.

"Stryker!" Ash shot a blast at him.

Instinctively, he rolled out of the way, thinking Ash had intended to hit him. It was only after it passed him that he realized Ash was aiming for a demon. Stryker flipped to his feet and ran for War.

He didn't make it. Two of the Keres caught him about the waist and threw him back to the ground. There were hundreds of them. Overwhelmed, he glanced to Katra who was being beaten down by them. As she reached to drain one, three more would appear.

He felt the color fade from his skin as he saw the same realization on Ash's face that he felt.

They couldn't win this.

Not with Ker in the fight. Her ability to replicate negated anything they could do. The Greek gods were surrounded. Both Ash and Nick were pinned down every bit as badly as he was.

War laughed, his voice ringing out. "Bow down to me and I might let some of you live . . . as my slaves."

Zephyra came out of her chair as she saw the imminent death of Stryker. "No," she breathed, her heart shattering. She couldn't lose him now. Not after she'd just learned to love him again.

She looked up at the ceiling as anger burned through her. The gods had played with their lives enough. "You bitches better back off my man," she growled at the Fates.

Her resolve set, she went to Apollymi to do the one thing she'd sworn she'd never do . . . beg a favor.

Tory paced the small area in front of Savitar's office while Simi and Xirena watched TV. She had a bad feeling that she couldn't shake. Something was wrong, she knew it.

A fissure went through the hallway. Turning, she hoped to find Acheron there. Instead, it was a woman whose head didn't even reach Tory's shoulders. Tory stepped back, ready to battle her.

"Relax," the woman snapped. "My name is Zephyra and I'm Stryker's wife."

Tory gaped at the angry-sounding declaration. "Why are you here?"

"Our men are about to die, and if you're even half the

woman I'm sure you are, you'll want to help me save them."

She had a moment's hesitation as she realized that this could very well be a trap of Stryker's. But Zephyra's demeanor was too sincere and there was fear in her eyes Tory was sure couldn't be faked. "Absolutely."

"Then come." She held her hand out.

Tory didn't hesitate to take it. In the next moment, they were in New Orleans again. That wouldn't have been so bad had they not landed in the middle of a bloodbath.

Gasping, she ducked as a screaming bird woman dove at her head.

Zephyra growled as she manifested a sword to fight the Keres with. "Jared!" she called, summoning her slave to her side.

He appeared instantly.

"Save Stryker."

His eyes glowed red as he saw Nick fighting. He headed for him.

"Stop!" she shouted. "Leave him be. Your only focus is War and keeping Stryker and my daughter safe."

His skin marbled red and black as he flashed to his true form. Snarling, he showed her his fangs. "The Malachai—"

"Obey me."

Jared hissed, but in the end, he had no choice except to do as she commanded.

Nick did a double-take when he saw Jared heading for War. The Keres tried to bring him down, but instead of falling as the rest of them did, Jared stood his ground. He manifested a tall staff and used it to drive the Keres back.

Nick watched and then imagined a similar weapon

for himself. To his amazement, it appeared. He felt the power of it vibrating down the wood. Acting on instinct, he swung it at the Keres. As soon as it connected, it dissolved them.

So this was one of his powers . . .

Stryker paused as he watched Nick taking out some of their enemies. At least until he saw Zephyra. Then he could think of nothing except getting to her.

Before he could take a step, War seized her and pulled her toward the Italian monument.

They were just about to head out of sight when Savitar appeared behind them and head-butted War. Zephyra turned on War with a kick so fierce that Stryker felt the impact of it. As War reached for her, Stryker was there to catch him and shove him back.

Ash grabbed him while he was off balance and Katra flashed in behind him. She kicked War.

Cursing, War slammed her to the ground and wrenched his arm free.

Stryker caught him. "Where's Medea?"

He laughed. "Kill me and she dies, too."

"Mache has them," Ash said. "He's the only one missing."

Stryker slugged War. "Where?"

War kicked Stryker away from him as a dozen Keres moved in to attack.

"How do we stop them?" Stryker asked Ash and Savitar.

"We have to find the one true Ker," Savitar said. "Stop her and the others will fall."

Stryker scoffed. "Care to tell me which one she is?"

"That one," Zephyra said, pointing to the one attacking Nick.

Stryker scowled. "How do you know?"

"Instinct."

Perhaps, but it wasn't until Ker headed for Tory that Stryker saw his opening. He exchanged a knowing look with Ash before they rushed Ker together.

As soon as they had Ker on the ground, the others vaporized. War shrieked in outrage before he sent a blast at Tory. Jared intercepted it. He hissed as it smoldered through his body and sent him to his knees. Nick attacked then, rushing for War.

Ker bit Stryker. He reached for her throat, but before he could choke her, Ash had her subdued.

War was another matter. He wouldn't go down. Not for any of them.

Ash shook his head at Savitar. "Three months to subdue him, you said."

Savitar nodded.

Stryker cursed. "I don't have three months."

"Me neither." Stryker frowned at the childish demon's voice as Acheron's demon Simi appeared. She slammed something against War, who snarled at her.

Stryker pulled the demon back before War could hurt her. War reached for him, but the moment he did, his hand turned to stone. Frowning, Stryker watched as it crawled up the god's arm all the way to his body until he was nothing more than a frozen statue whose face was a mask of fury.

"What is that you hit him with?" Zephyra asked Simi.

"Aima," Acheron answered. It was the same substance Stryker had once used to freeze him. Hopefully, War didn't have any friends who'd be willing to bring him the antidote after this.

Wiping her hands together, Simi grinned. "Your mama-akra sent that to you, *akri,* to hurt the heathen-god. Now it's Dimonique time. The Simi can't be bothered with no Greek god messing with the one who pays the plastic bills." She held her hand out to Ash. "Can the Simi have that black metal card she loves so much?"

Ash pulled his wallet out with a short laugh. "Sure, baby." He handed over the black American Express card.

"But where's Medea?" Zephyra asked.

They all looked to Jared who held Ker on the ground.

"I'll never tell you," she snarled.

Zephyra's heart stilled at those words and the thought of never seeing her child again. "Jared? Do something."

She saw the resistance in his eyes before he let out a long, tired breath. "Nim? Human form."

His demon pulled out from under his collar to take the form of a small adult male. The instant he saw Simi, he ran and tripped.

"Nim!" Jared snapped. "She won't harm you."

Nim looked less than convinced as he crawled on the ground to the other side of Jared. He crouched beside him. "What does Jared need?"

He met Zephyra's gaze. "Find Medea."

"Why can't you just pull the information out of her?" Zephyra asked Jared.

"There are too many voices in her head speaking too many languages for me to differentiate any real words. She's blocking me on purpose." He looked at Nim. "Find Medea for me."

Nim's eyes glowed red as he touched Ker and she shrieked in anger. "Medea in the hole with that god who died."

"What hole, Nim?"

"Deep one in the ground."

Sucking her breath in sharply, Zephyra started for the demon. "This is worthless."

Stryker pulled her to a stop. "I think I know where they are." He glanced past her to where Hades stood. "Tartarus."

Her throat tightened as she realized the significance of that. Once taken there, no one could leave without Hades's permission.

Zephyra turned to look at the god of the Underworld.

"I owe you nothing," Hades spat at Stryker.

"But that's not true of me," Acheron said as he stepped forward. "Let them go, Hades."

A tic worked in Hades's jaw. "Ma'at I can't keep anyway. Her soul doesn't belong to me."

Ash narrowed his gaze. "What about Medea?"

Hades growled. "Take her. But this clears our slate. Understood?"

Somehow that seemed too easy to Zephyra. "What about Mache?"

Hades laughed evilly. "If your demon is right and he's in my domain . . . he will regret it."

Jared rose with Ker. "What of her?"

Hades glared at the spirit of violent death. "Bring her down. I have plans for her." And by the tone of his voice, those plans weren't pleasant ones. "Bring her down."

Stryker took Zephyra's hand as they followed the Greek god out of the human world and into Tartarus. Ash brought the statue of War down and returned him to the place where he'd rested for centuries. Ker was taken to a small cell and locked inside.

"I'll deal with you later," Hades promised.

Ker spat at him and slammed her hand against the

door. "This isn't over. I'll be free again and we'll celebrate your funeral march."

Stryker ignored her threats as he looked at Nim who was clutching a small stuffed pink bunny. "Where's my daughter?"

Nim pointed to a small door.

Unsure, Stryker started toward it, then paused as he heard an explosion so loud it temporarily deafened him.

The door slammed into the far wall where it fell back and pounded a man into the ground.

"Stop!" Hades shouted.

The door slammed into the man three more times before it obeyed him.

As the smoke cleared, Stryker saw Menyara. With her arms folded, she left the room and cast a menacing glare at Mache who was bleeding profusely while the door held him in place. "That'll learn him to keep his hands to himself." She turned back to her cell. "Medea, love, your parents are here."

Acheron shook his head as he took Tory's hand into his. "Feeling rather stupid for having worried now."

"Don't," Menyara said. "Until you negated War's powers, we were stuck here. That poor fool didn't realize until it was too late and I had a chance to hurt him back."

Zephyra ran to her daughter and grabbed her into a tight hug before she pulled back to make sure nothing had happened to her.

Nick stepped forward, his face troubled. "What about my mother? What did War do to her?"

Hades put his hand on Nick's shoulder. "There's nothing he could do. Ker could show you the souls to weaken you, but they have no power over them. Your mother is back where she belongs, as are the others."

Ash cast his glance in the direction of the Elysian fields.

"Ryssa thinks of you," Hades said quietly. "And she's happy, Acheron. She doesn't blame you at all. That was Ker playing with your emotions."

"Thank you."

Hades inclined his head before he looked at Stryker. When he opened his mouth to speak, Stryker held his hand up.

"I only want to know if she's with her husband and children."

"She is."

"Then I'm at peace."

Zephyra frowned at the catch in his voice that belied those words. But perhaps he was right. He couldn't change anything, so why torture himself?

His head hung low, Nick turned to leave. Menyara went with him while Jared hung back, glaring after them.

"If he kills Nick, Jared will die, too," Menyara's voice echoed around them.

"What?" Zephyra said.

Menyara paused. "It's true. So think before you send him after my Nick again."

Zephyra narrowed her gaze on Jared. "Why didn't you tell me that?"

His features were blank and hollow. "You know why."

Because he wanted to die, too, and that was one thing she could never allow him to do. "For that you won't have a moment's freedom for your service." Zephyra squeezed Medea's hand. "Take him to Kalosis. I'm sure your father has a hole adequate for his punishment."

Nim took a step toward Jared, but Simi stopped him. "Wait."

He stepped back, his face a mask of fear, unsure of her intent.

Smiling gently, she pulled a small bear out of her coffin-shaped purse and held it out to him. "It's a Teddy Scare," she said. "Much more fierce than your bunny." She placed it in his hand before she flounced toward Acheron. "QVC time, *akri*." She disappeared.

Jared stared after her as if amazed by her act of kindness. "You should go with Acheron, Nim."

Nim shook his head defiantly, then returned to Jared's body. Jared cursed. "I really hate demons."

Medea's gaze held a trace of sympathy before she placed her hand on his arm and took him back to his captivity.

Tory peered into the room where the statue of War was now encased. "Do you think he'll go free again?"

Hades cut a chiding glare to Stryker. "I'm sure there's another asshole out there who'll free him."

"But not this one," Stryker said. He looked at Ash. "Thank you for your help."

"I would say anytime, but . . ."

Stryker held his hand out to him. "Enemies forever."

"Or at least until you learn to leave the humans and Dark-Hunters alone."

"When you leave my Daimons alone, I'll stop, too."

"I can't let the Daimons kill the humans."

"And I can't stand by and watch my people die over a curse my father gave them. So long as the curse stands, we hunt."

"Then our war is far from ended." Ash shook his hand, then took his leave with Tory.

Stryker draped his arm over Zephyra's shoulders. "You ready to go home?"

She nodded.

Without another word, he took her back to his palace in Kalosis. As soon as they were alone, he glared at her. "You were supposed to stay out of the fight."

"And let you get my daughter killed? Never."

"*Your* daughter?"

She folded her arms over her chest. "My daughter."

"So we're back to that, are we?"

"Absolutely. Besides, I had no intention of watching you die."

Stryker arched a brow at that. "No?"

"No. I would much rather kill you myself."

Menyara paused at the picture of Cherise holding Nick on his first day of school. The frame was set on his nightstand next to his bed. "Your mother was so proud of you."

Nick didn't speak.

Turning, she watched as he grabbed a bottle of Scotch and opened it. "Did you learn anything tonight?" she asked.

"Such as?"

"How much you need to know your powers."

He took a deep swig before he answered. "I knew that before the fight, Mennie."

"Yes, but are you willing to learn now?"

He paused. "What do you mean?"

Her resolve shone in her eyes as she cornered him. "You are part demon and part human. In order to function in this world, you will have to be taught by someone who has powers similar to yours."

"And that is?"

"Acheron."

Nick scoffed. "Ash is a god."

"Yes, but before he was a god, he was half human and half Charonte. Only he has the powers to help you."

Stunned, Nick dropped the bottle straight to the floor where it shattered.

EPILOGUE

Two Weeks Later

Zephyra sat in Stryker's chair as she listened to the sound of faint music playing. For the last fortnight, she and Stryker had been after the gallu to use them to convert more Daimons, but they were proving difficult.

In the meantime, there were only a few dozen gallu Daimons while the rest of their army needed to continue to feed on the humans.

"We will get you," she whispered. Like Stryker, she had no intention of watching their people die while Apollo lived so blithely on. Especially given the fact that if Medea were to ever marry again, her children would be born Apollite.

And they, too, would be cursed . . .

The door opened.

She glanced up to find Stryker there with a sword in his hand. Scowling, she watched him as he crossed the floor and placed it on the desk in front of her. Without a word, he knelt by her side.

"What are you doing?"

"I promised that at the end of two weeks I'd allow you to kill me." He looked pointedly at the sword. "I'm keeping my word."

She arched one brow at that. "Really?"

He inclined his head to her. "You own my life, Phyra. I lay it in your hands."

She pulled the sword from the desk, then rose with it in her hand. She angled the perfectly balanced sword and admired the gleaming edge. "You would allow me to kill you?" She placed the point directly over his heart.

His gaze locked with hers. "On my honor."

She pressed the tip into his shirt, but not deep enough to pierce his skin. "Would you die for me, Stryker?"

"Is that not what I'm doing?"

"No. You're upholding your honor and that's not what I want."

"Then what do you want?"

"I want you to stand by my side and never, ever fail me again."

Sincerity burned bright in that swirling silver gaze of his. "I would never fail you."

"Swear it on your life."

His gaze hardened. "That I can never do."

She pressed the point in until it drew a bead of blood. "Why can't you?"

"Because you are my life," he said, his voice cracking. "And I can't live another day without you."

She dropped the sword to the floor. "I despise you for what you make me feel."

He pulled her into his arms until she was kneeling on the floor in front of him. "And what is that?"

"Weak and vulnerable. You are my soul, and I will never forgive you if you take that from me again."

He smiled at her. "Have no fear, love. I will always be right here with you."

As he dipped his head to kiss her, the door behind

him crashed open. Angry at the interruption, he turned to growl at Davyn.

However, the words died on his tongue as he saw the man's face. "What's happened?"

"We can walk in daylight."

Stryker's scowl deepened. "What?"

Davyn nodded. "I was caught out in the dawn while trailing after the gallu. I thought I was dead, but I'm not. For the first time in centuries, I saw the dawn and I lived. I lived!"

Stryker exchanged an amazed look with Zephyra.

"The gallu are immune," she whispered. "I never dreamed that their blood would allow us to walk in daylight, too."

"You never tried?"

She shook her head. "I didn't dare."

A slow smile curled his lips. "We have our freedom."

"The dawn of the Daimon is here and the end of mankind is beginning."

LOVE BYTES

time she tried to update a page on their Web site, it refused to let her.

She hated Perforce, and it hated her. But they were required to use it so that upper management could keep track of who made what changes to the Web site, and out of the entire network services department, Adrian was the only one who really understood the program.

"What's it doing?" he asked as he came to stand beside her.

Sam couldn't breathe as he leaned down to read her screen. His face was so close to hers that all she had to do was move a mere two inches and she would be able to place her lips against that strong, sculpted jaw.

"Scroll down."

She heard Adrian's words, but they didn't register. She was too busy watching the way his incredibly broad shoulders hunched as he leaned with one hand against her desk.

He glanced down at her.

Sam blinked and looked back at the screen. "I'm scrolling," she said as she reached for her mouse.

"There's your problem," he said as he read the gobbledygook. "You haven't enabled your baseline merges."

"And in English that would mean?"

Adrian laughed that rich, deep laugh that made her burn even more. He covered her hand with his on the mouse and showed her how to choose the right options.

He surrounded her with his masculine warmth. Sam swallowed at the disturbing sensation of his hand on hers as fire coursed through her. He had beautiful, strong hands. His long, lean fingers were tapered and perfect. Worse, every time she looked at them, she couldn't help wondering what they would feel like on her body, touching her, caressing her.

Seducing her.

His cell phone rang. Adrian straightened and pulled the phone from its cradle on his belt. He checked the caller ID, then flipped it open like Captain Kirk. "Yeah, Scott, what's wrong?"

"Radius is down," Scott, their network security specialist, said over the speaker phone, "and I can't get it up and running."

"Did you reboot?"

"Duh."

Adrian indicated her chair with his head.

Sam got up and watched as he set the phone aside, took a seat in her chair, and opened a DOS window on her computer. He tapped swiftly on her keyboard, then picked his phone back up. "It's not cycling."

"I know, and I can't fix it."

"All right," Adrian said with saintly patience. "I'll be up there in a few minutes."

He clicked off his phone, but before he could move his phone rang at the same time his pager went off and the overhead paging system called his name. Adrian answered his cell phone again and checked his pager.

"Did you get the hacker alert?" Scott asked.

"Hang on," Adrian said, then he reached for Sam's desk phone to answer his page.

"Hi, Randy," he said as he tucked the phone between his shoulder and cheek and started typing on her keyboard. "I'm in the process of switching the main databases over to my SQL. We should be ready to fly by five." He paused as he listened and switched her computer from the Windows over to Linux.

Sam watched in awe as he flawlessly entered line after line of stuff she couldn't even begin to follow or understand.

"No," Adrian said to Randy, "our customers won't notice at all, except the searches will take less time." He entered more lines as he listened to their senior director, Randy Jacobs, on the phone.

Another page went off for him.

Adrian nodded as he listened to Randy. "Yeah, I'll get to it. Would you mind holding for just a second?"

He picked up his cell phone. "Scott, it's not a hacker. It's an invalid SID. Someone is using a bookmark with an old Session ID attached to it."

"Are you sure?"

"Positive. I'm looking at it right now."

"Okay, thanks."

Adrian gave her a sheepish smile as he clicked off his cell phone and picked up the other line on her desk phone.

Biting her lips to keep from smiling at the chaos, Sam felt for him. At twenty-six, Adrian was known to everyone in the company as the boy genius. He had taken a billion-dollar corporation from the 1980s mainframe mentality into twenty-first century Web-based e-commerce. He had single-handedly built the entire programming side of their million-dollar business retail site, and put together a Web design team that was second to none.

Unfortunately, though, everyone in the company turned to him every time something went wrong with the site. Which meant he was always on call and always rushing from one department to the next, putting out fires and trying his best to explain extremely complicated things to people who had absolutely no idea what he was talking about.

Adrian came into the office every morning by five-thirty, and seldom went home before eight at night.

The stress on him had to be excruciating, and yet he was the most easygoing boss she'd ever known. She couldn't count the number of times a day someone was complaining, if not shouting, about something, or begging him to help them, and yet he never let the strain of it show.

"Scott," Adrian said at his cell phone, "go get a cup of coffee. I'm headed upstairs as soon as I finish with Randy." He returned to her phone. "I'm back, Randy." He listened for a few minutes more, then nodded. "All right," he said, pulling the Palm Pilot off his belt. "I'll put it on my schedule."

Sam watched as he added yet another meeting to his already booked calendar.

"Okay," he said to Randy. "I'm on it. See you later."

Adrian left the chair, then hesitated at the opening of Sam's cube as she resumed her seat. In a rare show of uneasiness, he picked up the wooden medieval knight her brother had given her. "This is new."

She nodded. "Teddy got it Thanksgiving when he went to Germany."

"It's neat," he said, putting it back on the shelf with the rest of the knights. She had been collecting them for years. She figured they were as close as she'd ever come to having a real knight in shining armor.

He glanced around her cube at the large Santa and snowmen cutouts she had pinned up, the small Christmas tree she had next to her monitor, and the stack of holiday catalogues by her keyboard. "You really love Christmas, don't you?"

Sam glanced down at her Santa and reindeer sweater and smiled. "My favorite time of year. Don't you like it?"

He shrugged. "It's a day off, I guess."

Still Adrian hesitated, fiddling with her nameplate.

How odd. It was so unlike him to be fidgety. This was a man who made million-dollar decisions and held meetings with the stars of the *Fortune* 500 without even a minor qualm.

What on earth could he be nervous about?

"Would you mind if I asked a giant favor?"

Her heart pounded. *Oh, baby, ask me anything!*

"What'cha need?"

He dropped his gaze down to her nameplate as he slid it back and forth in its holder. "Since Heather has totally screwed up my clothes again, I was wondering if you'd mind going shopping with me after work? I'd take Randir, but even I can tell *his* clothes don't match."

"I heard that!" Randir said laughingly from the next cube.

Sam smiled. The guys in her department teased each other mercilessly, and it was what she loved most about her job. Everyone got along well and no one minded the incessant quips and taunts that were hurled about as often as Adrian got paged.

"Anyway," Adrian said, ignoring Randir's interruption. "Would you mind? I'll buy you dinner."

Yes! Her heart skipped a beat as she did her best to appear calm, while inside, what she really wanted to do was turn cartwheels. "I don't mind."

"You sure?"

"Positive."

"Great," he said with a slight smile. "Then I guess I better go to Scott before he hyperventilates."

"Okay, see you later."

Adrian took one last look at Sam as she returned her

attention to her monitor. He clenched his teeth as he watched her fingers stroking the keys on her keyboard.

That woman had the lightest touch he'd ever seen, and he ached to feel those hands on his body. Ached to take them into his mouth and nibble every inch of them.

Worse, what he really wanted to do was pick her up from that chair, take her into his office, and toss everything on top of his desk onto the floor before laying her down on top of it.

Oh, yeah, he could already taste her lips as he peeled the thick sweater and jeans off her body. Feel her hot and wet for him as he coaxed and teased her body into blind ecstasy.

His groin tightened in pain at the thought.

Stop it! he snapped at himself. He was her team leader, and she was one of his best employees. Company policy stringently forbade dating between management and staff, and violation of that policy meant immediate dismissal.

Yeah, but the woman made him seriously hot.

Dangerously hot.

She always wore her long, dark hair pulled back from her face where it fell in thick waves down to her waist. He'd spent hours at night fantasizing about that hair draped on his chest, or spread out across his pillow.

And she had the palest eyes he'd ever seen. She'd told him once they were green, and it pained him that he had absolutely no idea what that color meant.

But from what he could see, green had to be beautiful.

Her eyes were a bit large for her pixie face, and they were always bright and teasing when she looked at him.

He could stare into those eyes for an eternity.

Adrian ran his gaze over her lush curves, and he hardened even more as raw, demanding desire tore through him. Sam had once complained about her weight, but he couldn't find any fault with it. After growing up with a skinny, frail mother and sister, he couldn't stand to see a woman with no meat on her bones.

Her full, voluptuous body made him absolutely crazy with unspent lust. And for the last year, he'd been forced to learn to live with a raging erection every time he got near her, or heard the sound of her smooth Southern drawl.

Sam paused and looked up at him. "Did you need something else?"

Yeah, I need you to smile at me.

Touch me.

Better still, I need you to climb me like a ladder . . .

"No," he said as another page sounded for him.

Adrian turned away from her and answered the page with his cell phone as he headed upstairs to tend Scott's antsy twitters.

Sam clenched her hands as her computer clock showed ten after five. An anxious tremor went through her as she feared Adrian might have changed his mind about going out with her.

Taking a deep breath for courage, she shut down her computer, then walked the short distance to Adrian's office.

He had his back to her as he typed like lightning on his keyboard while talking on the phone. "It's switched," he said. "Everything is clear . . . No, I ran the logs, and as of yesterday, we've cleared seven hundred thousand dollars in orders since the end of October . . . Yeah," he said with a light laugh. "Merry Christmas to you, too."

He hung up the phone, and she saw him rub his hand over his eyes as if he had a headache. His cell phone rang. Without breaking stride, he answered it.

"Hi, Tiffany," he said to their marketing director. "Yeah, I'll be here for a few more minutes. I was planning on implementing your changeover after Christmas since there's a good chance it could slow down site access." He listened as he worked and Sam shook her head.

The man was simply amazing. She didn't know how he managed to stay on top of everything, but he did.

He pushed his chair back from his computer desk and swung it around to the desk in front of her. As his gaze fell on her, he smiled that wolfish grin that made her blood race. She felt a vicious stab of desire straight through her middle.

Reaching for a stack of reports, he flipped to one of the middle pages. "Okay," he said to Tiffany. "I'll take care of it first thing in the morning."

He clicked off his phone. "Sorry about that," he said to Sam. "I didn't know you were standing there. Just give me a sec, I'll get this finished, and we can leave."

Sam let out a relieved breath. Thank goodness, he hadn't changed his mind. She moved into his office and took a seat against the window as she waited for him. "Have we really done seven hundred thousand dollars off the site since Halloween?"

He nodded. "We should easily hit a million by Christmas." He flashed her another smile. "Should make for nice bonuses."

Money, she didn't care about. So long as she made enough to cover her car and rent, she was completely happy. But she was glad for Adrian's sake. Their business-to-business e-commerce Web site was his pride and joy, and he took a lot of flak from the higher-ups when the site didn't perform the way they thought it should.

Sam looked up as Tiffany stalked into Adrian's office. "Adrian," Tiffany whined as she glanced at Sam without acknowledging her. Thin, tall, and gorgeous, Tiffany should have been a model. All the leggy blonde had to do was bat her eyelashes, and every guy in the building would drop what he was doing and rush to her side.

And every time Sam got near her, she felt like a warted troll in comparison.

"Adrian," Tiffany said again. "I got an e-mail from a customer wanting to know why he has to enter in his password every time he wants to order something. He wants us to fix it so that he can just do a one-click order option. What should I tell him?"

Adrian didn't pause in his typing as he answered. "That it's a safeguard to save his butt should one of his disgruntled employees get ticked off and decide to order several thousand dollars' worth of merchandise and charge it to his account."

Tiffany rolled her eyes at Adrian's sarcasm. "Well, he says—"

"I don't give a damn what he says," Adrian said calmly.

Sam bit her lip as Tiffany's face flushed bright red. That was Adrian's only flaw. The man didn't pull punches, and he always spoke his mind, consequences be damned.

"Those safeguards are there for his protection," he continued, "and I'm not about to change it since he'll be the first one to whine when he gets burned."

Tiffany stomped her foot. "Would you look at me when you're talking to me?"

Sam arched her brow as Adrian turned around with a look on his face that should have sent Tiffany running. To his credit, all he said was a simple, "Yes?"

"I need a more tactful answer for him than that." She narrowed those blue eyes at him. "Look, I know you think you own this Web site, but the last time I checked, you were just another flunky here like the rest of us."

He took a deep breath as both his pager and phone went off. "I tell you what," he said in a self-controlled tone, "since I'm a flunky here like everyone else, why don't you come in at midnight tonight to post a press release because the man who signs our checks wants it to go live exactly at that time?" He picked his phone off his belt.

He checked the caller ID, flipped it open, and said, "Scott, it's not a hacker. I'm validating the PHP."

Adrian hung up the phone. "Now, Miss Klein, if you want a more tactful response, then please forward the e-mail to me and I will respond to it myself."

Tossing her hair over her shoulder, Tiffany glared at him. "I want a copy of your response."

"Yes, Mom."

Tiffany's nostrils flared. Turning on her red high heels, she stalked out of his office. But as she left, Sam heard her muttering under her breath, "What a friggin' geek."

She couldn't tell if Adrian heard it. He merely checked his pager, then grabbed one of the reports and swung his chair back around to his computer.

"You must get tired of all this," she said quietly.

"I'm used to it," he said simply as he started typing again.

Sam shook her head. Poor Adrian. He wasn't even allowed to get sick. She remembered last summer when he had pneumonia. He'd been forced to drag himself in to work to fix some problem no one else could solve.

The man needed a break.

And how she wished she dared get up from her chair, go over to him and massage those broad, tense shoulders for him. She could just imagine the feel of his lean muscles under her hand, the sight of his handsome features relaxed.

He would be breathtaking.

Sam, you have got to quit fantasizing. Boy genius doesn't even know you're alive.

Even though it was true, she wished things were different between them. Adrian was the first guy she'd ever met whom she really could see herself having kids with. She'd love to have a houseful of tall brainiacs who were fast on a comeback.

It was a full ten minutes before Adrian finally logged off his computer. He got up to shrug on his faded blue ski jacket.

"C'mon," he said to her. "Let's make a mad run for the door before someone catches me."

She laughed, knowing it wasn't a joke.

He locked his office, then they headed outside to the dimly lit parking lot.

"Why don't you ride with me?" he asked as she started for her silver Honda. "You're the only person in the department who hasn't ridden in the Vette."

Oh, don't tempt me, you cruel man. She hadn't ridden in his Corvette because she couldn't stand the thought of being so close to him and not being able to touch that wonderful body. "Yeah, but you'll have to bring me all the way back here."

"I don't mind."

Sam bit her lip as her pulse raced. *Don't do it! Don't torture yourself.*

But one look at his chiseled features in the streetlight and she was hooked. "Okay," she said with a nonchalance she didn't feel.

He opened the passenger side door for her, then closed it after she got in. Sam drew a ragged breath at his consideration. She'd never had a man do that for her before.

Adrian got in the other side, and she had to bite back a laugh at the sight of him cramming his long body into the car.

"Don't say anything," he said as he put the key in the ignition. "Heather already told me I look like a grasshopper in a peanut shell."

She couldn't help laughing at that. "Sorry," she said, clearing her throat as she caught his sideways glare. "I wouldn't have laughed if you hadn't said that."

Sam leaned back in the black leather seat as she inhaled the warm, spicy scent of him. Good heavens, but that masculine smell made her giddy and hot. She would love nothing more than to lean over, cup the back of his neck with her hand, and kiss the daylights out of those full, sensuous lips.

Adrian started the car and did his best to ignore just how good Sam looked sitting beside him. He ached to reach his hand over to where she had her legs slightly parted and caress her inner thigh.

Oh, yeah, he could already feel the denim and her flesh in his palm. And then, he imagined where he'd like to take his hand next.

Up her thigh to cup her between her legs.

Grinding his teeth, he could see them locked in a kiss, feel her hands sliding over him as he undressed her.

It had been a long time since he'd made out in a car, but for the first time since high school, he found the idea appealing.

A surge of lust ripped through him as he shifted uncomfortably in his seat.

She'd taken that stupid clip out of her hair and brushed her bangs with her hand so that now her hair fell around her face, framing it to perfection. And it was torturing him.

Pulling out of the lot, he headed toward Hickory Hollow Mall. He hadn't even gone a mile when he noticed Sam tensing in her seat. "What's wrong?" he asked.

She flinched as he changed lanes. "You know, Adrian, this isn't a video game, and cars don't evaporate if you hit them. Jeez, you drive like you have a death wish."

He laughed and backed off his speed. "Come on, half the fun of this car is pushing its limits."

She crossed herself. "I hope you have a good life insurance policy."

He did, but there wasn't anyone to reap the benefits of it. And it was one of his biggest regrets. He'd never been the kind of guy to date much. Taking care of his mother, sister, and work left him very little time to socialize.

Not that it mattered. As soon as he opened his mouth and said something, most women got a blank, dazed look on their faces and stared at him like he was speaking a foreign language.

But not Sam. She understood even his most obscure references.

"Adrian!" she snapped as a semi cut them off. "That's a truck!"

He hit the brakes. "Don't worry, I don't dare die before I put the Christmas press release up. And even if I did, I'm sure Randy would be at the funeral home with a laptop asking me to take care of some last-minute thing."

"You're not funny," she said, even though she was smiling. "Do you really have to go in later and do that?"

"Unfortunately, yes." Adrian pulled onto Bell Road. "Want to eat first?"

"Sure."

"What are you in the mood for?"

"Anything."

"How about Olive Garden?" he asked, knowing it was one of her favorites.

"Sounds great."

Adrian pulled into the lot, then went to open the door for her. But by the time he got to her side, she was already getting out. She looked up and smiled. "And they say chivalry is dead."

"You have a hard time letting anyone do anything for you, don't you?" he asked.

"What can I say? My brothers broke me in well."

Adrian shook his head. "I can't believe your mother didn't nag them into doing more for you."

"She might have, had she ever been home, but since she had to work all the time after my dad left, it was pretty much just us."

Adrian tucked his hands into his back pockets to keep himself from subconsciously reaching out to touch her.

God, how he wanted her. She barely reached his shoulders and every time he stood this close to her, he had the worst desire to pick her up in his arms and bury his face in her neck, where he could inhale the sweet scent of her skin.

Clenching his teeth, he tried to banish the thought of

laying her down on his bed and spending the rest of the night exploring her body. Slowly. Meticulously.

He opened the door to the restaurant and let her enter first. As she passed him, his gaze trailed down the back of her body and focused on her round hips. His groin instantly hardened. Thank God he wore baggy jeans.

The hostess led them to a booth in the back. Adrian hesitated as Sam sat down. His first impulse was to sit beside her, but he knew it wouldn't be appropriate. The only time he got to do that was when all of them went out to lunch, and then he always made a point of being the one to sit closest to her.

His gut tightening as another wave of desire hit him, he forced himself into the opposite booth.

"It's weird to be here without the guys," she said as she glanced over the menu.

Adrian stared at her as she read the menu. He didn't know why she bothered since she always ordered the Manicotti Formaggio, and he loved the way she said it. It rolled off her tongue like smooth whisky.

Sam tightened her hands on the menu as she felt Adrian's gaze on her. Unnerved by its intensity, she tried to cross her legs, but ended up kicking him under the table. "I'm sorry," she gasped as he grimaced.

"It's okay," he said, reaching beneath the table to rub his leg. "I tend to take up a lot of space."

"Don't knock it, I'd kill to be tall."

"I don't know why. I think you're a perfect size."

She glanced up at his unexpected compliment. He cleared his throat and dropped his gaze to his menu.

After they ordered, they sat in awkward silence.

Sam sipped her drink as she tried to think of something to say to him. Normally, they never had a bit of trouble finding things to talk about and laugh over. But tonight, she was just a little too aware of him. A little too nervous about being alone with him, knowing there was no one here to see her if she were to reach over and touch his hand.

No one to see if she . . .

"Did you decide to call that guy about the programming position?" she asked, remembering the résumé he'd given her to review that morning.

"I did, even though my first impulse was to toss it."

"Why?"

"Dear *Ms.* Cole," he said, curling his lip. "I hate it when someone gets my gender wrong. It's the reason I called you so fast when you submitted your résumé. You're the only one who hasn't made that mistake. I knew you had to be brilliant."

She smiled. "Yeah, well, I have to say I was stumped, which is why I wrote 'Dear Adrian.' I figured you had to be a guy, since there are so few women programmers, but just in case you weren't I didn't want to tick you off."

"Thanks, Mom," he muttered bitterly. "It wasn't bad enough she passed along the oh-so-wonderful color-blind genes, but she had to curse me with a godawful name to boot."

"If you hate it so much, why don't you use your middle name?"

"Because it's Lesley."

Sam felt her jaw go slack. "Your mother named you Adrian Lesley Cole?"

He nodded. "She *really* wanted a daughter. When the nurse told her she had a son, she told the nurse to check again. 'That just can't be right,'" he said in a falsetto, mocking a thick Southern accent.

Was he serious?

"You know," she said. "I really like the name Adrian. I think it suits you."

He snorted. "Gee, thanks for the affront to my manhood."

"No," she said with a laugh. There was absolutely *nothing* feminine about him, or his features. "You just have a classical, romantic look to you, like the hero from some period movie."

He looked a bit sheepish at her compliment. Sam dropped her gaze down to his hands again and watched the way he trailed the empty straw wrapper through his long fingers.

Oh, she loved those hands of his.

How she wished for the courage to reach over and cover them with hers. But she was terrified of what he might do. Terrified of him rejecting her, because in her heart, she knew she'd already fallen for him.

She needed to be able to see him every day. Needed to feel his presence even if it was at a distance.

No, she would never chance running him off. He was her boss, and she would have to satisfy herself with just being his friend.

As soon as they finished dinner, Adrian drove them up the street to the mall. Sam led him through the men's section of Dillard's, looking for things she thought would be hot on him.

She paused as she found a stack of button-fly jeans. "You know, these would look great on you."

Adrian didn't miss the gleam in her eyes. He hated button-fly, but if Sam liked them . . .

"I need a thirty-two waist and a thirty-six inseam."

"Oh, my God, you're tall."

He laughed. "I know and it's a bitch to find them. But if you can locate a pair in this mess, I'll try them on."

She did. Adrian tucked them under his arm as he followed her around and did his best not to be too obvious in his ogling of her.

"You're not going to put me in anything weird, are you?" he asked suspiciously as she stopped to look at a rack of V-neck sweaters. "I might not be able to see colors, but I know guys don't wear pink, or pastels. And please, nothing in bright yellow because I can't stand light-post jokes."

"I wouldn't do that to you. I'm thinking blacks and dark blues. Maybe red. You look really good in red."

He smiled. "Really? How good?"

"*Very* good." She plucked at his shirtsleeve. "But I don't like your plaid shirts. They make you look like a lumberjack."

She'd noticed him! Adrian wanted to shout in happiness. He couldn't believe she'd actually been looking at him.

"So, what do"—he had to bite back the word *you*—"women want on a guy?"

"Not those baggy jeans," she said, looking at his rear and making him even hotter. Harder.

His breathing tense, it was all he could do not to pull her to him and find out exactly what those lips of hers tasted like.

"I don't know who came up with the idea," she continued, "but ew. Women like to see a man's . . ."

He arched a brow.

"Never mind. I'm having a weird case of déjá vu."

"Why?"

"I used to buy clothes for my brothers and we'd always get into similar discussions." She ran her gaze over him. "No offense, but you could really use a makeover."

Adrian hesitated. Maybe if he let her, she might be a little more receptive to his . . .

You're her boss.

Yeah, but he liked her more than he had ever liked any other woman. She made him laugh . . . made him happy every time she looked up at him.

Better still, she made him burn.

"You feel up to it?" he asked before he could stop himself.

"You'd let me?" she asked in disbelief.

"Sure, just so long as you don't paint my fingernails pale pink."

She frowned at that. "What?"

"Heather did that to me in high school as a joke. One night while I was sleeping, she sneaked into my room and painted my fingernails. I didn't notice until I got to school the next day and people started laughing."

"Why is your sister so mean to you?"

He shrugged. "She doesn't mean any real harm. She's just impulsive, and never seems to think before she acts."

Shaking her head, Sam searched through a rack of black button-down shirts as she thought about what he'd said. "She really painted your fingernails?"

"Yup."

"My brothers would have killed me."

"Yeah, well, she's my kid sister. My mom always said my one job was to protect her, not pulverize her."

Affected by his protectiveness, she reached out without thinking and touched his arm.

Her heart stopped.

Holy cow!

Up until now, she'd thought he was on the skinny side like his sister, but there was nothing thin about that arm. His biceps were harder than a brick even while relaxed.

"Okay," she said, trying to distract herself from that delectable muscle. "Makeover with no nail polish."

Sam picked out several shirts and more jeans, then sent Adrian to try them on. She was busy looking through another rack when she felt someone behind her.

Turning around, she froze. Adrian was standing at the mirror outside the dressing room with his sweater lifted while he tugged at the back of his jeans. "I don't know about this," he said.

She only vaguely registered his words. Because she was captivated by him. The faded denim cupped a rear so tight and well formed that it made her ache to touch it.

He was wearing a thin, black V-neck sweater that clung to his broad shoulders, biceps, and pecs. And worse, the hem of the sweater was lifted up to where she could see his hard, flat stomach and dark brown hairs curling becomingly around his navel.

Oh . . . My . . . God. The man had the body of a well-toned gymnast. Why he had kept that yummy body hidden was beyond her.

"Buddy, you got abs!" she said before she could stop herself.

Adrian met her gaze in the mirror. "What?"

She closed the distance between them and lifted the shirt hem a tad higher as she stared in awe at that body.

"You got abs! A whole six-pack of them." She looked up at him. "You didn't get those on the computer."

"Well, no. I do other things on occasion."

No kidding.

And right then, there was a whole series of other things she wanted to do to him. Starting with those hard abs and working her way up and down that luscious, tanned body. "If I were you, I'd burn all those baggy jeans and oversized shirts as soon as I got home."

"You like these jeans?"

Biting her lip, she nodded.

Suddenly, Adrian liked them, too. But what he liked most was the hunger he saw in her eyes, the feel of her hand against his stomach. It sent chills all over him.

It was all he could do not to kiss her.

Worse, an image of her lying naked beneath him tore through him. He shuttered his eyes as his breathing faltered. He wanted her so badly, he could already taste the moistness of her lips. Feel the softness of those full breasts in his hands.

It was a such a raw, aching need that it sliced through him.

Sam looked up and caught the heated look in his eyes. He had his lips slightly parted. And she became all too aware of the fact that she was still holding his shirt in her hand, and was so close to his hard belly that she could feel his body heat.

Her breasts tightened as a wave of lust singed her.

Please kiss me. . . .

But he didn't. He swallowed and took a step back.

Sam sighed. What was she thinking? Smart, gorgeous guys like Adrian didn't date short, fat co-workers. They were friends, plain and simple. There could never be anything between them.

By the time they finished, Adrian was almost a thousand dollars poorer, but he had an entire new wardrobe. And if it would keep Sam staring at him like she was doing, he decided it was worth every penny.

He changed into a new T-shirt, sweater, and jeans before they left.

Their next stop was MasterCuts. "What's wrong with my hair?" he asked as he sat down in the chair.

"Nothing, Shaggy-Doo," Sam said playfully as she brushed her hand through his hair. His entire body erupted into fire as he savored her light touch against his scalp. "I love the tawny color and curls. With the right cut, you would stop traffic."

Sam watched from the side of his chair as the beautician trimmed his silken curls into a shorter cut that looked incredibly sexy and stylish.

Oh, yeah, now he was cooking. She stared in awe as the woman moussed his hair.

"Now that is a great look," Sam told Adrian. "You get rid of that goatee and watch out."

"Now you hate my goatee?" he asked, aghast.

"For the record," Sam said as she met his gaze in the mirror, "all women hate goatees."

The beautician concurred. "She's right. They're nasty."

Adrian stroked his goatee with his thumb. "Really? You don't think it's manly?"

"Do you think a billy goat is manly?"

"Oh, thanks, *Heather*."

Sam's eyes twinkled.

Adrian paid for the cut and for the bottle of mousse Sam insisted he'd better use, but personally, he'd rather stick a pair of tweezers in an electrical outlet.

All too soon, the night was over and he had to drive her back to her car.

"Thanks," he said as she got into her Honda. "I really appreciate your taking pity on my clothes tonight."

"It was my pleasure."

God, he wanted to kiss her. He stared at her lips, trying to imagine what they would taste like. He'd give anything to have a single night with her. To sink himself deep between her soft thighs as she held him close and moaned in his ear.

Then again, one night with her would never be enough.

"You be careful," he said, his voice hoarse. "How far is Spring Hill from here?"

"A good fifty minutes."

"Jeez, I shouldn't have kept you out so long. Do me a favor and call my cell phone and let me know when you get home, okay?"

"Okay."

Adrian forced himself to close her car door. He stepped away from her car as she started it. The light from the control panel lit her face as she buckled herself in.

In that moment, he ached for something he knew he could never have.

Her.

She looked up and waved. He returned the gesture, then watched as she drove off.

His heart heavy, and feeling twice as lonely as he had before, he got into his car.

Adrian froze as he reached for the ignition. He could still smell her floral scent in the air. Taking a deep breath, he relished it and dreamed of being able to bury his face in her neck where he could just breathe her in all night.

And in that moment, he made a decision.

Right or wrong, company policy be damned, he was going to find some way to make her his.

2

"Hey, Sam, could you come here for a minute?"

Sam cringed as Tiffany waylaid her outside of the breakroom at ten A.M. "What do you need?"

Tiffany huffed in agitation. "Adrian isn't here yet—"

"That's because he was here from eleven-thirty last night until three o'clock this morning. I imagine he's sleeping in."

"Whatever. I have to respond to the Waverley Valley customer, and he has yet to send me his e-mail."

Sam pursed her lips to keep from laughing. Oh, he'd written the e-mail all right. He'd answered the customer's complaints, point by point, with the most hilarious sarcasm she'd ever read. The last line of it had said, "All hail the goddess Discordia the day we let Lord Bone-Head's twenty-two teenage employees have unrestricted ordering capacity on our system."

Adrian was a riot.

And at the bottom of the e-mail, he'd pasted in the much more professional response that he had sent to their customer.

"I know he wrote it," Sam said seriously. "I'm sure he'll forward a copy as soon as he gets in."

"Well, he better, or I'm telling Randy about it." Tiffany glanced down the hallway, did a double-take, then gaped.

Sam turned her head to see what was going on.

She froze at the sight.

Oh, my.

Like all the other women in the hallway, Sam was transfixed by Adrian and that sexy, loose-limbed swagger of his as he came toward her. Dressed all in black, except for the hint of his white T-shirt peeking out of the V of his tailored black button-down shirt, he was dazzling.

The black leather jacket she had talked him into looked even better on him than she had imagined it would.

His goatee was gone and the new haircut gave a deeply poetic look to his chiseled features. He wore a pair of Wayfarer sunglasses, and when he smiled, she saw deep dimples that had been masked all this time by his thick whiskers.

The man was *seriously* hot.

Regina, the receptionist, was headed to her desk when she passed him. Turning her head to watch him, she stared so intently at his rear that she walked straight into the wall.

Oblivious to the gaping women around him, Adrian made straight for Sam.

"Good morning," he said, flashing those dimples as he took his sunglasses off.

"Morning," Sam said, amazed at how normal her voice sounded given the amount of havoc his new look had on her senses. Now that he was this close, she could smell the leather and his Old Spice aftershave. Yum. Her entire body burned.

"Oh, Adrian!" Tiffany gushed as she twirled a strand

of blond hair around her index finger. "We were just talking about you."

Adrian arched a brow at her. "What did I do now?"

"Oh, it was nothing bad. I was just asking about that silly old e-mail, but I know you're busy. So, you take your time and when you're ready, I'll take care of it for you."

My, how her tune has changed, Sam thought irritably. *Why is it, you find a good man, clean him up, and then the vultures start swooping in?*

Life was not fair.

"I sent the e-mail last night," Adrian said.

"How strange," Tiffany said with an obviously practiced frown. "I didn't see it in my in box."

"Did you forget to change it over from your personal e-mail account to the company servers again?"

"Oh," Tiffany said, stroking him lightly on the arm as she giggled and preened. "How silly of me. You know, I just can't keep all this computer stuff straight in my head. I'd really appreciate it if you'd show me how to fix that."

"I'll send Scott down."

His phone rang. Adrian answered it while Tiffany ran a hungry look over his body.

Sam wanted to choke her. "Don't you have something you need to do?" she asked Tiffany.

Tiffany glared at her until Adrian hung up, then she smiled sweetly at him. "You know, if you've got a minute, right now—"

"Actually, I don't. I need to talk to Sam. Excuse us?"

"Oh, absolutely. I'm sure you *guys*—no offense, Sam—" she said, sweeping a hard look to Sam before giving Adrian a worshipful smile, "have computer problems to talk about. I'll see you"—she punctuated the word by touching Adrian on the chest—"later."

Sam had to force herself not to clobber Tiffany.

As soon as they were alone, Adrian bent down to whisper in her ear. "I did put the right colors together, didn't I?" he asked.

"Oh, yeah," Sam breathed as two women who were staring at Adrian collided behind him.

He let out a relieved sigh. "I was having a bad Heather flashback as I came in the door and three women looked at me and started giggling."

Sam could well imagine that. She felt giddy herself.

Adrian stroked his chin with his hand. "And I'm not sure about the face. I've had a beard or mustache since I turned seventeen. I feel really naked."

At that moment, she wished he *were* naked. Naked and in her arms doing the Wild Thing with her. "You shouldn't."

"You're sure I don't look like a girly-mon? Because I really don't want the guys up in design to start following me around."

"Oh, no," she said with a laugh. "There's nothing girly about the way you look."

"All right, but if the guys start harassing me, I might have to fire you."

She laughed at the empty threat.

His phone rang again and Regina paged him.

"It starts already," Sam said.

"Already? Hell, it started two hours ago, which is why I came on in," he mumbled as he flipped open his phone and headed toward his office.

Sam bit her knuckles as she watched him walk away. She ran a lecherous gaze down his lean back and well-shaped rear. An image of those flat abs tormented her, and it was all she could do not to follow him into his office, lock the door, and keep him there until they were both sweaty and spent.

"Yo, A-dri-an!" Scott called as he passed by Sam's cube.

Sam cringed, knowing how much Adrian hated for someone to do that to him.

"What?" he snapped as he stuck his head over Randir's cube.

"Oh," Scott said. "You're not in your office. I was wondering what we're doing for lunch today?"

"We haven't discussed it."

"Well, it's eleven-thirty and I'm starving. Let's discuss it."

Adrian peeped over the cube wall to look at her. "Sam, you coming?"

"Depends on where you go."

"Well," Scott said to Adrian, "I was wondering if your sister's working at Chik-Fil-A today. I'm kind of broke, so if she'd spot us again, I'd really appreciate it."

"You mooch," Randir said. "I say we take him out back, and shoot him."

Adrian laughed as he picked up his phone and dialed it. "Hey, Mark? This is Adrian. Is Heather working today?"

"Hey, Sis," Adrian said after a brief pause. "Scott's broke and wanted to know if you'd feed him again? Okay, we'll see you shortly." Hanging up, he looked at Sam. "Chik-Fil-A?"

"Sure, I'll go."

"I'll drive," Jack said from the cube opposite her. "I have the minivan today. But I warn you, it's full of toys."

The six of them gathered their things and headed for

the door. Adrian fell in beside her, then reached an arm toward her.

Sam froze in nervous anticipation as it appeared he was about to put his arm around her, then he bent it up quickly and raked his hand through his hair.

Disappointed, she did all she could do not to pout.

Adrian cursed at himself as he realized what he'd almost done. And at work no less . . . Jeez. What was wrong with him?

But then, he knew. Sam had been sneaking looks at him all morning.

And he'd loved every minute of it.

Jack unlocked his van. Sam took the seat behind the driver's and Adrian quickly sat beside her. When she looked up and smiled, he felt like someone had sucker-punched him right in the gut.

"I really like that jacket," she said to him.

"Oh, Adrian," Scott teased from the front passenger seat as Jack started the van, then backed up. "You're just so cute today," he lisped. "Can I have a ride in your special Love Bytes machine after work?"

"Would you guys leave him alone?" Sam said.

"It's all right," Adrian said as he picked up a Game Boy from the seat and turned it on. "I'll just fire his ass after lunch."

Adrian played Centipede while Sam and the guys exchanged insults. He listened to them, all the while glancing sideways at Sam. Man, how he loved the way her eyes sparkled when she laughed.

As soon as they reached the mall, they piled out and headed to the food court. They had just entered the area when Sam caught sight of Heather standing beside a table with a guy dressed in a leather motorcycle jacket. He had three days' worth of black stubble on his face, and a death grip on Heather's arm.

Sam held her breath.

Rage descended on Adrian's face as he rushed toward them.

"Josh," Heather said in a pain-filled voice, trying to pry the man's hand off her upper arm. "You're hurting me."

"I'm going to do more than that if—"

"Let her go," Adrian growled as he grabbed Josh's hand and removed it from Heather's arm. He shoved the man back.

Josh raked a sneer over Adrian's body, but there was fear in his eyes as he took in the size of Adrian. "Look, pal, this is between me and my woman."

"No," Adrian said, "it's between you and my baby sister. And if you touch her again, it's going to be between you and me."

A wave of apprehension crossed Josh's face as he looked from Adrian to Heather. "I thought you said Adrian was a geek."

"He is," Heather said. "But he's a really *big* geek."

Josh angled a finger at Heather. "You remember what I said."

"Let me tell *you* something," Adrian said with a killing glare. "If I find you near my sister again, I'm going to play Picasso with your body parts."

Heather postured. "And he can do it too, he has a black belt."

Josh snarled at the two of them, then stalked off.

"Jeez, Heather," Adrian said as he turned to face her. "Can't you ever find a decent guy?"

"He's not always like that," Heather said dismissively. "He can be really sweet, sometimes."

Adrian's face turned hard, cold. "I better not find you near him again, and I mean it."

"Back off, Adrian. It's none of your business. You know, I'm not eleven years old anymore, and I don't need you coming to my rescue all the time."

"Fine," he snapped. "Then stop calling me every time you get into a jam."

"Fine," Heather snarled back at him. "Mom's right, you are just like your father. Worthless and mean."

Sam held her breath as a dark, angry pain descended over Adrian's face.

It was then Adrian must have remembered they were there, listening, because he looked to his left, saw them and locked his jaw.

Without a word, he walked off.

The guys stayed in the food court to comfort Heather while Sam ran after Adrian. He was halfway down the mall before she finally caught up to him.

"Hey?" she said as she pulled him to a stop with a gentle hand on his arm. "You okay?"

Adrian stared at her as he felt her soothing touch all the way through his body. "Why does she have to act that way?" he asked rhetorically. "I'll never understand you women, and why you're only attracted to pricks who run all over you, then turn on you if you dare open your mouth to defend yourself."

"Not all women are attracted to men like that."

"Yeah, right. Prove it."

Before he knew what she was doing, she stood up on her tiptoes, reached her arm around his neck, and brought his head down for a scorching kiss.

Adrian's head swam at the softness of her lips, of the feel of her tongue against his. He cupped her face with his hands and closed his eyes to better savor the moment.

She had her hand buried in his hair, sending chills the entire length of his body. He felt himself harden even more as a wave of her sweet feminine scent permeated his senses.

In that moment, he couldn't think of anything except taking her home, stripping her jeans and sweater from her body, and keeping her that way until breakfast.

Sam didn't know where she'd found the courage to finally kiss him, but she was glad she had. She'd been dreaming of it all day long. And now that she'd actually done it, it was all she could do not to moan from the incredible taste of his lips. The warm, masculine smell of him.

Until it dawned on her what she was doing. She was kissing her boss less than five miles from work, in the middle of a mall crowded with Christmas shoppers where four of their co-workers could see them any second.

Pulling back, she let go of him. "I'm sorry," she whispered. "I shouldn't have done that."

But Adrian didn't let her get away. He caught her in his arms and pressed her against the store window behind her. Then, he kissed her so fiercely that she thought she might faint from it.

It was raw, demanding, and it made her so hot that she couldn't breathe. Couldn't think as she felt his heart pounding rapidly in time with hers.

Good Lord, the man knew how to give a kiss. Every part of her throbbed and ached for him. And when he ran his hands down her back to press her closer to his hips, she felt his hard erection against her stomach.

He wanted *her*.

In that instant, she felt she could fly.

"Neither should I," he whispered against her lips. "But the bad thing is, I want to do it again."

So did she.

He took a step back and put his hands in his jacket pockets.

"What are we going to do about this?" she asked tentatively.

"I don't know." He looked around them. "You probably should get back to the guys before someone sees us."

She took a step toward the food court, then noticed he hadn't budged. "Are you coming?"

He shook his head. "I'm not hungry. I'll go play at Radio Shack while you guys eat. Just pick me up on the way out."

"I'll stay with you."

He smiled. "I appreciate the thought, but Ms. Hypoglycemic can't go without lunch."

It was so like him to think of her, and that was one of the things she loved best about him. "All right."

He caught her hand before she left him, then kissed the back of her knuckles. "Thanks for coming after me."

"You're very welcome."

He let go and she felt a strange vacant hole in her stomach. Glancing back at him and the striking image he made smiling at her, she headed to the food court.

Sam waved at the guys as she went over to Chik-Fil-A and ordered a value meal.

"Is Adrian okay?" Heather asked.

"No. You embarrassed him."

"Well, you know, it's not my fault. He always has to act like he's Mr. Macho out to defend my honor all the time. It gets really old."

"He loves you, Heather. What's he supposed to do? Sit around and let you get hurt? Jeez, I'd kill for one of my brothers to do the things for me he does for you. I mean damn, girl, you let him go to work, knowing he's the boss, in ruined clothes while he *pays* you to embarrass him. I just don't understand you."

Heather looked away guiltily. "I do love him, you know. I just wish he'd quit trying to parent me all the time."

"Well, from what I've heard, he was pretty much the only parent you had growing up."

"I know," Heather said. "I remember when he was twelve and I was six, Mom couldn't afford a Christmas tree. I was crying on Christmas Eve because I didn't think Santa would come without one, so Adrian rode his bicycle down to the supermarket and talked the tree dealer into letting him work for one."

Heather sighed. "He's always doing really sweet things like that for me. I guess I really do take him for granted."

"Personally, I think a whole lot of people do."

Heather handed Sam her food.

"Wait," Heather whispered as Sam started to leave. She quickly bagged a sandwich, fries, and brownie. "Would you take this to him and tell him I'm really sorry?"

"Sure."

Sam made her way over to the guys who were eating. They were back to their usual bantering, but as she ate, she couldn't get the taste of Adrian's kiss out of her mind. That kiss had really done something to her.

Worse, she kept imagining him as a kid working on a cold Nashville parking lot so his baby sister would have a Christmas tree. It was such an Adrian thing to do.

And she wondered if anyone had ever done such a thing for him. But in her heart, she knew they hadn't.

Adrian took care of the world while no one took care of him.

Sam cracked open Adrian's office door. "Hey, I just wanted to let you know that I was leaving."

He turned around in his chair to face her. "Is it five already?"

"Five-thirty, actually."

"Oh." He rose from his chair and shrugged on his leather jacket. "I'll walk you out."

"Okay," she said, her heart pounding as every hormone in her body instantly fired.

There was an awkward silence between them as they walked down the hallway toward the side door where she parked.

"I, um . . . I had something I wanted to ask you," he said as he opened the door for her.

"Sure," she said in dread as she led the way across the lot to her car. "If you're worried about what happened this afternoon, don't be. I'm not going to tell anyone."

"Oh, I don't care about that. I mean, I care about that, but . . . shit," he breathed. "I never was any good at this. So, I'll just do what I do best, and blurt it out. Would you like to go to the Christmas party with me?"

Sam smiled as her heart raced even faster. "Yes, I would. But only if you bring the mistletoe."

His gaze dropped to her lips and she wondered if he was imaging the feel of their kiss like she was.

"Great," he said. "Pick you up at three?"

"Sounds good. I'll give you the directions to my house tomorrow."

"Okay." He bent his head down like he was going to kiss her again, then he quickly shot back upright. "We're still at work."

Adrian watched as she got in her car, and a chill went up his spine that had nothing to do with the cold winter wind and everything to do with her.

She was something else. And he liked it.

She rolled her car window down.

Adrian leaned down to where he could speak to her without someone overhearing them. "You know, I really want to kiss you right now."

"Me, too."

Ask her back to your place. It was on the tip of his tongue, but he didn't dare.

"You better get back in," she said. "It's cold out here."

No, it wasn't. Not when he was standing so close to her. "Yeah," he breathed. "You're probably freezing."

She reached out and touched his hand. "I'll see you tomorrow."

Adrian gave a light squeeze to her hand even though what he wanted to do was hold it tight.

Letting go, he walked away from her, and with every step he took, he cursed himself for the stupidity. Why hadn't he asked her back to his apartment?

But then, he knew. If he had her alone in his place, his hands would be all over her. It was too soon, and the last thing he wanted was to drive her away from him.

He'd never wanted anything in his life the way he wanted Samantha Parker.

Closing his eyes, he did his best to banish the image in his mind of her naked in his arms. The imagined feel of her breath falling across his neck as he lost himself inside her body.

"I want you, Sam," he breathed as he watched her pull out of the lot. "And one way or another, I'm going to have you."

3

"Sam?"

Sam looked up to see Adrian's head poking out of his office door. "Yeah?"

"In my office. Now."

She swallowed at his low, even tone. It sounded strangely like the one he used to crawl all over Scott when Scott did something stupid.

Worse, he'd been avoiding her all day. He hadn't even gone to lunch with them.

Had she done something wrong?

Nervous, she got up and took the five steps that separated her cube from his office.

As soon as she was inside, he closed the door.

Sam's heart pounded. This wasn't good. Adrian never closed his door unless it was time for a major performance talk.

Eyes dark and features grim, he turned toward her.

Sam expected him to tell her to sit, so when he cupped her face in his hands, and pressed her back against his wall, she was stunned.

His breathing ragged, he lowered his head down and captured her lips with his.

And it wasn't just any kiss. It was scorching and

demanding. Every hormone in her body jumped to attention. Closing her eyes, she relished the warm scent of him. The masterful feel of his tongue dancing with hers as his hands roamed over her shoulders and back, down to her hips. She wrapped her arms around his shoulders and moaned softly as her desire for him tripled.

He separated her legs with his thigh and cupped her buttocks as he set her down on that taut muscle. Sam groaned at the feeling of him between her legs. Her feet barely touched the floor as he surrounded her with warmth.

Her head light, she throbbed and ached for more of him.

Adrian knew he shouldn't be doing this, but he hadn't been able to stand it any longer. All day long, he'd been unable to think about anything other than the fact that she was only five feet away.

She was so intelligent, so much fun.

He wanted to devour her.

Adrian pulled back from the kiss to where he could nibble her lips as he buried his hand in her thick, dark hair. He laved a trail from her lips to her neck where he inhaled her.

He skimmed his hand up from her waist to the side of her breast. At the sound of her murmured pleasure, he felt his control slipping.

He ached for her. Burned for her in a way he'd never burned before and all he could think of was being inside her.

"I want you, Sam," he whispered.

Sam gave him a chiding stare. "I thought I was in trouble."

Adrian shook his head as he lost himself in those

light eyes of hers. "I think I'm the one in trouble. Serious trouble."

He dipped his head to kiss her again.

His cell phone went off.

Growling, he answered it. "Scott, I'm in the middle of a damn important meeting. Send an e-mail."

Someone knocked on the door.

"Just a minute," Adrian snapped, then he brushed her cheek with his fingers, even though what he really wanted to do was lay her down on his desk and alleviate the vicious, throbbing ache in his groin.

Not to mention the one in his heart.

His breathing ragged, he let go of her. "I better let you get back to work."

She nodded, then kissed him hard on his lips.

The knock sounded again.

She smiled. "Duty calls."

Sam spent the rest of the day dreaming about that kiss. And as she watched people traipse in and out of Adrian's office, she felt like cursing. Couldn't they just leave him in peace?

"Hey!" Randir said as he came around her cube. "It's snowing really bad outside."

Sam looked up with a start. "What?"

"Oh, yeah, the roads are freezing." Randir stuck his head in Adrian's door. "I'm going home."

Adrian came out of his office. "Tell everyone to head out."

Since she lived fifty minutes away, Sam dialed her oldest brother's cell phone.

"Don't you dare head home," Teddy said sternly. "The

roads are awful. I had to leave my Blazer at the bottom of the hill and walk home. Is there some place in La Vergne you can bunk for the night?"

"I guess. Thanks." She hung up.

"Why are you still here?" Adrian asked.

"My brother said the roads are frozen solid. Looks like I'll be spending the night on the cot in the first-aid room."

Adrian frowned. "You can't do that."

Like she had any choice, she thought wistfully. "Sure I can. I have the vending machines and the security guard for company. I'll be fine."

"Why don't you come home with me?" he asked stoically.

Sam hesitated as her heart pounded. If she did that, she had a really good idea what would happen.

But then, how bad would it be to make love to him all night?

She bit her lip in indecision. "I don't know."

At the hurt look on his face, she quickly added, "I bet you get stuck here with me. I'm sure the Corvette isn't any better in this weather than my Honda."

"I'm not in the Vette. I drove my Bronco in."

She arched a brow. "I didn't know you had another car."

"Yeah. I love the Vette, but she's temperamental and she hates snow." He took her jacket off the peg inside her cube and held it open for her. "C'mon. I promise I'll behave."

Her stomach knotted in excitement and fear, she shrugged her coat on. "Okay."

Adrian led her out of the building, across the virtually

empty parking lot to an older-model black Bronco, and opened the door for her.

After he got in and started the car, Sam sat beside Adrian with her heart in her throat. She was so nervous, she was actually trembling. It'd been a long time since she'd been with a guy. A long time since she'd gone to a guy's place.

And she'd never loved a man as much as she did Adrian.

Should I make a move on him? Or should I wait for him to do something?

What if he thinks I'm fat? He was so well toned and she was . . . well, fleshy. What if it turned him off?

Good grief, her doubts and fears plagued her silly.

Adrian tried to think of something to say as he drove the ten-minute commute to his apartment.

But he couldn't.

His hands were actually sweating inside his gloves. He hadn't taken a girl home with him since college.

Should I make a move on her? Or should I wait for her to do something?

Is it too soon?

He didn't want to scare her off. He really liked her. And the last thing he wanted was for her to bolt for the door.

But he couldn't stand the thought of not having her.

By the time he pulled up next to his Corvette, his stomach was absolutely knotted.

"Do you have a roommate?" she asked as he walked her to his door.

"With the hours I keep? No one would put up with me." He unlocked the door and let her in.

Sam entered the living room, then froze. She'd never seen anything like it in her life.

"Good Lord, it looks like a Circuit City showroom," she said as her gaze darted over the big-screen TV, three leather recliners, DVD player, double-decker VCR, two computers, and a stereo bigger than her car.

His walls were stark white and completely bare. But at least the whole apartment was amazingly clean and well kept.

"Jeez. Adrian, you live like a bear in an electronic cave."

He laughed as he locked the door, then set his keys, security badge, and wallet in a bowl on the breakfast counter.

He shrugged his coat off and hung it up in a closet to her left. Sam took hers off and handed it to him.

"Should I ask about the three recliners?"

He shrugged. "Sometimes the guys come over to watch a game."

"So, why don't you have a couch?"

He looked offended by the very idea. "I'm not sitting my ass down next to another guy. Jeez, Sam, I thought you were raised with five brothers."

"Oh, yeah, how could I forget?" she said as she rolled her eyes at him. "The male and his territory."

He laughed as he gave her a brief tour of his place.

"Do you really need a PlayStation 2, Dreamcast, and Nintendo 64?" she asked. But what really amused her was the small TV next to the big one. She arched a questioning brow.

"Sometimes I play games while I'm watching the big TV," he said as if there were nothing unusual about it.

Sam smiled, until she glanced down at one of the chairs. Then she sobered. "You know, Adrian, you're quite a guy."

He gave her a puzzled frown.

"There's not many men who let their underwear watch TV while they're at work," she said, glancing to the pair in the seat of the chair closest to the window.

"Oh, jeez," he moaned as he grabbed them and rushed to the laundry room in the kitchen.

"I'm sorry," she said as she followed after him. "I didn't mean to embarrass you. I think it's funny. Besides, I used to have to do my brothers' laundry, and all I have to say is—"

He turned around at the same time she took a step forward. They collided.

Adrian's breath left his chest as soon as her breasts touched his arm. She looked up at him with her lips parted and before he could stop himself, he took advantage of it.

Sam wrapped her arms around his shoulders as she kissed him with all the passion and love flowing through her. And in that moment, she knew what was about to happen between them.

This was the moment she'd spent the last year dreaming of.

Scared and excited, she couldn't wait.

Adrian deepened his kiss as his hands roamed freely over her back, pressing her closer to him. Growling low in his throat, he pulled back from her lips and buried his mouth against her neck.

Sam hissed in pleasure as his hot tongue, lips, and teeth nibbled and suckled her. Chills swept through her entire body as her breasts tingled in response to his expert, masculine touch. Heat pooled itself into an aching throb between her legs.

The scent of leather and Old Spice tormented her unmercifully. Gracious, how she wanted this man.

No one had ever made her feel the way he did. Desirable. Beautiful.

And best of all, needed.

Tonight, she would show her love to him. Tonight, she would hold nothing back and she would hope for a time when perhaps he might love her in return.

Adrian's vision dulled as he inhaled the warm, sweet scent of her skin. And he wanted more of her.

He wanted all of her.

That need foremost on his mind, he ran his hand over her breast, and squeezed it gently. He moaned at the softness, and at the feel of her hardened nipple through her Santa sweater.

To his amazement, Sam answered the caress with one of her own as she reached down between their bodies and cupped him in her hand, through his jeans. Adrian growled as she stroked him, teased him, making his entire body quiver and burn for her.

She was bold with her caresses, and more than generous with her lips.

His body on fire, Adrian returned to her mouth as she unbuttoned his jeans, then slid her hand beneath the elastic band of his briefs to take him into her hand.

He sucked his breath in sharply between his teeth as he hardened to the point of pain.

"You are a big man," she whispered against his lips as she gently stroked his shaft.

"You're the only one who does that to me," he whispered. He ran his hands under her sweater, over her smooth, soft skin, to the back of her bra where he released the catch.

His breath caught as her breasts spilled out of the satin bra and into his hands. He reveled in the feel of those taut nipples in his palms and he couldn't wait to taste them. To run his tongue over the tiny ridges as he breathed her scent in.

Her soft flesh filled his hands past capacity and he loved it.

Then, she untucked his shirt and ran her hands over his chest and back, clutching at him in a way that made him dizzy.

The damned phone rang.

"Do you need to answer it?" she said breathlessly.

"To hell with it."

"What if it's work?"

"To hell with it."

She laughed.

He heard his answering machine pick up.

"Adrian?"

He flinched as he heard his mother's nasal, Southern drawl.

"Adrian, this is Mom. Are you there? If you are, pick up, honey. I need to talk to you."

His hormones instantly iced by the sound of his mother's voice, he pulled back. "I better answer it or she'll call every ten minutes from now on and start beeping me."

Devastated by the interruption, Sam licked her lips and tried to pull herself together as Adrian left her and picked up the cordless phone from the counter. He tucked his shirt back in and buttoned his pants.

"Hi, Mom," he said coolly as he left the kitchen, then went to his bedroom and closed the door while Sam straightened her own clothes.

"Adrian, where have you been? I've been calling for an hour."

Sam went over to his answering machine to turn it off so that she wouldn't overhear their conversation, but it had so many unmarked buttons, she didn't know which one to press.

"I was at work."

"I wish you'd give me your work number. I need to be able to get a hold of you when something comes up."

"What do you need now, Mom?"

"I need you to come over and salt my driveway, so that I won't get stuck here tomorrow."

"Jesus, Mom, it's a forty-minute drive and the roads are iced over."

"I know, that's why I need you to come over, right now."

Sam frowned at his mother's insistence.

"Mom, I can't. I'm busy."

His mother gave a dramatic sigh. "Busy doing what? Playing with your stupid computers again? All I ask is a little, tiny favor and this is the thanks I get. Do you know, I was in labor for thirty-six hours with you? I almost died giving birth."

"Yes, Mom, I know."

"Don't you take that tone with me, young man. I gave my life to you kids, and the least you can do is take care of me in my old age."

"You're only forty-seven."

"Don't you dare get smart with me. It's not like you have anything better to do. God forbid you should actually date and marry someone, and give me a grand-child."

"Would you please lay off me, Mom? I'm not in the mood."

"Fine," she said in a sarcastic tone that made Sam want to choke her. "You just stay there, and let me fend for my-self. You're just like your worthless father."

"Would you leave Dad out of this?"

"You're just like him, you know. Selfish and worthless. It's a good thing you don't have a girlfriend. You'd prob-ably just knock her up, and leave her, too."

Sam's heart lurched. Poor Adrian. It was a good thing he didn't have another phone or she'd pick it up and give his mother a piece of her mind.

"Just my luck," his mother continued. "To get stuck with an ungrateful son. I knew you should have been a girl. That's fine, though. I'll just call Heather and get her to do it."

"Jeez, Mom, Heather can hardly drive when the weath-er's clear and she lives farther away than I do."

"What do you care? At least I can depend on her."

"All right," Adrian snapped. "I'm coming, okay? Don't get her killed because you need your driveway salted."

"Oh, good."

Sam gaped at the sudden change in the woman's voice. Now that she was getting her way, she actually sounded nice.

"Love you, sweetie."

"Me, too." By his tone, Sam knew he had his teeth grit-ted.

The answering machine clicked off. Sam shook her head. She'd never heard anything like that in her life.

Adrian came out of the bedroom with his jaw ticking. "I have to go out for a little bit."

"Adrian, you can't do that. What if you have a wreck and get killed?"

"Trust me, I'm not that lucky."

"You're not funny."

He shrugged his heavy ski jacket on. Sam zipped it while he fixed the collar. "You be careful," she said, standing up on her tiptoes to kiss him.

Adrian nibbled her lips as warmth spread through him. Only Sam had ever said that to him. "I will. Lock the door behind me."

As soon as he was gone, Sam sighed. Adrian reminded her of a tolerant lion with cubs hanging off him while they nipped his skin. How could he stand it?

Shaking her head, Sam went to get herself a Coke. She opened the fridge and stared in disbelief. It was bare except for an almost-empty gallon of soured milk and a six-pack of beer.

Frowning, she opened his kitchen cabinets, taking inventory. One plate, two mismatched bowls, a cookie sheet, one medium-sized pot, three glasses, two coffee cups, coffee, and two half-empty boxes of cereal. That was it.

Unbelievable. She'd had no idea he lived like this. And now that she thought about it, she realized he didn't even have a Christmas tree in his apartment.

The phone rang again.

Sam ignored it until the answering machine picked up.

"Adrian?" Heather said. "Hey, I need you to call me back as soon as you hear this, okay? Um, I need you, big brother. And please don't yell at me. I had to write a check out for tuition today or else they'd cancel my classes. And I don't have the money to cover it. I'm also two weeks overdue on my rent again. I really need twelve hundred dollars by tomorrow. I swear, I won't ever again ask you for money. I know I said that last time, but I mean it this time. Anyway, please call me tonight. Love you."

Sam ached for him. When he had told her he watched out for his sister and mother, she'd had no idea just what a challenge the two of them were.

"That's *it*," she muttered as she grabbed her coat out of the closet. "It's time someone did something for you."

It was almost three hours later when Adrian finally got home. His head throbbed from his mother's incessant criticism. And the woman wondered why no man would ever stay with her for more than a few months.

If he had any sense, he'd take off, too. But he refused to do that to Heather. His sister could barely look after herself, let alone watch after their mother.

Pushing the thoughts out of his mind, he opened the door. He frowned as he caught a whiff of something really good.

Must be his neighbor's dinner again, he thought as he closed and locked the door. He hung up his coat.

"Sam?" he called, not seeing her in the living room.

"I'm right here," she said from the kitchen.

Adrian turned, then froze as his breath left his body. Sam was standing at the sink wearing nothing but one of his flannel shirts. It was huge on her, reaching all the way to her knees.

The sight floored him.

"I hope you don't mind," she said as she pulled at the collar. "I fell on my way back and got mud all over my clothes."

"Fell?" It was then he realized the warm, delicious aroma was coming from his stove. Damn, the thing actually worked. Who knew?

He frowned. "What did you do?"

She moved toward him with a coffee cup in her hands. "Here," she said, handing him hot chocolate. "I'm sure you're frozen."

He had been until he saw her half-dressed. Now, he felt as if he were on fire. "Where did this come from?"

She smiled. "I walked down to the market on the corner."

He was stunned. He'd never in his life come home to such a warm welcome.

And in that moment, he knew he loved her.

Setting the cup down on his breakfast counter, he pulled her into his arms and held her close.

Sam trembled at the contact. He ran his hands down her back, then to her bare hips.

"Oh, God," he breathed. "You're naked under there."

Sam laughed. "I know."

Adrian's thoughts scattered as he touched her bare buttocks. Her skin was so incredibly soft, while he was harder than he'd ever been before.

Bending down, he scooped her up in his arms and carried her to the bedroom.

Sam wrapped her arms around his neck, amazed he was able to carry her so easily. And when he laid her on the bed, she smiled, knowing this was what she'd wanted since the first time she'd seen him greeting her in the lobby for her interview last year.

She got up on her knees and pulled his shirt over his head. Her gaze feasted on the sight of all that strong, tawny skin as she ran her hands over his delectable flesh.

Good gracious, the man had a gorgeous body, and she couldn't wait to taste every inch of it.

The way he watched her with his eyes dark and hungry, his breathing ragged, made her burn even more for him. How could a man like this want *her*?

Sam hesitated as she placed her hands on the top button of his jeans. "I want you to know that I'm not easy," she whispered.

"It never crossed my mind," he said as he cupped her face in his hands. He moved to kiss her, but she pulled back.

She met his confused gaze. "I've only been with one other guy. My college boyfriend."

"Okay," he said, dipping his head toward hers.

She laughed as she dodged his lips again. "Would you listen for a second?"

He arched a brow at her.

"I wanted to let you know that I'm not on the pill or anything."

Adrian went rigid. Cursing, he took a step back from the bed. "Well, since we're confessing things, I have to tell you, I haven't been with a woman since college, either. And I threw out my condoms last year after it occurred to me that they were older than I was." Adrian retrieved his shirt from the floor.

Damn it, he was so hard it hurt. And all he could think of was taking her, consequences be damned.

But he couldn't do that. He wasn't about to take a chance on getting her pregnant. In spite of what his mother thought, he wasn't his father.

It figures. Whatever made you think you could have a woman like her, anyway?

Sam frowned as he stalked out of the room. She started to call him back, then reconsidered. He needed to eat first.

She went after him. "You hungry?"

Adrian nodded, but by his face she could tell food was the last thing he wanted.

Sam served him a bowl of chili.

Adrian stood at the counter while he ate it.

Bemused, Sam watched as he refused to look at her. And the only words he uttered were a very brief compliment on how good her chili tasted and a simple thank-you.

As soon as he was finished, Adrian placed the bowl in the sink, then went to sit in his recliner.

Picking up his remote for the stereo, he clicked on his CD player. He had to do something to distract himself from those luscious legs peeking out from under her shirt. He rotated the discs to Matchbox 20.

Suddenly, he felt Sam beside his chair. He glanced at her, then did a double-take as he saw her shirt unbuttoned all the way to her navel. Even worse, the swell of one breast was so obvious that it sent a wave of heat straight through his groin.

"Don't tease me, Sam," he said hoarsely.

With a tight-lipped smile, she lifted up the hem of the shirt to gift him with a glimpse of the dark curls at the juncture of her thighs before she climbed into his lap.

"Sam," he groaned as she reached to unbutton his pants. His entire body burned and, worse, her feminine, floral scent was making him insane. If she didn't get up, he was going to have her regardless of his common sense. "Please don't."

She took his hands in hers and led them to her breasts.

Adrian leaned his head back and moaned at the softness of her bare breasts in his hands.

Sam kissed him then, and he felt something strange in her mouth.

Adrian pulled back to see her with a wrapped condom between her teeth.

The smile on her face was devilish as she removed the package. "I bought them at the store, just in case."

Growling low in his throat, he kissed her fiercely.

Sam gasped as he rose to his feet with her still in his lap. She wrapped her arms and legs around him as he carried her back to his bed with his hands firmly gripping her bare bottom.

He set her on the bed, then pulled his shirt over his head again as she finished unfastening his jeans. She removed his clothes from him.

Sam gaped at the sight of his lean muscles as she saw him naked for the first time. Every single inch of his lean, hard body was toned and perfect. Never had she seen anything like it.

Her face burned as she saw the size of his erection.

She ran her hands over the veins on his forearms, over the strength of a body she'd never dared hope to touch. His skin was so soft, his muscles so hard. It reminded her of velvet stretched over steel.

She'd never imagined her programming genius would have the body of a Greek god. But he truly did.

Adrian hesitated as he stared at her in his bed, wearing his shirt. She was beautiful there. So soft, warm, and giving.

His desire surged through him like lava as he joined her in the bed and laid her back against the mattress. He rained kisses over her face and neck as he did his best to control himself.

His body demanded he get down to business with her, but his heart wanted to savor her for as long as he could. Even if it killed him.

Adrian groaned as she rolled him over onto his back and straddled his waist. He liked her feistiness. But most of all, he liked her on top of him.

She leaned over his chest and ran her tongue along the edge of his jaw, sending a thousand needlelike chills over his body as she rubbed herself against his stomach.

It shook him all the way to his soul.

"I'm so glad you got rid of that goatee," she whispered in his ear a second before she ran her tongue around the curve of his jaw.

Adrian held her against him. "If I'd known you would do this, I'd have shaved it off the first week you came to work."

She laughed.

He buried his lips in the curve of her shoulder, inhaling the sweet scent of her skin. His head swam from the moistness of her on his stomach.

Needing her in a way that terrified him, he unbuttoned her shirt and pulled it from her shoulders. "You are so beautiful," he breathed as he saw her naked.

Her curves were every bit as full and lush as he had imagined. And her breasts . . .

He could stare at those luscious breasts all night long.

His breathing ragged, he reached up and cupped them in his hands. She trembled in response, delighting him even more.

He dropped his gaze down to the moist curls that were driving him crazy, the moist curls that covered the part of her he couldn't wait to have.

Sitting up, he kissed her furiously as he skimmed his hand from her breast, down her smooth, soft stomach to the tangled curls and into the sleek, wet cleft.

Sam hissed at the pleasure of his long, lean fingers stroking her intimately. She'd never felt anything better, until he slid them inside her. In and out, and around, those fingers tormented her with a fiery pleasure she feared might actually consume her.

Shamelessly, she rubbed herself against him, wanting him in a way that went beyond the physical.

Her body on fire, she pushed him back against the bed, then moved to kiss a trail down his chest.

Adrian hissed as Sam brushed her lips against his taut nipple and when she drew it into her mouth he thought he would die from the pleasure of her tongue on his skin.

He buried his hands in her hair, cupping her face gently as he let the love he felt for her wash over him. She was so giving, so kind. Never in his life had anyone taken care of him. Never had anyone cared.

But Sam did, and it rocked him all the way to his heart.

"Touch me, Sam," he breathed, wanting to feel her hand against him again.

She moved herself lower, trailing her tongue and lips down his abdomen, to his navel, his hip, where she tormented him mercilessly with little nibbles that rocked his entire body.

Delirious from her touch, he closed his eyes in painful anticipation as she finally brushed her hand through the curls at the center of his body. She cupped him in her hand.

Adrian arched his back, growling at the softness of her fingers stroking his shaft.

"Yes," he moaned, writhing from the unbelievable sensations that ripped through him.

And before he knew what she was doing, she moved her head lower and licked a slow, torturous path from the base of his shaft, all the way to the tip.

Adrian hissed at the unexpected, blind ecstasy that tore through him.

Sam smiled as she felt him shivering around her. Her only thought to give him more pleasure, she took him into her mouth.

She knew she was making him crazy, and she loved every minute of it. Adrian deserved to be loved by someone who wouldn't take him for granted, and she wanted to show him just how much he meant to her. Just how much she needed him.

Adrian clenched his fists in the sheets at the incredible sensation of her tongue and lips covering him. No one had ever done that to him before, and he couldn't believe just how good it felt.

His body trembling, he couldn't stand not tasting her in return.

He had to have her. Now!

Sam lifted her head as Adrian sat up. His eyes dark and shuttered, he moved until his body was lying in the opposite direction of hers. He ran his mouth and tongue over her stomach as he skimmed a hand down her hips, blazing a scorching trail of heat.

His touch literally burned her from the inside out as

he trailed it up her inner thigh, urging her to open her legs for him.

He nudged her legs farther apart, then buried his lips at the center of her body.

"Adrian!" she breathed as he tormented her.

Sam moaned at the sensation of his mouth on her as he nibbled and licked. His tongue and fingers swirled around her, intensifying her pleasure.

Trembling, she returned to torment him the same way.

She writhed as he continued and as she tasted him.

There was such fire and magic in his touch. It scorched her in a way that was indescribable. No wonder she loved this man.

She gave herself to him without reservations or fear. There was something so special in this equal sharing, equal giving. It touched her profoundly and she knew in her heart that she would never be the same.

Sam's head was light as he gave careful consideration to her, and when he slid two fingers inside her body and stroked her, she moaned in ecstasy.

Biting her lip, she closed her eyes as his fingers delved deep and hard inside her, swirling around with the promise of what was to come while he laved her even faster.

Sam's entire body shivered and jerked involuntarily in response to his touch.

Her head spun from the intense sensations. The pleasure was so incredible, so extreme, as it built inside her until she could stand no more.

Suddenly, her entire body exploded as white-hot ecstasy tore through her in ever-increasing waves. Sam cried out as her release came.

Panting, she couldn't move.

"That's it," he said, his skin covered in sweat. "I have to be inside you."

Sam pulled back from him and reached for the condom a few inches from her.

Adrian tensed as she gently slid the cool condom over his hot, swollen shaft. Then she cupped him in her hand. Her touch singed him as his body quivered in response.

How could such tiny hands wreak so much havoc on him?

Needing to feel her more than he needed to breathe, Adrian pressed her back against the mattress, then separated her thighs with his knees.

You are about to violate your Web designer.

He didn't know where that thought came from, but it ripped through his mind as he pressed the tip of his shaft against her core.

What was he doing?

"Adrian?" she asked as she looked up at him with a frown. "Is something wrong?"

"Are you sure you want this?" he asked as he looked down at her. "If anyone finds out, we could get fired."

"Then I'll find another job," she said, lifting her hips toward his.

Joy ripped through him. Taking her hand into his, he stared into her eyes, then drove himself deep inside her body.

They moaned together.

Sam couldn't believe the fullness of him as he rocked his hips against hers. He went so deep inside her, she could swear he touched her womb as fierce, hot stabs of pleasure tormented her.

She wrapped her legs around his lean waist and savored the feel of his muscles flexing in and around her. She ran her hands down his back, over the chills that covered his body as she met him stroke for stroke.

He was spectacular.

"You feel so good," he breathed in her ear as he rocked his hips, hard and fierce, against hers. "I could stay inside you forever."

She was sure she didn't feel half as good to him as he felt to her. He lowered his upper body to where she could nuzzle his neck as he thrust into her.

Sam wrapped her legs tight about his hips, then she rolled over with him.

Adrian looked up, startled, as he found himself beneath her. She took his hands in hers and placed them on her hips. Then, holding them in hers, she lifted herself up to the tip of his shaft, before she lowered herself onto him.

He growled at the feel of her body on his as she rode him fast and furiously. He'd never felt anything like it.

"You're making my toes curl," she breathed.

"I plan to make more than that curl before the night is over," he said as she released his hands and leaned forward.

Adrian ran his hands over her breasts, cupping them gently as she continued to stroke him with her body.

Why had he waited a year before kissing her?

It terrified him when he thought of how close he'd come to never acting on his desire. What if he had let her get away without ever having tasted her lips? Her body?

And in that instant, a wave of possessiveness washed over him. He would never let her go.

She belonged to him.

Sam watched Adrian watch her. His dark eyes were shuttered, but the look of pleasure on his face tore through her.

She ran her hand over his stubbled cheeks, grateful that she had finally kissed him. This moment far exceeded any fantasy she'd ever had about him.

Her body aching with bliss, she could feel her pleasure mounting again with every forceful stroke she delivered to him. She moved her hips faster as Adrian lifted his hips to drive himself even deeper.

"Oh, my goodness," she breathed as her body became even hotter as massive, wrenching stabs of pleasure tore through her.

Adrian rolled over with her then, and placed her beneath him. His eyes wild, he quickened his pace.

Sam moaned at the feel of him sliding in and out, fast, deep, hard.

And then suddenly, an indefinable ecstasy exploded through her body in resounding ripples. Sam gasped at the same time Adrian threw his head back and roared as he delivered two more long, deep thrusts to her. His entire body convulsed around her as he released himself.

He collapsed on top of her and buried his face in her neck.

Sam held him there, cradled in her arms and legs as she just listened to him breathe. She felt his heart pounding against her chest and sweat covered them both.

This was a perfect, peaceful moment that she wished she could hold on to forever.

"That was the most incredible experience I've ever had," he whispered in her ear as he cradled her gently in his strong arms.

"No kidding," she said as she ran her hands over his hard biceps, then kissed him tenderly on his chest. "You know, I've never done that before."

"Done what?"

"Orgasmed."

Adrian smiled. He was glad he'd been the man who had shown her the full depth of her sexuality. Cupping her head in his hand, he pulled her lips to his for a scorching kiss.

The phone rang.

"I swear, I hate those things," he snarled.

"Oh," Sam said as she let go of him. "I forgot to tell you Heather called."

Carefully, he withdrew from her. "Then I'm sure that's her," he said, reaching for the cordless phone on his nightstand.

"Hi, Heather," he said in a tone that was half a growl.

Sam could hear just a hint of Heather's chattering on the other end.

"Damn, Heather. What do you do with your money? I pay you two hundred and fifty dollars a week to do my laundry and buy groceries for me, and half the time you don't even do it."

She heard Heather chattering again as Adrian ran his hand through his hair and clenched it tight.

Adrian got out of bed and reached for his pants as he listened to her. Biting her lip, Sam admired the perfect shape of his buttocks as he stooped over.

"Give me a break," he said as he fastened his jeans. "I worked three jobs in college and no one ever . . ."

He went rigid. "I'm sorry," he said. "Just stop crying, okay? Heather, please stop crying."

Sam sat up as he walked out of the room.

Frowning, she pulled her shirt on and followed after him.

He wiggled his mouse at his computer. "I'm doing it right now," he said in a gentle voice. He cursed again.

"You only have two dollars in your account, did you know that? What are you living on?"

His jaw ticked, but his voice was patient. "All right, I'm transferring two grand over to you, but this is it, Heather. I work too damned hard just to give it away to you because you decide you need a Christmas vacation in Daytona for a week."

He clicked the phone off and tossed it on his desk.

Sam moved to stand behind him. She ran her hand over his back. "You are a wonderful man."

"I'm an idiot," he said under his breath. "I don't know why I put up with them."

"You love them."

"I wonder sometimes. God, I'm just so tired of everyone needing me all the time."

Sam went cold at his words. His dependability was what she loved about him most, and in truth that was what she wanted. Someone she could depend on who wouldn't disappoint her. She was tired of unkept promises.

Sam, you fool. No one is ever going to put you first. When are you going to realize that?

Her father had done what Adrian's had; he'd abandoned them. And her worst fear was to fall in love with some thoughtless, woman-chasing jerk who dumped her for a trophy girlfriend the minute she passed the age of thirty.

She didn't want a little boy, she wanted a man.

And she had hoped Adrian would be that man.

"Is something wrong?" he asked.

She shook her head, then brushed her hand over his whiskered cheek.

Please don't disappoint me, too. The words were on the tip of her tongue. But she didn't dare utter them aloud. Didn't dare give him any more ways to hurt her.

He already held a place in her heart where only he could destroy it.

"Why don't we go back to bed?" she whispered.

He looked up at her with those dimples flashing. Then, he scooped her up in his arms and ran with her back to the bedroom.

4

"Hi, Adrian," Sam said as soon as he answered his cell phone.

"Hey, sweet, what's wrong? You sound upset."

God, how she loved the sound of his deep, caring voice. It comforted her on a level that defied explanation.

"My brother forgot to pick up my mom's Christmas tree and she's having a hissy fit. I'm over here at the lot and there's no way I can make it back home and get ready in time. Is it okay if we just hook up at the hotel?"

"Sure. Is there anything I can do for you?"

She felt tears well at his offer. This last week had been the best of her life. After they had returned to work, they had kept quiet about their relationship, but it hadn't been easy. More nights than not, she'd left work first, then gone over to his apartment to fix dinner and wait for him.

He'd even given her a key.

"Thanks," she said, "but I've got it. I'll see you at the hotel."

"I'll be waiting for you in the lobby."

Worried, Adrian paced the hotel lobby. The temperature outside was steadily falling, and the news had been calling for a bad snowstorm later that evening. He'd tried to call Sam a dozen times to warn her not to come out this far, but she'd turned her cell phone off.

The door opened.

Adrian looked up and felt his jaw drop as Sam swept in.

She was wearing a Renaissance-style dress with a high waist, long flowing sleeves, and ballerina slippers. Her hair was down around her face and she had a light ribbon braided across the top of her hair with flowers. She looked just like Guinevere.

And he loved it.

No, he corrected himself, he loved her.

Sam paused as she caught sight of Adrian staring at her. He looked gorgeous in his black jeans and sweater. He'd even gone to the trouble of fixing his hair and she knew how much he hated doing that.

Better still, his entire face lit up as his gaze met hers.

"My lady, you are beautiful," he said as she drew near him. He took her hand in his and kissed the back of her knuckles.

The warmth of his hand startled her. He took her coat from her hands and offered her his arm.

Feeling like a heroine in a romance novel, Sam took his arm and allowed him to lead her into the party.

"Wow, Sam," Randir said as he saw them. "You clean up good."

She laughed. "Thanks, I think."

While Adrian went to get her something to drink, she took a seat at the large, round table with the guys from her department.

"Oh, Adrian," Scott teased as soon as he returned. "You're just so thoughtful. Want to go get me a Coke?"

"No," Adrian said as he sat down beside Sam.

Sam did her best to appear nonchalant and distanced from Adrian, but it wasn't easy when all she wanted to do was lean back into his arms and have him hold her like he did in the early morning hours.

How she loved curling up with him in his favorite recliner, watching TV or listening to music while they fed each other popcorn. Naked.

She'd never been overly comfortable with her body, but Adrian seemed to love it and she loved him for it.

He gave her a meaningful look, then slid his gaze toward the lobby. "I need to go make a call."

Sam waited until he was out of sight before she excused herself to go to the bathroom.

She met Adrian in the lobby, where he pulled her into a hidden, dark corner. "Why are we here?" he asked as he pressed her back against the wall.

She trembled at the strength of his chest against her breasts as he cupped her face in his hands and stared down at her with heat in his eyes. "Because it's a free meal?" she asked impishly.

"I'd rather be at home, making love to you."

"Mmm, me, too."

He kissed her then.

"Hey, Adrian!"

They both went tense at hearing Randy's voice.

Adrian stepped out of the corner while Sam pressed herself against the wall, hopefully out of Randy's sight.

"Hi, Randy. How's it going?"

"Great. I meant to tell you that Greg Wilson is going to applaud your team tonight after dinner. We hit the million-dollar mark for the Christmas season this morning. Congratulations. Greg says he's going to double your bonus and give you a raise."

"Thanks."

"So, what are you doing out here?" Randy asked. "C'mon, let's go say hi to Greg. I know he wants to shake your hand."

Sam listened with pride. Greg Wilson was on the pompous side, but he owned one of the largest privately held corporations in the country. For him to want to spend six seconds in your company was a big compliment.

As soon as the coast was clear, she went to the ladies' room.

She had barely closed the door on her stall when she heard Tiffany and a gaggle of her girlfriends sweep into the bathroom.

"Did you see Adrian?" Tiffany said to them.

"Are you kidding?" Barbara Mason said breathlessly. "How could anyone miss such a baby doll?"

"I heard that." Sam didn't recognize that voice.

"Yeah, well," Tiffany said in a loud whisper, "I'm going to nail that boy tonight."

Her friends laughed as Sam saw red. Tiffany better lay off Adrian, if she wanted to keep that perfect nose of hers.

"Right," Barbara said in disbelief.

"I am," Tiffany bragged. "I rented a room upstairs and as soon as I see him, I'm going to get him up there and have my wicked way with him."

They left the bathroom.

Sam clenched her fists. How dare she.

Her eyes narrowed, she left the bathroom and went after Adrian to warn him.

There was no need.

Tiffany had him cornered outside the ballroom. Worse, they were locked in a fiery kiss with Tiffany's hands on his waist and neck.

Sam froze at the sight as pain tore through her.

Her first impulse was to tear them apart and slug Tiffany. And if she wasn't so stunned, she might have actually done it.

But she couldn't move.

Not while her heart was slowly splintering into a million pieces.

And what hurt her most was the fact that Adrian would kiss Tiffany out in front of everyone while he wouldn't even so much as touch her hand when anyone was around.

Her tears swelled, but she blinked them back. She wouldn't give either one of them the satisfaction of seeing just how much damage they had done to her.

God, she was such a stupid fool. How could she have thought Adrian was any different than her own father?

Tiffany pulled away, and handed him a card key. "It's room 316," she said seductively. "I'll see you in twenty minutes."

Sam went numb as even more pain washed over her. How could he?

He's a man! Look at Tiffany.

How on earth could you ever compete with that?

Heartsick and aching, Sam rushed back to her table. She gathered her purse and coat.

"You okay?" Randir asked.

"No," she said, swallowing her tears. "I need to go home. I'll see you guys Monday."

Adrian waited and waited for Sam. Where was she? Had she gone back in when he wasn't looking?

He went to check, and as soon as he saw her coat was

missing, a feeling of dread washed over him. "Where's Sam?"

Randir shrugged. "She went home."

"What?"

"She said she didn't feel well."

Adrian pulled his phone out of its cradle and dialed her cell phone.

No answer.

Cursing, he ran after her.

A heavy snowfall had started as he reached his Bronco, got in, and went to find her.

Sam wept the whole way to Spring Hill. She didn't really notice the icy roads until she had to turn onto Nashville Highway to reach her house. Her car started skidding.

Terrified, she held her breath until she landed safely in a ditch.

Her heart pounding, she was glad she hadn't been physically hurt. She picked up her cell phone to call her brothers, then saw the battery was dead.

"Damn it!" she snarled as she slammed her fist against the steering wheel. "What next?"

Angry and hurt, she wiped her eyes, then shoved open her door and started the five-mile walk to her rented house.

Adrian's heart raced as he realized how hazardous the roads were becoming. Sam's little Honda was about as safe in weather like this as his Corvette.

Why had she left? It didn't make any sense to him.

He turned onto Nashville Highway and saw her car in

the ditch. Terrified at the sight, Adrian pulled to the side of the road and got out. Running up to her car, he saw it was empty.

She was out walking in 26 degrees?

He shook his head as he remembered her thin shoes and dress. She would freeze to death. Damn her independence. Couldn't she ever let anyone do anything for her?

He ran back to his Bronco. Getting in, he tried to start it.

"No!" he snarled as the starter clicked without firing the engine. He tried again, but still the car refused to start.

Pulling out his cell phone, he called the only other person he knew who lived in Spring Hill.

"Hey, Trey," he said as his friend picked up. "I need a huge favor from you."

Sam was absolutely freezing. Her shoes were soaking wet and she had all but lost the feeling in her feet.

Worse, she still had a mile to go to get home. And over and over again, all she could see was Adrian kissing Tiffany.

"Why, Adrian?" she breathed, clutching her coat tighter around her. "Why wasn't I good enough?"

Suddenly, she heard a strange clip-clopping sound coming from behind her.

What on earth?

It sounded vaguely like hooves. Turning around, she saw . . .

No, it couldn't be.

Sam blinked, not trusting her eyes.

The image only got clearer as the snowfall became heavier.

It was a knight. A knight in black leather.

Frowning, she watched as Adrian rode up to her on the back of a white stallion. Her mouth wide open, she looked at him as he reined to a stop by her side.

"Methinks milady damsel doth be in distress."

She shook her head at his fake medieval English way of speaking. Those deep, dark, chocolate-brown eyes stared at her with a heat that instantly warmed her freezing bones.

"Adrian?" she gasped.

"Sir Adrian," he corrected with a smile. He reached his hand down to her.

Without thinking, she took it and allowed him to pull her up to sit before him on the medieval-style saddle. He wrapped her up in two blankets as he adjusted her in front of him.

"What are you doing here?" she asked in disbelief. "I thought you were with Tiffany." As she said the name, her rage ignited.

"Tiffany?" he asked with a frown. "Why would you . . ."

She saw the color darken his cheeks.

"Yes," she snarled at him. "I saw you two. And you took her room key."

"Didn't you see me give it back?"

Sam hesitated. "You gave it back?"

"Yes. A few minutes after she left."

"You kept it a few minutes?" she snarled. "You skunk. How could you do—"

He stopped her words with a heated kiss.

"Don't yell at me, Sam," he said as he pulled back. "It wasn't my fault. I was waiting for you when she grabbed me from behind. At first, I thought it was you. Then she swept around me and put a lip-lock on me so fast I didn't know what to do. In case you haven't noticed, women don't usually do things like that to me. She caught me off guard."

"You looked like you were enjoying it to me."

"I was too stunned to move. And when she handed me the key, it took a full minute before it dawned on me what it was."

"A full minute?"

"I know you don't believe me, but if I wanted Tiffany, then why am I out here on a horse, freezing?"

"I don't know. Why are you here on a horse, freezing?"

"Because I love you, and I wanted to come to your rescue."

Sam choked on a sob. "Really?"

He tilted her chin up to look at him. "Don't ever doubt me, Sam. You're the only woman I've *ever* wanted to take care of."

Coming from him, that meant something.

She smiled as he kicked the horse forward toward the setting sun.

And in that moment, Sam knew she had the best Christmas present ever. She had her knight in shining leather.

EPILOGUE

Christmas Day

Adrian let out a tired sigh as he pulled up to his apartment, just after noon. He'd spent most of the morning at work, alone, doing his best not to call and disturb Sam. She was spending the day with her family, while his had fled. Heather had gone to Daytona, and his mother was on a cruise in Alaska with her latest boyfriend.

But then, there was nothing unusual about that. He hadn't had a family Christmas since he was fifteen.

For the last eleven years, Christmas had meant nothing more than a heated TV dinner eaten in front of bad television shows.

"I hate Christmas," he muttered as he got out of his car and went to his apartment.

He opened his door. Then, he froze dead in his tracks.

Someone had put a small Christmas tree in his living room and decorated it.

Frowning, Adrian closed the door and took his coat off, then went to the tree where a medieval-looking note card was tied with a ribbon to a branch.

He flipped it open.

Milord, Knight in Shining Armor, methinks thou hast a present in thy chamber.

He smiled at Sam's writing. She must have stopped by

while he'd been at work. How he wished she'd called him. He'd love to see her today.

Oh, well, she'd be at work tomorrow.

Holding the card to his heart, he went to see what she'd left for him. He opened the door to his bedroom and went stock-still as his jaw fell open.

Sam was lying on his bed dressed in a teddy that made his mouth water, and she had a bow tied around her neck.

"Where have you been?" she asked with a seductive smile as she closed the book she'd been reading and put it on his nightstand.

Adrian couldn't speak, since his tongue was hanging on the floor.

Her smile widened as she left the bed and moved to stand in front of him. "Carpet got your tongue?" she asked.

He smiled.

Cupping her face in his hands, he stared in awe. "I thought you were going over to your mom's."

"I am, for dinner. But I wanted to surprise you."

Adrian pulled her to him and kissed her until he couldn't stand it anymore. He wanted her in a way he had never wanted anything else.

And that flimsy outfit that barely covered her and left nothing to his imagination was making him way too hard for comfort.

Growling, he pulled his clothes off in record time, then tossed her over his shoulder and deposited her gently on the bed.

Sam laughed.

Adrian ran his hand down the curve of her thigh, amazed at how much he loved her.

Sam kissed Adrian's bare shoulder as he reached into his nightstand for a condom.

He turned to her then, but instead of handing the condom to her as he normally did, he kissed her.

She felt something strange in his mouth.

Pulling back, she frowned as he pulled a ring out from between his teeth and handed it to her.

"I was going to give this to you tomorrow at dinner," he said, looking a bit sheepish. "But since you're here . . ."

Completely stunned, Sam couldn't breathe as she stared at the ring. It was a one-carat, heart-shaped diamond engagement ring in a medieval-style setting that made her heart pound.

Tears welled in her eyes as she blinked in disbelief. "Are you sure about this?"

He ran his hand down her arm. "You're the only thing in my life I've ever been sure about," he whispered before he took the ring back.

He left the bed and went down on one knee beside it, then took her hand into his.

Tears fell down her cheeks at the sight of Adrian naked on the floor.

"Samantha Jane Parker, will you marry me?"

She launched herself at him and knocked him flat against the floor. "Of course I will."

He laughed as she straddled his bare stomach.

Adrian placed the ring on her left hand, then he kissed it. "I love you, Sam."

"I love you, Adrian," she whispered, knowing in her heart that she had finally found her one, true knight in shining armor. And she was never, ever going to let him go.